THE SOUND AND THE FURRY

Also by Spencer Quinn

THE SOUND AND THE FURRY

A CHET AND BERNIE MYSTERY

SPENCER QUINN

PAPL
DISCARDED

ATRIA BOOKS

New York   London   Toronto   Sydney   New Delhi

ATRIA BOOKS

A Division of Simon & Schuster, Inc.

1230 Avenue of the Americas

New York, NY 10020

First Atria Books hardcover edition September 2013

ATRIA BOOKS and colophon are trademarks of Simon & Schuster, Inc.

For information about special discounts for bulk purchases, please contact Simon & Schuster Special Sales at 1-866-506-1949 or business@simonandschuster.com.

The Simon & Schuster Speakers Bureau can bring authors to your live event. For more information or to book an event, contact the Simon & Schuster Speakers Bureau at 1-866-248-3049 or visit our website at www.simonspeakers.com.

Manufactured in the United States of America

10 9 8 7 6 5 4 3 2 1

Library of Congress Cataloging-in-Publication Data

Quinn, Spencer.
  The sound and the furry : a Chet and Bernie mystery / by Spencer Quinn.—1st
Atria Books hardcover ed.
    p. cm.
  1. Dogs—Fiction. 2. Private investigators—Fiction. I. Title.
  PS3617.U584F57 2012
  813'.6—dc23

                                                    2012005329

ISBN 978-1-4767-0322-0
ISBN 978-1-4767-0326-8 (ebook)

This book is dedicated to Bernie Weiner, in memory.

ONE

"O ne thing's for sure," the lawyer said, handing Bernie our check, "you earned every cent."

Bernie tucked the check in—oh, no—the chest pocket of his Hawaiian shirt, just about his nicest Hawaiian shirt, with the hula dancers and the trombones, but that wasn't the point. The point was we'd had chest pocket problems in the past, more than once. And possibly more than twice, but I wouldn't know, since I don't count past two. What I do know is that checks have a way of falling out of chest pockets.

"What's he barking about?" the lawyer said.

Bernie glanced at me. "Just wants to get rolling," he said. That wasn't it at all: what I wanted was for Bernie to put that check in his front pants pocket where it would be safe. But then I realized that I did kind of want to get rolling. Wow! That was Bernie, knowing my own mind better than I did. And I knew his exactly the same way! Which is just one of the reasons why the Little Detective Agency is so successful, especially if you forget about the finances part. We're partners. He's Bernie Little. I'm Chet, pure and simple.

"You did a nice job, Bernie," the lawyer said. "Those motel pics? Perfecto. Might have another case for you in a couple of weeks."

"More divorce work?" Bernie said.

"That's my beat."

Bernie sighed. We hated divorce work, me and Bernie. None of the humans involved were ever at their best, or even close. Get me to tell you sometime about the Teitelbaum divorce and what Mrs. Teitelbaum did at the end, a nightmare except for the fact of that being the night I got my first taste of kosher chicken. There's good in everything.

The lawyer had one of those human mouths where the corners turned down. You see that a lot, but not on Bernie: his mouth corners turn up. Now the lawyer's mouth corners turned down some more.

"Aren't you divorced yourself?" he said.

"So?" said Bernie. He has a way of saying "so" that makes him seem a little bigger, and Bernie's a pretty big guy to begin with.

"Nothing," the lawyer said. "Nothing at all. Just sayin'."

Bernie gave him a long look. Then he reached for the check and jammed it into one of his front pants pockets. Life is full of surprises, sometimes not so easy to understand. I put this one behind me as fast as I could, my mind shutting down in a very pleasant way.

We hopped into our ride, a real old Porsche painted different shades of red, but Bernie says I'm not good with red, so don't take my word for it.

"That left a bad taste in my mouth," Bernie said. "How about a little spin?"

What was this? Bernie had a bad taste in his mouth? I felt sorry for him. At the same time, I let my tongue roam around my own mouth, and what do you know? Up in the roof part, hidden away in one of those hard ridges? Yes! A Cheeto! Not a whole Cheeto, but pretty close. I nudged it loose with the tip of my tongue and made quick work of it. Riding shotgun in the Porsche, Cheetos practically falling from the sky: we were cooking.

Bernie stepped on the pedal, and we roared out of the strip mall lot where the lawyer had his office, the tires shrieking on the hot pavement. Roaring and shrieking: the Porsche had a voice of its own, a voice I loved. We zipped past a lot of strip malls—we've got strip malls out the yingyang here in the Valley—and hit the freeway. Freeways we've also got out the yingyang, all of them packed day and night; this one took us past the downtown towers—their tops lost in the brownish sky we sometimes get in monsoon season, a season with a strange damp smell all its own, although there hadn't been a drop of rain yet, not in ages—across the big arroyo and up into the hills, traffic thinning at last. Bernie let out a deep breath.

"Think there's anything to that?" he said. "Me hating divorce work on account of my own divorce? Some kind of—what would you call it? Hidden psychological connection?"

What was Bernie talking about? I had no clue. I put my paw on his knee, for no particular reason. The car shot forward.

"Hey, Chet! What the hell?"

Oops. Had I pressed down a bit too hard? I laid off.

"It's all right, big guy. Sometimes you don't know your own strength."

Whoa! Don't know my own strength? Had to be one of Bernie's jokes. He can be a funny guy with jokes—take that time he found some pink streamers and stuck them on the handle grips of a bunch of bikes parked outside a biker bar and then waited for the bikers to come out. And that was just the beginning of the fun! But take it from me: I know my own strength.

We topped a rise and cruised over a long flat stretch, the highway shimmering blue in the distance like it was covered in water. Not true, as I'd learned many times and now was learning again.

"Thirsty, Chet?"

Yes, all of a sudden. How did he know? Bernie slowed down, dug my bowl out from under the seat, filled it from a water bottle, and set it on the floor in front of me, all of that with one hand on the wheel and sometimes not any. Bernie was the best driver in the Valley. That day he went off the cliff—in the Porsche before this one, or maybe before that one, too—it wasn't his fault at all. Once he'd even been offered the job of wheelman for the Luddinsky Gang. We'd busted them instead. The look on their faces!

I stopped panting, leaned down, and lapped up the water.

"Better?" Bernie said.

Totally. I sat up straight. We rounded a curve and spotted some dudes in orange jumpsuits picking up trash by the roadside, a sheriff's van idling behind them, yellow light flashing. Bernie eased off the gas. We'd put a lot of perps into orange jumpsuits, and you never knew when you'd bump into an old pal.

"Hey," Bernie said. "Isn't that Frenchie Boutette?"

The little roly-poly dude at the end, poking at a scrap of paper, missing, taking a short break? He glanced our way, recognized the car, easy to tell from how his eyebrows shot up. Yes, Frenchie for sure. We pulled over.

"Frenchie! How's it going?"

Frenchie looked at Bernie, then at me, and backed away.

"Don't be shy," Bernie said. "We're not going to bite you."

"Think I'm fallin' for that line again?" Frenchie said. "Slipped your mind how Chet bit me that last time, down in Arroyo Seco?"

"Come on, Frenchie. How can you call that a bite?"

"Because of all the blood," Frenchie said.

"Barely a scratch," Bernie said. "Booze thins the blood. And why did you try to run away in the first place?"

"Because I didn't want to do time. Why else? Like maybe I was training for the Olympics?"

Bernie laughed. "Haven't lost your sense of humor."

A sheriff's deputy came over, shotgun pointed down, although not completely down. Weapons are something I keep a close eye on.

"What's goin' on here?" he said.

"I was just saying that Frenchie hasn't lost his sense of humor."

"Bernie?" the deputy said.

"Hey, Waldo," said Bernie. "How's it going?"

"Hundred and seven in the shade and I'm out here with the scum of the earth—how do you think it's going?" Deputy Waldo said, the shotgun now pointed directly at the ground, just the way I like. "This Chet?"

"Yup."

"Heard about him." Deputy Waldo gave me a close look. Right away, just from a change in his eyes—tiny eyes and pretty cold until this moment—I could tell he liked me and my kind. "A pretty big dude," Waldo went on. "What's he weigh?"

"Getting him on the scale's not easy," Bernie said.

I remembered that game! Bernie tried to pick me up, maybe with some idea of standing with me on the scale. Lots of fun, but no one picks me up, amigo.

"A hundred plus," Bernie was saying. "And he's strong for his size."

"You got him from the K-9 program?"

"Basically."

"He flunked out—was what went down?" Waldo said. "Hard to believe."

"A long story," Bernie said.

And not one I wanted to dwell on at that moment. Flunked out on the very last day, with only the leaping test left, and leaping was my very best thing. The good part was I actually couldn't dwell on it for long, on account of the details growing hazier in my mind every day. I was pretty sure a cat was involved, and maybe some blood—but I might have been getting it all mixed up with Frenchie's blood. I'd never meant to do Frenchie any harm, just grab him by the pant leg, which was how we usually ended cases at the Little Detective Agency, but Frenchie had strangely chubby calves, and all of a sudden I'd found myself . . . best not to go there. Sometimes things happen before you even know it—let's leave it at that.

Meanwhile, Deputy Waldo was saying, "Is he allowed any treats?" He handed Bernie the shotgun, fished through his pockets. Allowed? That was a new one on me. "Don't have any dog treats as such," Waldo said. "But here's a Slim Jim, kind of a weakness of mine."

Not a whole Slim Jim—one end completely chewed off—but one thing was clear: Deputy Waldo and I were peas in a pod, although peas, in or out of the pod—and I had experience with both kinds—didn't do it for me at all. Also I was kind of confused on the weakness part. The very next moment, I was fully occupied, and none of that—peas, pods, weaknesses—mattered the least little bit.

When I tuned back in, Frenchie was talking to Waldo. "Wouldn't have another one of those hangin' around by any chance?"

Waldo took the shotgun back from Bernie. "You askin' me for a Slim Jim?"

"Very politely."

"Why would I give you a Slim Jim? You're the laziest son of a bitch on the whole goddamn crew." Waldo turned to Bernie. "Was he always a lazy son of a bitch, or is this just a special treat for me?"

My ears perked up at that. More treats? And how could Frenchie be the one to hand them out? There were no pockets in his orange jumpsuit, and he gave off not a whiff of treat, his scent being mostly a not unpleasant mixture of dried sweat, dandruff, and soft butter. Uh-oh, and something else, not good, a dried-up mushroomy smell that our neighbor, old Mrs. Parsons—now in the hospital—gave off, too, somewhat stronger in her case. Did Frenchie have what Mrs. Parsons had?

"His talents lie in other directions," Bernie said.

"Talent? He's got talent?"

"Frenchie has a head on his shoulders."

When they get praised, some humans gaze at the ground and do a foot-shuffling thing. Frenchie did it now.

"Puttin' me on, Bernie?" Waldo said.

Bernie shook his head. "Frenchie came up with this scheme for conning disabled Vietnam vets out of their benefits. One of them was a friend of ours, which was how we got to know Frenchie in the first place."

"He's not in for armed robbery?" Waldo said. "That's what he tells everybody."

"Armed robbery?" Bernie said. "Frenchie Boutette?"

Waldo turned to Frenchie, the shotgun barrel rising slightly, unsteady in the motionless air. "Conning disabled vets? That's despicable."

Frenchie raised his hands, plump little hands that reminded me immediately of his calves. I was suddenly very aware of my teeth and not much else. "Hardly any of those stup—of those heroic vets—lost anything worth thinking about. Bernie caught me practically right out of the gate."

Bernie gave Frenchie a hard look. "And Chet," he said.

"And Chet, of course. Goes without saying."

"I like hearing it said just the same," Bernie told him.

"Won't let it happen again," Frenchie said. "I've got nothing but respect for the Little Detective Agency." All at once, Frenchie went still, his eyes blanking in that strange way that means a human's gone deep in his own mind. They do a lot of that, maybe too much. No offense. "Bernie?" he said.

"Yeah?"

"Can we, uh, talk for a moment or two?"

"Sure. We're talking right now."

Frenchie shot Waldo a sidelong glance and lowered his voice. "I mean in private."

"Okay with you, Waldo?" Bernie said. "Frenchie wants to talk to me in private."

"Sure," Waldo said. "There's the T-Bone Bar and Grill in Dry Springs, not more than fifteen minutes' drive from here. Why don't you take Frenchie out for a beer, on me?"

Frenchie blinked. "Dressed like this? I'm not sure that's—oh." He turned to Bernie. "He's foolin' with me, right?"

"You're wrong, Bernie," Waldo said. "He's a moron." Waldo waved the back of his hand at Frenchie and walked away.

"If I'm such a moron," Frenchie said, "how come I got fourteen hundred on my SATs?"

"You took the SATs?" Bernie said.

"Manner of speaking," said Frenchie. "My kid brother Ralph took them for me, so it's basically me, DNA-wise. Ralph's what I wanted to talk to you about."

"You're looking to get him busted for the SAT scam, cut some kind of deal for yourself?" Bernie said.

"My own flesh and blood?" Frenchie said, putting his hand over his chest. "And even if I could, you know, get past that, the law wouldn't be interested in Ralph. He's a total straight arrow. The SAT caper was the only time in his whole life he even came close to the line. Which is how come I'm worried about him now."

"He's crossed the line?"

"Hard to imagine," Frenchie said. "But something's wrong for sure. Ralph's gone missing."

TWO

We moved to the other side of the road, away from Deputy Waldo and the work crew. A breeze rose in the distance. It stirred up a dust devil, a tumbleweed ball, and some scraps of paper and blew them in our direction, all of that stuff sort of dancing in a stopping-and-starting way. A few moments later, I felt the breeze in my face, like a hot breath: this was one of those breezes that come off the desert in summer. The air grew hotter and strangely heavy, pressing down like a weight. A scrap of paper came to rest at the feet of one of the prisoners across the road. He poked at it with his stick, but the breeze caught it again and carried it away. I considered chasing after that scrap of paper, but why? Did Bernie want me to? Then I would, goes without saying, but probably not just for fun, not in this heat. I turned to him.

"What do you mean," he was saying to Frenchie, "by missing?"

"Missing?" said Frenchie, sounding surprised. "Like nowhere around."

"But how would you know?" Bernie said.

"Huh?"

"Aren't you the one who isn't around?"

"You on something, Bernie? I'm right here in front of your face."

"But somewhat out of circulation."

"Oh, that," said Frenchie. "Don't mean I don't hear nothin'. My mama calls me every week. She hasn't seen Ralph in days and neither have Duke or Lord."

"And they are?"

"My brothers, of course. Other brothers, asides from Ralph."

"You have brothers named Duke, Lord, and Ralph?"

"What I said."

"And Frenchie is . . ."

"Just my nickname out here in the west on account of coming from Louisiana and all."

"Your real name being?"

"Baron."

"Baron Boutette."

"Correct."

"Are Duke and Lord like Ralph?"

"More like me."

"Not straight arrows."

"Not super straight, no," Frenchie said. "But here's something you need to understand about the whole family, from my mama on down—we don't go in for violence, hardly ever. It's a family tradition kind of thing. Our roots run deep."

"You're saying your mother's a crook?" Bernie said.

"That's harsh, Bernie. She's hardly done any time at all and she bakes the best pies you ever tasted."

"What kind?"

"You name it, but I'm partial to her sweet potato pie." Frenchie laughed. Human laughter is normally one of the nicest sounds there is, but Frenchie's laugh reminded me of crows. What's up with birds? Ever look at their little eyes, so unfriendly? Soaring around the big blue sky all the time: they should be in a better mood. "And not just because of the time," Frenchie was saying, "that she got a hacksaw to Lord inside of one."

"She hid a hacksaw in a sweet potato pie?"

"Didn't do much good—we're not so hot with tools, none of us excepting for Ralph. But Lord traded the saw to another inmate so at least he had smokes."

"And the lucky inmate?"

"Shot while escaping. But we're gettin' off topic here. The whole family's worried sick about Ralph. You're good at finding people. Can you find him?"

"No."

"No? Just like that, no? You dint even wait to hear the details."

"We do this for a living, Frenchie. We're not cheap—eight hundred a day plus expenses, against a two-thousand-dollar retainer. How are you going to come up with that?"

Frenchie took a quick glance across the road, where Deputy Waldo had a big bottle of water tilted up to his mouth and the guys on the crew had all paused to watch him drink. He lowered his voice. "Let me worry about the money."

"That never works. I have to worry about the money."

Hey! What about me? Didn't I worry about the money, too? And even both of us worrying about the money wasn't enough because we still didn't have any. Hawaiian pants were part of the problem. The night Bernie had that idea! Hawaiian pants, just like Hawaiian shirts, except they were pants! We were going to be rich! Bernie got so excited, he started dancing in the kitchen. And then I joined in—not dancing exactly, more like bounding around and then racing from room to room and back to the kitchen, skidding to a stop, tiles popping up all over the place. Now all the pants are filling up our self-storage in South Pedroia. Once we drove down there and had a look at them. We stood in the open doorway, light flowing over the clothing racks, the kind of indoor light you get sometimes that's full of golden dust. We haven't been back.

Frenchie lowered his voice some more. "How about I get you three grand by tonight?"

Bernie got a look in his eyes like he was going to smile. His smile is one of the best things going. I gave his face all my attention, but no smile came. "Sure, Frenchie," he said. "You do that."

Our place is on Mesquite Road. We've got the canyon in back, open country all the way to the airport in one direction and up to the Rio Arroyo Bridge in the other, and long ago, Bernie says, when his great-grandfather owned this whole stretch of the Valley it was all like that, nice and empty, but now houses lined both sides of the canyon and were even starting to creep down the sides in some places. Bernie has this dream—I know because once after he had a few drinks he told me about it—that one day we'd wake up and it would be the old way again. I checked first thing every morning for a long time after that, but now I often forget.

As we pulled into the driveway, Iggy started up inside the Parsonses' house next door. *Yip yip yip. Yip yip yip.* That was Iggy, a yipper through and through. Iggy's been my best pal for almost longer than I can remember—and sometimes actually longer, if that makes any sense—but he doesn't come out to play anymore, partly on account of some sort of electric fence problem and partly on account of the Parsonses being so old now, what with Mrs. Parsons in the hospital and Mr. Parsons on a walker. I could see Iggy standing in the side window, front paws against the glass and his weird stubby tail going crazy down below. I barked at him, a low rumbly bark that couldn't have been friendlier. That seemed to get Iggy going, not my intention at all. His yipping rose higher and higher in a way that hurt me deep in my ears. I barked louder, sending a message. It did no good.

"Chet!" Bernie said. "What the hell? Get in the house."

Me? This was on me? How come? I went inside, not realizing at first that my own tail was down, practically dragging on the floor in the front hall. I got it up, pronto, nice and high. Bernie always says never let them see you something or other, it might come to me later, but the point is: tail up.

We had drinks in the kitchen, bourbon for Bernie, water for me. As he filled the bowl at the sink, he clinked his glass against it and said, "Cheers." He took the check out of his front pants pocket, looked at it for a moment or two, and then—oh, no, tucked it away in the chest pocket of his shirt, just when I thought we had everything under control.

Bernie sat down at the computer. I went for a little roam around the house, ended up in Charlie's room. His mattress was bare. Charlie is Bernie's kid, and we don't see him much, Charlie now living with Leda, Bernie's ex-wife and her new husband, Malcolm, up in High Chaparral Estates, probably the fanciest neighborhood in the Valley. I hopped on the mattress and sniffed around, Charlie's scent—a bit like Bernie's, but without the funky part—real easy to pick up. I had a notion to lie down even though I wasn't tired, but then I heard the clink of Bernie adding more ice cubes to his drink, or possibly pouring another, and I went back to the kitchen.

Yes, a brand-new drink topped up pretty high. Bernie turned to me.

"Did a search for Ralph Boutette," he said. "And guess what?"

I waited.

"No hits."

Bernie sipped his bourbon. I went over to my water bowl, lapped up a sip or two of my own.

"See what this means?"

I did not. And even if I had, I was much more interested in the sound of a car approaching on our street. Was it slowing down as it neared the house? Yes. That made it even more interesting. I glanced at Bernie to see if he found it interesting, too, but he showed no sign he heard a thing. Human ears: a puzzler. Sometimes they're so small—take Suzie's ears, for example, Suzie being Bernie's girlfriend, but she'd taken a job far away and now Bernie's sleeps were restless—that it's not fair to expect them to do much hearing, although Bernie's ears aren't like that, not even close, so what's the story?

"With missing people," he said, "you get hits. Police department hits, reward hits, newspaper hits."

He rose, dropped more ice cubes into his glass, and tossed me one, which I caught in midair and crunched up in no time. Nothing like an ice cube to make your teeth tingle. My insides, still hot from the day even though we had the A/C on—never blasting, which was one of our things, at least Bernie's—started cooling down nicely. I had no complaints, in fact, felt tip-top.

"So therefore?" Bernie said.

I went still. The way we have the work divided up here at the Little Detective Agency, Bernie handles the so therefores, and what comes next is always important. But in the stillness I heard a car door close with a soft *thump* out on the street, and then came footsteps on our stone path, footsteps with a little *click-click* that meant high heels. I forgot about whatever I'd been waiting for and trotted to the front door. Leda often wore high heels, Suzie almost never. Other than that, I had no ideas.

Knock knock. Leda's was much quicker than this one, Suzie's more solid. I barked.

"Chet?" Bernie called.

Knock knock.

"Someone at the door?"

Oh, Bernie. I barked again. What else could I do?

He came into the hall: flip-flops, shorts, T-shirt, drink in hand.

Knock knock.

Bernie heard it this time. He put down the drink, smoothed his hair, opened the door.

Bernie's always the smartest human in the room, but the woman standing on the step was the kind of woman who could make it a close call. Not because of her brain so much, more on account of her shape, her little dress, the look in her eyes, the makeup around them. And the smell, a dead giveaway—although there was nothing dead about it—but maybe just to me. In a contest between the human sense of hearing and the human sense of smell there are only losers, no offense. But the point is a certain kind of woman has a bad influence on Bernie's braininess.

"Bernie Little?" she said.

I left out the voice.

"Um, yeah."

She became aware of me, a little late in the game in my opinion. "I'm not that comfortable around dogs," she said.

"You can be totally comfortable with Chet," Bernie said.

"He's so big."

"But very gentle."

She gazed at me, a narrowed, making-up-the-mind look in her eye. That just happens to be a look that bothers me, no telling why. I barked—not the low rumbly friendly kind, or the angry kind, or the kind where I'm warning you once and for all; this was just the hi-it's-me kind, but in a big way.

She jumped back. "Oh my God. Is he going to bite me?"

"Never. That wouldn't happen. He never bites. Cool it, big guy, for Christ sake."

Christ came up a lot, but I'd never met him; something to look forward to, maybe. I cooled it. At the same time: never bites? What was with that? There were dudes—true, not many and always the worst kind—now breaking rocks in the hot sun who knew different.

"How—how can I help you?" Bernie said.

"My name's Vannah," she said. "Vannah Boutette. I'm Frenchie's wife."

"Frenchie has a wife like—" Bernie cut himself off; why, I didn't know. I'm always interested in what he has to say.

"Yes?" Vannah said. "Go on."

"Uh, nothing," Bernie said. "Nice to meet you. I'm Bernie."

"We've already gotten past that," Vannah said. "Aren't you supposed to be smart? I've got three grand in cash which I'd like to give you without getting my goddamn arm bit off, if possible."

Bernie glanced at her arm. A nicely shaped female human arm, perhaps, but not much there to sink your teeth into.

"Come in," said Bernie.

THREE

Vannah Boutette crossed her legs, uncrossed them, crossed them again. Bernie's gaze went to the ceiling, the floor, back to her legs. We were in the office, just down the hall from the kitchen, Bernie at the desk, Vannah on the couch, me on the rug, a comfortable, nubbly rug with a circus elephant pattern. I was fond of the pattern, had once gotten to know a circus elephant named Peanut quite well, but no time for that now.

"You work out of your home?" Vannah said.

"Any problem with that?" Bernie said.

"Why would I have problem with that? I work out of my place, too."

"Yeah? What line of, uh . . ."

"Let's call it importing," Vannah said.

"What kind of goods?"

"Good goods, bad goods, everything in between." Vannah glanced around the room, taking in the hat stand with Bernie's baseball cap collection—he'd pitched for Army before throwing out his arm, and even so could still fling the tennis ball a country mile, whatever that might be—the basket of kids' blocks lying

The Sound and the Furry

in one corner—the room was meant for a little sister or brother
that never came along—and the waterfall pictures on the walls.
Humans get an oh-my look on their face when they're impressed.
I wasn't seeing it on Vannah's. What if she knew that the biggest
waterfall picture hid the safe, and that in the safe were Bernie's
grandfather's watch, our most valuable possession, plus the .38
Special? We hadn't had any gunplay in way too long.

"You get eight hundred a day plus expenses?" Vannah said.

"Yup."

"What if I said seven?"

"Try it."

"Seven."

"Nice meeting you."

Vannah laughed. "Frenchie mentioned your sense of humor.
He thinks the world of you."

"He does?"

"Which is why you're his first choice for finding Ralph."

"You know Ralph?"

"Why wouldn't I know Ralph? He's my brother-in-law."

Bernie nodded. He's a great nodder, has different nods with
different meanings. This one could have meant anything.

"He was best man at the wedding," Vannah went on.
"Frenchie's and mine."

"Where did you two tie the knot?"

"I hate that expression."

"Sorry."

"Don't you? It's so negative. Why not say shackled together
and be done with it?"

"I see your point."

"Married yourself?" Vannah said.

"Not at present."

"All the better."

Bernie looked at her, tilting his head how he does when he's seeing someone in a whole new way. The last person he'd used the head tilt on was Truffles Siminoni—a B-and-E type specializing in high-end restaurants—who'd immediately thrown up his hands—I love when they do that!—and said, "All right, you got me."

Did Bernie hope Vannah Boutette was about to cop to something? Would I soon be grabbing her by the pant leg, not so easy since she wasn't wearing pants? How was I going to do that, exactly? I realized my tongue was hanging out maybe a bit too much, and possibly drooling; I curled it back up in my mouth and sat up straight, a professional through and through.

"Frenchie and I got married at his mom's place in St. Roch," Vannah said, which didn't sound criminal to me, or even at all interesting.

But Bernie's eyebrows went up. Have I mentioned his eyebrows? Nice and thick and expressive, with a language all their own. Bernie was interested, no doubt about it. So, therefore, I was interested. Whoa! Had I just done a "so therefore"? My very first? Chet the Jet!

"St. Roch?" Bernie said.

"Down in bayou country," Vannah said. "That's where they're all from, the Boutettes. I didn't see the point of a church wedding. Been there, done that. More than once."

"Understood," Bernie said. "There's no right way of doing it."

"You can say that again."

But Bernie did not. Instead, he said, "I meant no single one right, um—"

"Whatever," said Vannah. "Here's a picture of Ralph." She rose, crossed over to the desk, took a photo from her purse—I caught a glimpse of a roly-poly glasses-wearing dude—and laid it in front of Bernie.

"Except for the, uh, shape, he doesn't look much like Frenchie," Bernie said.

"Tell me something I don't know," she said. Which Bernie could have done, no problem, but he kept his mouth shut. "Ralph turned out different from the others in just about every way."

"What does he do?"

"He's an inventor, I guess you'd say."

Inventor? A new one on me. I knew investor, especially of the golf-course subdivision type: we've sent one of those up to Northern State Correctional, me and Bernie. That was as far as I could take it, maybe farther.

"What has he invented?" Bernie said.

"Gizmos," said Vannah.

"Like?"

"Things. He gets them patented and sells the patents."

"I'm a little lost," Bernie said. Which made two of us: don't forget we're a lot alike in some ways, me and Bernie.

"What's your problem?" She gazed down at him.

He gazed up at her. "I ran a quick online search, came up with no hits for Ralph Boutette. That makes no sense if he's got patents."

Vannah blinked. "You think I'm making this up?"

"I don't think anything," Bernie said, which was one of my very favorites of all his lines; no one was funnier than Bernie. Him not thinking anything! "I'm just trying to figure this out."

Vannah glanced around, looked at me. "Maybe the patents are in his company name?"

"Which is?"

"Not sure, exactly," she said. "But something with Napoleon in it."

"Napoleon?"

"Ralph's dog."

"What sort of dog?"

"Huh? Does it matter? A horrible little dog, pug, maybe."

"Horrible in what way?"

"Hell, every way. And the dog's missing, too, come to think of it. One day they weren't on the houseboat anymore, just vanished off the face of the earth."

"Ralph lives on a houseboat?" Bernie said, turning to the keyboard and tapping away.

"Lives, works, everything."

"Here we go," said Bernie, eyeing the screen. "Napoleon Industrial Products, twenty-two hits."

"See?" said Vannah.

"Through a glass, darkly," said Bernie.

"Huh?" said Vannah. I was sort of with her on that, but not really. I'd never cross over on Bernie.

"Nothing," Bernie said. "What's the name of the houseboat?"

"Little Jazz."

Bernie put his hands on the desk, leaned back. *"Little Jazz?"*

"That's what I said."

"Named after Roy Eldridge?"

Vannah shrugged. "Never heard of him, but the Boutettes know a ton of people down in bayou country, so anything's possible."

Was I following this right? Vannah didn't know Roy Eldridge? His trumpet did things to my ears, the best kind of things, especially when he played on "If You Were Mine" with Billie Holiday, which we blast in the Porsche just about every single day.

"Tell you what," Bernie said. "We'll take the case."

Because Vannah didn't know Roy Eldridge? Bernie was full of surprises, just one of the lovable things about him.

"Yeah?" said Vannah. She was surprised, too, no doubt about it.

"Yeah," Bernie said.

Vannah opened her purse again, handed Bernie a fat roll. Not the fattest in my experience, but it was always nice to see a fat roll coming our way. "Count it," she said.

"I trust you," said Bernie.

"You do?"

"On the three grand being here," he said.

For a moment, Vannah's forehead wrinkled up, like she was going to get mad. Then she laughed. Bernie laughed, too. Then he started counting the money. Vannah laughed some more.

"Three grand on the nose," Bernie said, although he didn't put it anywhere near his nose. "This money clean?"

Interesting question. I actually picked up a whiff of shrimp coming off those bills. Had Bernie done the same? That would have been a shocker. Bernie had a nice-size nose for a human, but it didn't do much, as I'd learned many times. But why had he just brought noses into the conversation? I got the feeling I wasn't quite in the picture. It didn't bother me at all!

"Do you care?" Vannah said.

"Yeah," Bernie said.

"Then it's clean."

Bernie stuffed the roll in his—oh, no—chest pocket, somehow dislodging the lawyer's check already in there. The check wafted down under the desk and out of sight.

"Okay," Bernie said, leaning back in a relaxed sort of way, "tell me everything you know about Ralph's disappearance, starting with how you heard about it."

Vannah returned to the couch, maybe crossing, uncrossing and recrossing her legs again. I'm pretty sure that happened but not totally, on account of how worried I was about that check. I moved over to the desk, a desk with sides that came fairly close to the floor, meaning I had to crouch down on my belly and wriggle forward to squeeze underneath. Even just getting my head under wasn't that easy. I had to push up with the muscles at the back of my neck, actually sort of lifting the whole desk somewhat off the floor, just to get started.

". . . last week," Vannah was saying. "Sometimes he takes his Zodiac up into the bayous so the boys went looking."

"The boys meaning Lord and—hey, Chet, what's going on down there?"

Bernie reached down, his hand feeling around. For a moment, all those fingers seemed to be moving like tiny humans with minds of their own, a real scary thought that I hoped would never come again. Then they found my head and started giving me a nice scratch. Nice scratches are always nice, but wasn't I down here wriggling under the desk for a reason? I tried to think. I thought: *Nice scratches are always nice.* I closed my eyes and enjoyed the moment. The sound of their voices flowed over me, quite pleasant, especially Bernie's.

"Right, Lord and Duke," Vannah said. "Not boys except in the good ol' way. The point is there was no sign of Ralph anywhere."

"Has he ever done anything like this before?" Bernie said.

"Gone missing, you mean?"

"Or made himself scarce," Bernie said. "He sounds like a loner. Loners have a way of going off by themselves."

"Ralph's a loner for sure," said Vannah. "But it was Mami's birthday last Tuesday and he didn't show. No way he'd ever be disrespectful like that."

"Mami being?"

"Their mother," Vannah said.

"Frenchie mentioned her."

"Head of the clan."

"A criminal sort of clan, if I understood Frenchie properly."

Then came a silence, maybe not the friendly kind. The lovely scratching—right in the perfect spot between my ears, impossible for me to get to myself—stopped. I opened my eyes. And right in front of my face, was it possible? Yes, a bag of Cheetos, practically full! How could that have happened? How long had it been there? I didn't worry about any of that. This was turning out to be one of the best days of my whole life. All I had to do was—

"Chet! What the hell! Cool it right—"

Then came a crash, kind of big, and the next thing I knew Bernie's desk was sort of on its side. That was very wrong and if I had played any part in it, that was wrong, too. Bernie was on his feet gazing down at me with not the best look on his face. Vannah's eyes were opened wide and she seemed to have jumped into the small space between the couch and the wall. And the bag of Cheetos? Now nowhere in sight. But on the rug, practically right at my feet, lay a small scrap of paper, somewhat like a . . . a check? The check! I remembered the check! And in no time at all I'd snatched it up, stepped forward, and offered it to Bernie.

"What's this?" Bernie said. He took the check, smoothed it off, wiped away some moisture that might have gotten on it. Then he gave his head a shake like he wasn't seeing right, patted his chest pocket, pulled his shirt forward so he could peer down into the pocket—a button snapping off his shirt at that moment, which I snatched right out of the air and swallowed, not even thinking twice; was I on a roll or what?—and then his face softened in a lovely way and he said, "Good boy."

"What's going on?" Vannah said.

"Nothing," said Bernie, standing the desk back up. "Nothing at all."

"You're still taking the case?" Vannah came out from behind the couch.

"Why wouldn't I be?"

"Just wondering about the nuts and bolts," Vannah said, losing me completely. Nuts and bolts weren't our department: when they came springing out of the Porsche, we always went right to Nixon Panero, our ace mechanic. "Specifically do you, ah, put the dog in a kennel when you're on the road?"

Kennel? Me? I tried to fit those two together in my mind and couldn't.

"Chet in the kennel?" Bernie said. I could see on his face that he couldn't fit them together either. "Chet and I are partners." His voice hardened in a thrilling way that made the fur at the back of my neck stand straight up. "Maybe Frenchie can fill you in on his capabilities."

Vannah held up her hand. "Whatever you say. No offense."

What a very proud moment in my life! And not spoiled at all by the fact that I now puked up Bernie's shirt button; a tiny thing, but it had disagreed with me.

"Let's go celebrate," Bernie said when Vannah was gone. "Money's burning a hole in my pocket."

Oh, no—anything but that. We'd had some bad experiences with fire, including one very scary night involving a firebomb and a crummy motel down Mexico way. I sniffed the air, detected no smoke or any hint of fire at all, so it had to be one of Bernie's jokes. There was no one funnier than Bernie, in case that's not yet clear.

We went to the Dry Gulch Steakhouse and Saloon, one of

our favorite restaurants in the whole Valley, with a patio where me and my kind are welcome. Sergeant Rick Torres, our buddy from Valley PD Missing Persons was there, and Bernie started telling him about the new case.

"Took it for three reasons," Bernie said. I tried to concentrate, but my steak tips were ready: I could smell them on the other side of the swinging door that led to the kitchen.

"Money, money, money?" said Rick.

"Four, if you include the money," Bernie said. "Reason number one," he began, but then the waitress arrived with my steak tips on a paper plate. She set it on the floor, me sort of helping her, and I missed the rest of whatever Bernie had to say.

FOUR

Night had fallen by the time we left the Dry Gulch patio and walked out to the Porsche, although night never actually falls, in fact, it rises from the ground up. The sky darkens the very last. Here in the Valley it never goes completely black, just dialing down to dark pink, especially in the direction of the downtown towers. I was sort of thinking about all that, but not hard, when I noticed a shadowy dude standing near our ride.

I didn't bark or make a sound, just stiffened a bit. Bernie felt it even though we weren't touching, and right away peered over at the Porsche. The dude came forward, a tall dude wearing a dark suit and a small-brim cowboy hat, walking the way dudes in cowboy boots walk, his hands empty and out where we could see them.

"Bernie Little?" he said.

"That's right," Bernie said, stopping an empty space or two from the Porsche. I stopped, too.

"And this must be Chet," the dude said. "Heard a lot about him."

Bernie said nothing. Silence is a tool. He's told me that, and more than once. I love it every time he tells me, no matter what it means.

Silence, silence, and then the dude filled it in. Filled it in with talk, which is what usually happens. Once or twice a special silence of Bernie's has gotten filled in with gunfire, but this dude's hands were still empty. "My name's Rugh," he said. "Cale Rugh. I'm with Donnegan's, Houston office."

"Uh-huh," said Bernie, Donnegan's being a sort of competitor, but way bigger. We'd met some of their agents at the Great Western Private Eye Convention a while back. Bernie gave the keynote speech, and it couldn't have gone better—the Mirabelli brothers and all those other guys at the back and down the sides plus a few in front must have been real tired to have zonked out the way they did—but I didn't remember this dude.

"Somewhere we could go for a quick talk?" Rugh said.

"Here is good," Bernie said.

"It's confidential."

"We'll talk in low voices."

Rugh smiled, showing a lot of white teeth, not small for a human. His eyes showed nothing. "They warned me about you."

"Who's they?"

"Colleagues. They said you're a difficult son of a bitch. But you know what I told them?"

"That anyone who's any good in this business is a difficult son of a bitch," Bernie said.

Rugh's smile faded. A tall dude and even taller with the small-brim hat, but he seemed to shrink down toward Bernie's size. Not that Bernie's not tall—don't think that for a moment.

"I'm not going to do all your lines for you, Cale," Bernie said. "What's on your mind?"

Rugh took a quick glance around. We had the parking lot to ourselves. "We'd like you to consult on a case for us. A month's work, more or less. We'll double your rate—not your actual bargained-down rate but your asking. Makes thirty times sixteen hundred—forty-eight grand. Plus expenses. I've got a retainer check for ten grand in my pocket, if ol' Chet here will let me reach for it."

Bernie laughed. What was funny? Why wouldn't I let him give us a check? I was totally in favor. Let's see it, dude.

"Don't need to see it at the moment," Bernie said.

What was that? Why not?

"I think the case'll interest you," Rugh said, or something like that, hard for me to concentrate on account of that check remaining out of sight. All of a sudden we had checks, practically out the yingyang, but they were still giving us problems. Rugh said something about Alaska, mines, the environment, most of which went by in a kind of buzzing tangle, but mines were a big interest of Bernie's—we'd explored lots of old abandoned ones in the desert—and if the environment was about water, then Bernie was interested in that, too. As for Alaska, was that where Bernie said the old days were still around? Bernie was a big fan of the old days, in case that's not clear already.

"Who's the client?" Bernie said.

"That stays under wraps until takeoff," said Rugh.

"Takeoff?"

"Private jet. We're scheduled out of here at six a.m. sharp, nonstop to Fairbanks."

"Six a.m. tomorrow?"

"Yup."

Bernie shook his head. "It'll have to wait. We're on another assignment."

"Wait? It can't wait, Bernie. Thought I made the urgency of the situation crystal clear."

"Then we're out."

Rugh made a little breathing noise from his nose, actually a kind of laugh. I like the mouth kind better. "They mentioned this, too."

"Mentioned what?"

"That you're your own worst enemy. Come on, Bernie. What's this other case? Some grubby divorce shit?"

Bernie's head bobbed back the tiniest bit, kind of like he'd been hit. He hadn't been hit, and I knew that perfectly well, but just the same I got ready to do something about it, hard to explain. And at that very moment, I also felt Bernie's hand on my collar. My brown collar, in case you're interested: black is for dress-up.

"Even if it was grubby divorce shit," Bernie said, "which it happens not to be, we've committed to it, so that's that."

Rugh raised his hands, palms up. That's something I always like to see. "I apologize for the divorce crack. But we've all been there, let's not be naïve. Donnegan's has a whole department, for Christ sake."

"No apology necessary," Bernie said. "But we don't have any other departments here. We take 'em as they come in."

"Makes total sense," Rugh said. "And does you credit. You've got a great rep, maybe I should have put that front and center. But here's a thought— what if we took over this other case for you?"

"I don't think so," Bernie said.

"Whatever your quote was, we won't go over, if that's what's worrying you."

Bernie shook his head.

"A longtime client?" Rugh said. "Worried that we'll make off with one of your cash cows? We'll draw up a contract ruling that out. If you like, I'll meet with your client myself and—" something, something, but whoa! A cow was in the case, or possibly more than one? That wasn't good. I've had some experience with cows. It's not so easy to get them to do what you want them to do, especially if it involves moving. Also, they have a way of looking at you that I don't like one little bit.

"Thanks anyway, Cale," Bernie said. "But the answer's no."

Meaning Bernie's take on cows was the same as mine. I wasn't surprised.

Rugh flashed his smile again, the upper half of his face lost in the shadow of his hat brim. "Suit yourself, Bernie." He held out his hand, a big hand, maybe the slightest bit bigger than Bernie's. They shook. "Good luck with the case. I'm betting it's something really special."

"I wouldn't say that," Bernie said.

"No?"

We got in the car. Bernie waved. Rugh waved back. He watched us drive out of the Dry Gulch parking lot. I turned so I could watch him watch. He took out his phone and walked toward a big, dark-colored car. Someone was waiting in the driver's seat.

Back home, Bernie got on the phone, hit speaker.

"Mitch? Bernie Little here."

"Hey, Bernie. How they hangin'?"

"You say that every time," Bernie said.

"So?" said Mitch. "It's my regular form of greeting."

"With women, too?"

"You suggesting that's why I never get any?"

"It's on the list," Bernie said.

Mitch laughed. Fat guys have their own kind of laugh, and Mitch Crudup was a fat guy and also a good pal. For one thing, he liked sharing his food. Hadn't seen Mitch in way too long. "What can I do for you, Bernie?"

"Know an agent named Cale Rugh, supposedly working out of your Houston office?"

"No supposedly about it," Mitch said. "What have you done now?"

"Not following you, Mitch."

"Rugh's a heavy hitter, works out of special ops."

"Donnegan's has something called special ops?" Bernie said.

"Innermost sanctum," Mitch said. "Ex-CIA types, even a few ex-KGB, according to rumor."

"My knees are shaking."

I checked Bernie's knees. He was in his boxers so I could take a good close look. They weren't moving in the slightest! What was that all about? My gaze wandered to the wound on one of his legs. Poor Bernie! He got that wound in the war and sometimes—only when he was at his very tiredest—it made him limp, but not a lot, hardly even noticeable.

"Chet? What are you—"

All of a sudden, Bernie was looking down at me and I was . . . giving that wound a quick lick? Had he brought up something along these lines before? Quite possibly. But I only wanted to make it better. And the next moment, I saw in his eyes that he knew that, too. He gave me a pat. We were square, on the up-and-up, cool with each other to the max.

"Chet there?" Mitch said.

"Very much so," said Bernie, which I didn't quite get. You're here or you're not here, unless I'm missing something.

"Give him a treat for me."

Mitch: a gem.

"He just had a big dinn—Chet! Down!"

"He knows 'treat,' huh?"

"Among others."

Mitch laughed again. *Invite yourself over, Mitch. Bring a little something.* But Mitch didn't do that. Instead, he said, "What's special ops want with you?"

"Consultation."

"They wanted to hire you as a consultant?"

"What's so astonishing?"

"Did I sound astonished? Must be a bad connection. Nothing against you, Bernie—you're . . . how to put it? One of a kind. But I've never heard of Donnegan's hiring a consultant. Everything around here stays under the dome."

"What dome?"

"There's no actual dome," Mitch said. "It's more of a company metaphor. Point is, we don't go outside, no way, no how. What's the case?"

"It's out of state and involves mining. Names and all the intel were going to be forthcoming when I signed on, which I did not."

"You turned it down?"

"Yup."

"The money?"

"Nope. Money was good."

"Then what?"

"I'd already accepted another assignment."

"Divor—"

"Don't say it. Wouldn't matter what it was—we can only do a case at a time."

"And Cale Rugh couldn't come up with a workaround for that?"

"Not for lack of effort."

"I'll bet," Mitch said.

"You know him?" said Bernie.

"Met him once or twice. Those slow-talking Texans can be much smarter than they seem."

"I'm aware of that," Bernie said. "I was born in Texas myself."

"But you're not slow talking."

"Neither was he."

"Want me to touch base with him?"

"Nah," Bernie said. "I was just making sure he was legit."

"As legit as anyone in our business," Mitch said.

"Now I'm scared," Bernie said.

Mitch was still laughing when he hung up.

Bernie got out his old Army duffel bag, started throwing things into it. "Twenty-hour drive, give or take," he said. "Or we could fly and rent wheels on the other end. Flying means a crate."

He looked down at me. I looked up at him. Crate? That brought back memories, almost totally faded away. But not quite, amigo.

"We'll drive," Bernie said. He zipped up the duffel. "Lie down, big guy. Get some shut-eye. We leave at dawn."

I lay down at the foot of Bernie's bed and closed my eyes, followed his movements by sound as sleep came fuzzing all around me. He picked up the duffel with a soft grunt, carried it to the front hall, let himself out, walked onto the driveway, his foot crunching on something crunchy, maybe a twig. Then came a squeak from the trunk opening, the thud of the duffel getting tossed in, and—another footstep-on-a-twig crunch? I'd kind of been expecting the thump of the trunk closing. There it was: a thump. But not a trunk-closing-type thump. This was different, a thump I didn't like at all. The next thing I knew I was charging out the front door.

Oh, no! Bernie was on his knees behind the car, blood dripping down his face. A man with a ski mask covering his own face stood over him, a tire iron raised high. He didn't see me coming until it was too late. Too late for him, not for me. I caught his forearm between my jaws as he was swinging that horrible tire iron down at Bernie's head, caught it good and bit my hardest, my top teeth and bottom teeth meeting up deep inside his arm. He screamed, tried to twist himself free, and hey! Somehow got his other hand on the tire iron and whipped it sideways at my head. Whack! A black hole sprang up out of nowhere in my mind and started growing.

Fight it off, big guy, fight it off. That was Bernie's voice talking inside me. It hardly ever happens, but when it does I pay attention. I rose to my feet in the driveway—Bernie was rising, too, wiping blood from his eyes—and saw the masked guy running down Mesquite Road, supporting his bitten arm with his free hand. A motorcycle was parked next to my fire hydrant down the block; not actually mine, I suppose, but no time for that now. I took off.

The man mounted the bike, glanced back, and saw me coming. The engine roared. I dug in, my claws tearing into the pavement, still hot and soft from the day. My heart pounded like some huge engine of its own, driving away all traces of that black hole in my mind. The man's hand—the only useful one now—squeezed the throttle and the bike rose almost straight up in a wheelie, back tire screaming. I sprinted my very fastest, came real close to catching up, and at the last possible moment leaped the very most powerful leap of my whole life. I hit him on the shoulder, hit him hard. The bike went spinning across the road and the man flew high into the air, his mouth—visible through the mouth opening in the mask—a big round black hole of its own. He landed on his head and lay still.

FIVE

Fritzie Bortz, a highway patroller pal of ours—a pal even though he'd written us up once to make his quota, whatever that was, and then had done it again!—was the first cop on the scene. He pulled up on his bike, had some trouble with the kickstand, almost fell over. Fritzie was a pretty poor bike rider, had caused lots of accidents.

He dismounted, came over to us, his belly stretching his shirt and hanging over his belt in a friendly sort of way. The biker lay motionless on the road, mask ripped to shreds and face exposed. It was a face we didn't know. I did know that the smell of the living leaves very quickly and the biker's was totally gone already.

"What's with your forehead?" Fritzie said.

Bernie had his T-shirt in his hand, was pressing it against the cut on his forehead. "Nothing," he said. "How come you're here?"

"How come?" Fritzie said. "I'm a cop, Bernie."

"Pretty far from your beat," Bernie said.

"My beat is the whole Valley, freeway-wise," Fritzie said. "I roam the land. But the fact is I was on a break just over at Donut

Heaven when the call came in." He glanced down at the biker. "Dead?"

"Yup," Bernie said.

"What happened?" said Fritzie.

Bernie started explaining things. My name came up once or twice in what sounded like a very nice way, but my mind kept having thoughts about Donut Heaven, my favorite place for crullers, and don't get me started on the bear claws. Lucky Fritzie!

Fritzie gave the biker a closer look. "Think he's over seventeen?"

"Way over," Bernie said.

"Then I can't write him up on a twenty-eight dash nine sixty-four."

"What's that?"

"Helmet law violation."

"He's dead."

"I'd have to check on the finer points," Fritzie said.

An ambulance drove up, and then a couple of cruisers and an unmarked car. Some uniformed cops came over, plus Captain Stine wearing a dark suit. Captain Stine was a very watchful dude with deep dark eyes and a sharp kind of nose. He used to be Lieutenant Stine and had gotten to be Captain Stine on account of us, but in ways I couldn't remember exactly or even not exactly. The point is, we'd always been careful around him and still were.

"What's with your forehead?" Stine said.

"Nothing," said Bernie.

Stine gazed down at the biker. "Dead, huh?"

Bernie nodded.

"Take me through it."

Bernie took him through it. Meanwhile, the back doors of the ambulance opened up and out came Doc Devine, an EMT buddy of ours. Doc Devine had been an actual doctor back when we'd first known him, not pals at all at that time, and then had done a spell up at Northern Correctional by reason of us busting him—and now we were pals. What a world!

"Hey, Chet," he said, giving me a pat. "Lookin' good, big guy." I bumped up against him in my palliest way. Doc was a little dude, which I'd forgotten to take into account, but he didn't fall all the way flat down, so no harm done.

Meanwhile, Bernie and Captain Stine were squatting on either side of the biker. Stine snapped on surgical gloves, checked all the biker's pockets, finding nothing, and then rolled back one of the biker's sleeves. He raised the limp arm, shone a flashlight on the inside of his wrist, revealing a small tattoo.

"See this?" he said.

"A Q?" Bernie said.

"Stands for Quieros. Mean anything to you?"

"Besides the fact that *quiero* means 'I want'?" Bernie said. "Nope."

"Haven't heard of the Quieros?"

"Thought I made that clear."

Stine glared at Bernie over the biker's body. "Why are you like this?"

"Like what?" Bernie said.

"Like the way you are," Stine said. "A son of a bitch."

Bernie smiled. There was blood on his teeth, but not much. "Some combination of heredity and environment," he said.

Stine smiled, too. Had I ever seen him smile before? It was a small smile, and quickly gone, but his eyes joined in, which is always the best.

"Quieros sort of means I Wants," said Stine. "I think it's supposed to be funny."

"I don't get it," Bernie said. I was totally with him on that. We're a lot alike in some ways, me and Bernie; don't forget that.

"They're a gang," Stine said. "Kind of new, originally from Central America somewhere."

"And the name is the mission statement?" Bernie said.

"You got it," Stine said. "They have wants. Sure you haven't heard of them?"

"Why do you keep asking?"

"Because this guy just tried to take you out." Stine let go of the biker's arm. It fell heavily to the pavement, bounced up the tiniest bit, then lay still. "I always wonder about motive in situations like this. Maybe your mind works different."

Uh-oh. Was Stine saying something bad about Bernie's mind? Right there was why you always had to keep an eye on him. Didn't he know that Bernie was always the smartest human in the room? How could anyone miss that?

The biker's eyes were open. Bernie gazed down into them. The biker's eyes gazed back in a way that bothered me. Wasn't Bernie or Stine going to reach out and gently close the lids? Proper procedure at a time like this, in my opinion; I'd seen it done lots of times. But not now. "Haven't got a clue," Bernie said. "Car thief surprised in the act?"

"Seems unlikely," Stine said. "What with this Harley Softail on the scene"—he nodded his chin at the wrecked bike now lying in the gutter—"and no one to drive it away."

"Mistaken identity?" Bernie said.

"Can't rule it out completely," Stine said. "But just about, in the case of someone like you."

"Someone like me?"

"How about I revise that to someone in your profession? Can't help making enemies, no matter what a sweetheart you might be inside."

At least Stine hadn't missed that: Bernie was a sweetheart inside. But did we have enemies? I myself liked most of the perps and gangbangers we'd come across. And they liked us. Take Whispering Hex Voidman, for example, who on his very first day out on parole made a point of dropping in with some antler snacks just for me. Those antler snacks: a dream come true. And dreams coming true happens a lot in my life! I often dream about antler snacks, for example. Maybe you do, too. All of that probably fits together in a way that might come to me later. Too bad old Hex had boosted the antlers from Petco and ended up back behind bars by dinnertime, but that wasn't the point. The point was, I couldn't think of any enemies.

"What might be useful," Stine was saying, "is if you came up with an enemies list and we put our heads together over it."

"We could also turn the A/C way up and sit around the fire," Bernie said. I started panting, not sure why.

"Huh?" Stine said.

"That's another thing Nixon liked to do."

Stine rose. I listened for the knee crack that often happens when humans rise like that, and there it was. Little pleasures are all around. "Don't start," Stine said.

On what? The only Nixon I knew was our mechanic, Nixon Panero, and there was no fireplace in his shop.

Stine walked to one of the cruisers, leaned against it in a tired sort of way, took out his phone. Doc Devine came over.

"What's with your forehead?" he said.

"Nothing," said Bernie.

"Let's have a look-see," Doc said.

Bernie dabbed the wound with his T-shirt one more time, let

Doc have a look-see. I had a look-see, too. Poor Bernie. He had a deep gash on his forehead, still seeping blood.

Doc peered at the gash. "Gonna need stitches."

Stitches? I'd had stitches on my head once, back at a time Bernie and I had had a dustup with some no-good Russian dudes. Stitches on the head meant wearing one of those horrible cones around your neck for days and days. Bernie wasn't going to like that.

"Okay," Bernie said. "Let's do it."

"I can't do it," Doc said. "You have to go to the ER."

"You forgot how to stitch?" Bernie said.

"You know it's not that," Doc said.

"Then let's get it done."

Doc glanced around, lowered his voice. "It's illegal."

Bernie called over to Captain Stine. "Doc here's going to stitch me up."

"Doc?" said Captain Stine.

"Yes, sir?"

"When you're done I've got a couple skin tags you can snip off."

"No problem," said Doc. "Depending where they're situated."

Bernie and Doc went over to the ambulance. Bernie sat on the back bumper. Doc dabbed something on his forehead, threaded a needle. "This might smart a bit."

And Bernie, as I must have made clear already, was pretty damn smart himself, so this was going to go smoothly. In went the needle. Bernie's face showed nothing. I laid down on the road, curled up a bit, not sure why.

"All set," Doc said. "And a nice piece of handiwork, if I say so myself. You're going to look even more beautiful than before."

"That's a scary thought."

Uh-oh. Bernie was scared? Because of the neck cone? I didn't blame him. I waited for the cone to appear, but it never did. Fritzie mounted his bike, got it started after a few tries, and drove off. A wrecker rumbled up, loaded what was left of the Harley and took it away. The uniform cops snapped lots of pictures, picked bits of this and that off the street and dropped them in evidence bags, and then they left, too. Doc and the other EMT rolled the body onto a stretcher and slid it in the ambulance. Captain Stine got in the unmarked car, paused before closing the door.

"If anything happens that I should know about," he said, "I want to know about it."

"I hear you," Bernie said.

Stine gave him a long look. Was he wondering about Bernie's ears? That was my only thought. He drove away, the ambulance following. We were alone. Heat rose up from the pavement. Bernie's eyes seemed to be on something far away. He gave me a pat. I noticed for the first time that lights were on in the nearby houses. They went off one by one.

Bright and early the next morning we were on the road, heading straight into the rising sun.

"Best part of the day, big guy," Bernie said, as we passed the very last abandoned development and hit open country.

I couldn't have agreed more. I sat up my tallest in the shotgun seat, wonderful smells streaming by so fast I could hardly keep up: sagebrush—such a strong scent, always reminding me of Leda'a parmesan sage pork shoulder recipe, actually her only dish and not a favorite of Bernie's, meaning I always got lots; greasewood, which was kind of like mesquite but oilier; rocky smells like chalk and iron; plus all kinds of poop—javelina, buzzard, snake, coyote, cougar, goat, lizard, human. And all that was from just one sniff! I was having the time of my life.

"It's a big country, Chet," Bernie said after a while. And he was so right: it stretched on and on to where it finally met the sky. "You're going to see the Mississippi." I had no idea what that was, but I got excited just the same. Bernie glanced over at me. "Something to look forward to, I know," he said. "But that's not why I took the case."

No? Had I already heard something on this subject? I came close to remembering, so close it was almost as good as if I'd done it. Or even better!

"Three reasons," he said, which meant this wouldn't be easy, since I don't go past two, a perfect number in my opinion. "Put together, they add up to fate. First, there's the name of the town the Boutettes come from—St. Roch. St. Roch, big guy—patron saint of dogs. Second, Ralph Boutette's company is named after his dog, Napoleon, also missing. Third—"

The phone buzzed. Bernie hit the button.

"Bernie?"

It was Suzie. I missed her, and hearing her voice made me miss her even more, which was kind of strange because here she was, sort of. Suzie was Bernie's girlfriend, if I've left that out. We'd had happy times when she was a reporter for the *Valley Tribune*, but now she'd gone to the *Washington Post*, which was a no-brainer, Bernie said. Maybe if he'd used his brain, Suzie would have stayed and he'd be happier, Bernie's brain having proved itself time and time again in our work at the Little Detective Agency.

"Hey, Suzie," he said, and all of a sudden I could see Charlie in his face. Charlie's smell is always in his bedroom, but it fades between visits.

"Guess what," Suzie said.

"You're going to be on *The Tonight Show*."

Suzie laughed. "I actually might be on a local cable news roundup in September. But I'm calling because I've got the whole Labor Day weekend off. I was thinking of coming home."

Bernie turned to me, and quick and softly said, "I'm an idiot." Then he raised his voice back to normal. "That would have been great. Any interest in meeting up in New Orleans instead?"

"New Orleans? What's gotten into you?"

Bernie laughed and started in on a long explanation. Partway through I realized he was going over the case. What a great chance to wrap my mind around the whole enchilada! But instead, my mind drifted over to experiences I'd had with enchiladas, some better than others, and the opportunity slipped on by.

Bernie was at his cheerfullest when he hung up. "Practically a paid vacation, Chet—we're on a roll." He dialed up some music, cranked the volume. We listened to all our favorites: "Sea of Heartbreak," "Death Don't Have No Mercy," "After You've Gone," and of course "If You Were Mine." When Roy Eldridge hit that last part on his trumpet—the hair on the back of my neck standing straight up—Bernie said, "And that's reason number three—the name of Ralph Boutette's houseboat. *Little Jazz.* He sounds like the kind of guy we're going to like."

Wow! I couldn't wait. We zoomed across the big country. I felt huge.

Sometime later, Bernie said, "If we can find him."

Who was he talking about? Kind of a puzzler. But if people are missing, we always find them, here at the Little Detective Agency. Except for that one time on the trail of a little girl. We'd roared through the night, pedal to the metal, Bernie leaning forward like that would make us go faster. Both of us leaning forward, if you want the truth, and it did make us go faster. We got there too late just the same. I'm a pretty good forgetter, but I can't seem to forget the moment we opened that horrible broom closet.

I went back down to normal size; which is still pretty big, amigo.

SIX

I opened my eyes. Nighttime, which I'd already known just from the feel. I was curled up on the shotgun seat, air streaming by. Strange air, much heavier than in the Valley, and kind of wet, if that makes sense: wet air but with no rain. I glanced up at Bernie, caught sight of the black zigzag pattern of the stitches on his forehead, his skin all green from the light of the dash. He hardly looked like Bernie! I closed my eyes.

A dream rose up out of the darkness, a lovely dream that began with she-barking across the canyon in back of our place on Mesquite Road and the next thing I knew I was right there with her, the two of us in the shade of a sweet-smelling eucalyptus tree. Oh, what a moment! Why couldn't it go on forever? But it didn't and not only that, it took a quick turn for the worse. Bernie and Mr. Parsons were gazing down at me, and I was caught in a circle of light, just like a perp down at the station. Mr. Parsons showed Bernie a photo of a puppy.

"Spitting image," Bernie said.

"Right after I took that picture," Mr. Parsons said, "I heard a woman calling for him and the little critter took off."

"Catch the name?" said Bernie.

"Shooter," Mr. Parsons said.

He started laughing in his normal, friendly old-dude way, but then his laughter got scary and wild. Doc Devine came and threw him in the ambulance. Bernie gazed down at me, not pleased. Whatever it was, I didn't do it! I opened my eyes.

And there was Bernie, gazing down at me, yes, but not with not-pleased eyes, far from it. "Bad dreams, big guy? You were whimpering pretty good there."

Whimpering? Oh, no. I sat up straight at once, a total pro on the job and ready for anything, and that was when I noticed we were parked outside a small motel, empty night all around.

"Welcome to Texas, Chet," Bernie said, giving my head a kind of rumple. "Let's get some shut-eye."

I wasn't actually that keen on more shut-eye at the moment, but if Bernie said shut-eye, then shut-eye it was. I glanced around at Texas, saw not much.

"But first," he said, opening the cooler, "how about some chow?"

He had roast beef sandwiches in there? When had that happened? Bernie: just when you think he's done amazing you, he amazes you again.

Crack of dawn the next morning we were back on the road again, speeding toward the sun, which actually wasn't up yet, except for the first tiny blazing curve. The air got heavier and the land got greener.

"No one ever said 'Go east, young man,'" Bernie said. I myself certainly couldn't recall hearing it. Bernie: right again. "And it just feels wrong, like there's a magnet pulling at the tailpipe." That didn't sound good. Did it mean the tools would be coming out soon? I hoped not: we had bad luck with the tools.

I spotted a blue lake in the distance, and then another, forgot all about whatever had been bothering me. We had no lakes in the Valley except for Lago Linda, which was always dry. Also, from not too far away came the smell of the ocean. I knew that smell on account of the time we'd gone to San Diego. We'd surfed, me and Bernie! But the point was that wherever we were now they had water out the yingyang. Water was one of Bernie's biggest worries. I checked his face carefully for signs of worry and saw none, which made total sense. He probably hadn't smelled the ocean, but no way he'd missed those lakes, shining in the sun.

The phone buzzed. "Bernie? It's Vannah."

"Hi."

"How's it going?"

"No complaints."

"Where are you?"

"About a hundred miles east of Houston."

"You're making good time." No surprise there: we almost always had a good time. "Slight change in plan," Vannah went on.

"Yeah?" Bernie said. The expression on his face stayed the same and so did anything else you could see, but I felt him growing more alert inside, and actually smelled it, too, just a bit. The smell drifted up my nose and suddenly I was more alert, too, just another one of those hard-to-explain things that come along in life.

"Instead of heading right on down to St. Roch," Vannah said, "how about stopping off in the city? The boys are up there at the moment and they can give you a quick walk-through."

"The boys?"

"I'm sure I mentioned them. My other brothers-in-law? Lord and Duke? The boys?"

"I didn't realize they were underage," Bernie said.

Vannah laughed. "You're not married as I recall."

"Correct."

"Seeing anybody in particular?"

"I'm not, uh, actually what you'd call, um, available," Bernie said. But at the same time he said that, or maybe in the short space before "available," there came one of those phone bursts of high-pitched scratchy noise—which really hurts deep in my ears, by the way—followed by dead silence.

"Vannah? Vannah?" Bernie turned to me. "Lost her. Maybe I shouldn't have been so brutally honest, and she happens to be married herself, of course, but I'm starting to learn that with some women you've got to—"

The phone buzzed again, so I didn't find out what Bernie was starting to learn.

"Bernie?" Vannah said, sounding very friendly of all sudden. "Lost you there for a second. But now I've got you again." She laughed a low little laugh. "Know your way around the Crescent City?"

"I've been there."

"Good. The boys'll be waiting in Marigny at a place called Fishhead's."

"What's that?"

"A bar," Vannah said. "Mami kind of owns it."

"Are you going to be there?" Bernie said.

"Wish I could, but I'm stuck in the Valley. And kind of tied up at the moment."

A man laughed in the background. The high-pitched scratchy noise started up and we lost her again. This time she didn't call back.

Huge dark clouds appeared in the distance. Underneath lay a city with some towers, but not many and not as tall as ours back in the Valley.

"True I've been here before," Bernie said. "But only sort of. Four-day leave. I remember zilch." Traffic thickened around us and we slowed down. Still the middle of day, but the sky got very dark and headlights and taillights lit up on both sides of the freeway. "Was her name Bubbles?" Bernie said after a while. "Seems impossible."

What was this about? I waited for more, but no more came. We entered the city, swung onto an off-ramp and were soon on a street lined with small houses except for the corners, which had a bar pretty much on every one. A bolt of lightning sparked across the sky, its pattern a lot like Bernie's stitches. I smelled burned air, the kind of burned air that meant—*BOOM!* And there it was: thunder. Panting sounds started up right away.

"Easy, big guy," Bernie said.

The panting? Me? Probably had to be me. Bernie wasn't panting the least bit—he hardly ever did, just maybe sometimes when we were hiking in steep country—and no one else was around, except for a few dudes sitting on their front steps, one or two drinking out of paper bags. "It's only thunder," he said.

The thunder wasn't what bothered me. What bothered me was that burned air smell.

"Now you're barking? What's with you? Put a lid on it."

Nothing. Nothing was with me. Lid was what again? I shut myself up, or at least amped down to a low growl. There's only so much I can do. Hey! But it's a lot. And just like that, I was in a great mood, never better. More burned air, more thunder, more lightning? I hardly even noticed.

"Fishhead's," Bernie said, and there, sticking out over the sidewalk was a big sign that looked like the head of a fish, a grinning fish wearing a bandanna and an eye patch, very confusing. "Here we are."

He pulled over. As we hopped out—me actually hopping, Bernie a little slower which happened sometimes after long drives, what with his war wound and all—a big fat wet thing hit me right on the tip of my nose. I hadn't seen rain in so long—it hardly ever rains in the Valley—that I didn't realize what was going on until I was soaked practically through to my skin and Bernie was trying to raise the top on the Porsche. So much time had passed since the last time we'd needed the top that I'd forgotten how tricky it could be. The tools came out. Bernie said things I'm sure he didn't mean. A passing drunk offered to help. He turned out to be an expert. The top got raised. Bernie and I walked into Fishhead's, trailing our own puddles.

I've been in a lot of bars—comes with the job. And in all of them, even the very fanciest, you can pick up the scent of human puke first thing. Maybe not you. No offense. Fishhead's was no different. I sniffed around. Far from the fanciest, but Fishhead's wasn't the grubbiest either. In the grubbiest you find actual grubs, edible although I can't really recommend them. No grubs at Fishhead's: that's the kind of thing I know the moment I enter any new place. They did have roaches, spiders, of course—no getting away from them—and possibly a snake, but way down under the floorboards somewhere. The floorboards themselves were very worn and wonderfully soft against my paws. There was a small stage in one corner, a few rickety chairs and tables on one side and a long dark bar on the other. As for people: a gray-haired woman at a table, cigarette in one hand and a drink in the other; a big old white-bearded dude at the bar, wearing a straw hat, possibly the kind called a boater; the bartender, who had bright red hair and full sleeves on both arms, the inked kind; and a guitar player on stage. Hey! Was he singing "Baby Please Don't Go?" Kind of, maybe.

"Baby Please Don't Go" was one of our favorites. I liked Fish-head's right off the top.

We walked up to the bar.

"Nice pooch," the bartender said.

Some people called me pooch. Not sure what that was all about but I didn't mind.

"Thanks," Bernie said. "Lord or Duke in the house?"

"Who's asking?" said the bartender.

Bernie laid our card on the table. This was the new card designed by Suzie, the one with the flower; Bernie wasn't happy about it.

The bartender's fingertips were long and blue, hard to take your eyes off of. She tapped our card with one of those long blue fingertips. "Little Detective Agency?"

"Correct," Bernie said.

The singing stopped. "Vannah din't say nothin' 'bout no dog," the singer said, rising and leaning his guitar against the chair.

We turned to him. He had a straggly goatee, straggly long hair, kind of greasy—part from grease he put on, part from his own natural grease—and wore jeans and a muscle shirt that showed he had no muscles. He was a very skinny dude, in fact, as skinny as meth heads I'd known. Also, there was the problem of that goatee. Why would anyone want to look like a goat? I've had encounters with goats, none pleasant.

"Which one are you?" Bernie said. "Lord or Duke?"

The goateed dude squinted, at the same time letting his mouth fall open, maybe not his best look. But he was no meth head—his teeth were all there, not too crooked, not too stained.

"How'd you figure that out?" he said, proving he knew nothing about Bernie.

"Lucky guess," Bernie said.

The white-bearded guy at the bar laughed, a quick, explosive burst that sounded a lot like . . . yes, barking. What was the name of this town again? It was off to a great start.

Whoever the goateed dude was—most likely Lord or Duke if I was getting this right—turned on the white-bearded guy. "What's so goddamn funny?" Bernie himself had no beard. He'd tried once, back in the Leda days, and she'd put a stop to it pronto, maybe the only time she and I had lined up on the same side about anything.

"Sorry, Duke," said the white-bearded guy. "I just enjoy a little repartee now and then."

"What the hell is he talking about?" Duke said.

"Back-and-forth of a witty nature," said the bartender, mopping up a wet spot on the bar.

"Huh?" said Duke. "Where's his tab at anyways?"

The bartender checked a sheet of paper. "Two thousand seven hundred fourteen dollars and ninety-three cents," she said. "Not counting the two Bloody Marys today."

"Three," said the white-haired guy. "So far."

"What if I said pay up right this minute or you're cut off?" said Duke.

"I'd be shocked," the white-haired guy said.

"Damn straight," Duke said. "How 'bout horrified?"

"Not denying it, Duke. You pick an adjective, that'd be me."

"'Kay," Duke said, "just so we's on the same page."

"Same page, same paragraph, same line," said the white-haired guy. "Let me buy you a drink, Duke."

Duke thought about that; he was one of those humans whose forehead wrinkles up when thinking is going on, something I always watch for. "I could use a beer," he said.

"The Hammerhead Red?" said the bartender.

"Sounds 'bout right." Duke turned to Bernie. "Somethin' for you?"

"The same," Bernie said. When Bernie's enjoying himself all the darkness disappears from his eyes, leaving only light, like right now. "And I'm sure Chet would appreciate some water."

Sounded 'bout right. I've tasted just about everything somewhere along the way, but water's always been my drink and always will be. No question booze can loosen you up: I've seen it happen more times than I can remember, possibly lots more times. But I have this way of loosening myself up with no help. I'm a pretty lucky guy, in case that's not clear yet.

SEVEN

"Tell you what let's do," Duke Boutette said when we'd finished our drinks. "So's we can avoid goin' through all these things twice." He paused as though waiting for Bernie to jump in. When Bernie did not, Duke said, "Catch that—what's the word?"

"Reference," called the bartender from back of the bar. We were at a table near the stage, Bernie and Duke sitting on chairs, me on the floor, my eyes just above tabletop level, one of my favorite viewing angles. Above the table everything looked on the up-and-up. Below the table, one of Duke's legs was going a mile a minute, which turns out to be not that fast, just another thing I'd learned from Bernie. Out in the desert we'd topped two miles a minute plenty of times, Bernie hooting and hollering behind the wheel, me howling at the sky from the shotgun seat. You've got to make time for a little relaxation: that's one of my core beliefs.

"Right—reference," Duke said. "You catch my little reference, Bernie?"

"To Bob Dylan?" said Bernie. The name meant nothing to me. A perp? Couldn't rule it out. And if he was a perp, he'd be breaking rocks in the hot sun sooner or later. That was pretty much our game plan at the Little Detective Agency.

"Uh-huh," said Duke, not looking pleased, which was maybe easier for him than most, on account of the way his normal face was almost there already. "Fact is, ol' Bob was sitting at this very table, in your very chair, not two months ago."

"Yeah?" said Bernie.

"We got music in our veins here in New Orleans, brother," Duke said. "What was he drinkin'?"

"Pink lemonade," said the bartender. "Then he switched to chocolate milk."

"There you go," said Duke. "Show Mr. Little where that drummer of his put a fist through the wall."

The bartender pointed to a hole in the wall near the front door. At that moment, it opened and a uniformed cop walked in. He glanced around and said, "Hey." No one else spoke or even seemed to notice him. The cop headed over to the bar. The bartender poured him a shot of something. He slugged it down and walked out.

"Point is," Duke said, rising from the table, "we'll pay a little visit over to Lord's place and go through everything just the once."

The woman with cigarette in one hand and a drink in the other suddenly came to life. "And what if he's not there?"

The white-haired old guy laughed so hard his straw hat fell off.

"What's so goddamn funny?" Duke said. He stalked out of the bar. We went with him. Outside the rain had stopped and the street, the sidewalk, even the rooftops were steaming, a lovely sight. Back inside the bar, the white-haired guy's laughter seemed to have spread to the bartender and the lone lady drinker.

"Can you believe those banshees?" Duke said. "I'm gonna burn the place to the ground."

"Really?" Bernie said.

"Just an expression," said Duke. "More or less." He checked his watch, huge and gold, with lots of dials and jewels. "Up for a walk? It's only three blocks."

"Sure," said Bernie. "That sounds—" He looked at me. "Ch—et?"

That's a special way he has of saying Chet, and when he does I always pay close attention. Like now: I went absolutely still, with the possible exception of my tail. I'm totally at the controls of all the rest of me, but my tail has a—how to put it? Mind of its own? Whoa! What a scary thought, two minds in one body! What if . . . but I didn't want to go there. So I didn't, dodging some dark thoughts at the very last instant.

Bernie came closer. "What have you got there, big guy?"

I had something? News to me. Then Duke looked my way and started laughing. There was a lot of laughter in this burg, normally a good thing, but confusing at the moment. Bernie bent down and . . . what was this? Removed a straw hat, possibly the kind called a boater, from my mouth? He took it into the bar and returned without it. My confusion cleared up a bit. Have you ever noticed the whole world of smells you get inside a hat that's been worn for a while? I hope the answer's not no: that would be sad.

We walked a few blocks on steaming streets, little rainbows appearing and vanishing around every corner. Only a few blocks, and heat was something I was very used to, having spent my whole life in the Valley, but by the time we stopped in front of a small yellow house with green trim and a green door, I felt the way I do after one of our all-day rambles in the desert. Not that I couldn't have gone on much, much longer. Don't think that for a moment. I can go on for as long as you like. Maybe not as long as you like, but Bernie? Count on it.

Duke knocked on the door. A voice on the other side called, "Who the hell's there?"

"Me," said Duke. "Who else?"

"What do you want?"

"What do I want? I'm your fuckin' brother, God save me. Open up."

"Is this about Baron's crackpot idea?"

Duke glanced at Bernie, did a quick finger-circling thing at the side of his head. What did that mean again?

"Not sure what you're referencing, bro," Duke said. "But I have the gentleman in question right here."

"You're a moron," said the man on the other side of the door. "And Vannah is worse. Know what's dumber than a moron?" The door opened. On the other side stood a dude who looked a lot like Duke except more so, if that made any sense. He was smaller, leaner, stragglier, and more goateed, the big difference being that his goatee was salt-and-pepper, while Duke's was all pepper. He wore only his underwear—not nice clean boxers, like Bernie's, but tighty-whiteys that could have used some time in the washing machine. With him dressed that way, you didn't have to be an expert to spot his ankle monitor. But I am an expert, in case that's not clear yet.

Bernie eyed him for a moment and said, "Cretin."

"Huh?" said the even-more-Dukish dude.

"Cretin is dumber than moron," Bernie said. "Wasn't that the question? Not a particularly meaningful question, since those terms have no scientific basis."

"Huh?" the even-more-Dukish dude repeated.

"Lord," said Duke, "this here's the detective, Bernie Little. Bernie, my big brother, Lord Boutette."

Bernie and Lord shook hands. Lord's hand was smaller than

Bernie's—most always the case whenever Bernie shook someone's hand—but real strong-looking.

"Uh-huh," said Lord. "Nice to, uh . . ."

"Same," said Bernie. "And this is Chet."

Lord Boutette looked my way. "Is he gonna bite me?"

"Why would he do that?" Bernie said.

"Hell if I know," Lord said. "But he sure does look like he's fixin' to take a piece outta me."

"You've got nothing to worry about," Bernie said.

And whatever Bernie says is the way things are, which kind of mixed me up inside right about then, because—for no particular reason and coming from out of nowhere—I had felt a sudden and very strong, pretty much irresistible urge to take a piece out of Lord Boutette. A nice big fat piece, in fact. That couldn't happen and it was my job not to let it happen, no matter what. I clamped my jaws together tighter than tight, although maybe not completely tight. My teeth wanted to bite and bite hard, as though they—oh, no: don't tell me my teeth also had a mind of their own! What was happening to me? Then came Bernie's hand on my head, just a light touch. I felt better.

"I've had bad luck with dogs," Lord was saying.

"Yeah?" said Bernie. "Why do you think that is?"

Lord screwed up his forehead. There was a pause—like he was waiting for some action in there—and during the pause, Duke said, "Can we go inside, for Chrissake? I'm meltin' out here."

I watched Duke closely, ready for anything. Humans were capable of many surprises. You never knew.

"I guess," Lord said. "If you want."

"Is that the best you can do?" Duke said. "We're known for our hospitality down here."

"Put that where the sun don't shine," Lord said.

I couldn't quite keep up with that. The sun was starting to penetrate the steam now, but was it actually shining? Plus the sun never shone at night. That was as far as I could take it. Next thing I knew we were inside Lord's crib.

I'd seen worse. The kitchen, which was where we ended up, was kind of nice. It had one of those old stoves you sometimes see that stand on little feet, with space underneath, and in that space, would you believe it? Practically a whole strip of bacon, presently—but not for long, amigo—getting gnawed on by a nervous-eyed mouse. The little guy split in a hurry—and tried to abscond with the goods, abscond with the goods being cop talk for making off with the bacon. In the end, he barely absconded with himself. As for the bacon? Delish, and not really that old at all. Still plenty of crunch left, which is how we like our bacon, me and Bernie. This case, whatever it was about exactly, couldn't have been going more smoothly.

I looked around. Bernie, Duke, and Lord were sitting at the table, Lord pouring from a big square bottle. Bourbon: an easy scent to pick up, and one with which I was very familiar. Harder to pick up, but not what I'd call actually hard, was the scent of Vannah, a human female scent mixed with coconut, pears, and honey that's been left out with the top off the jar for some time. Not a bad smell, but I preferred Suzie's, which was all about soap and lemons and those little yellow flowers that grow beside the dry washes in the Valley. But back to Vannah. She'd left her scent in the room quite recently. Was it even possible she was in the house at this very moment? I wondered about that.

Meanwhile, Bernie was saying something about taking it from the top.

"Didn't Vannah go over all this?" Lord said.

"Can't have too much input in this business," Bernie said. Whatever that meant, it sounded brilliant to me. I went over and sat beside him.

Duke nodded. Then Lord nodded.

"Makes sense," Duke said.

"I guess," said Lord.

Duke stopped nodding. Lord stopped nodding.

"Where you want us to start?" Duke said.

"With the ankle monitor," said Bernie.

Under the table, one of Duke's legs started up again, and so did one of Lord's, namely the monitor leg. I felt the approach of an interesting thought about these two dudes. It came right up to the very edge of my mind and stayed there, just out of reach.

"What the hell?" said Lord.

Bernie remained silent. He was great at that!

"Lord's trying to say how come you wanna start with the tether," Duke said. "Ain't that right, Lord?"

"No, it ain't right. What I'm trying to say is it's nobody's goddamn business."

"But at the same time a matter of public record," Bernie said. "Kind of a contradiction there."

"Like how?" said Lord.

"Doesn't matter," Bernie said. "The point is your brother Ralph has disappeared and you seem to be under house arrest. Anyone doing my job would look for a possible connection—that's basic."

"Ain't no connection," Lord said.

"I can vouch for that," said Duke.

Bernie put down his glass and stood up.

"Where you goin'?" Duke said.

"Home," said Bernie. "We can't help you."

"Keep your shirt on," Duke said. "Tell 'im, Lord."

"Tell 'm what?"

"What you did, for Chrissake. Why you're hooked up to that ball and chain."

Lord gazed down at the ankle monitor. "That's what it is, all right. Never realized." He pounded the table. "That goddamn judge. I'll murder her."

Bernie gave him a look.

"Uh, only in my prayers, kind of," Lord said. And then he started in on the story of the monitor, all about some crime he wouldn't have even dreamed of committing, no matter what his disloyal brother thought, a crime maybe involving stolen shrimp and a grandmother with a sawed-off shotgun, but I missed most of it because of how closely I was watching Bernie's shirt, the one with the martini glasses and cigars pattern. Was he going to take it off? That wouldn't be like him in an interview situation, which I was pretty sure this was.

". . . your alibi?" Bernie was saying.

"Alibi?" said Lord.

Bernie rubbed his eyes, maybe a bit tired all of a sudden. "You must know the meaning of *alibi*," he said.

"Sure he do," said Duke. "We all of us learned it at Mami's knee."

Then everyone was laughing and Bernie didn't look so tired. "Let's have it," he said.

"Have what?" said Lord.

"Your alibi. If you didn't steal the shrimp, you were elsewhere at the time, and as soon as we verify that fact, you're off the tether."

"Elsewhere?" Lord said.

"Right. Where were you late on the Saturday night and early Sunday morning?"

"That's a tough one," Lord said.

Bernie sat down.

"See," said Lord, "I might have had a drink or two."

"You're having a drink or two right now," Bernie said.

"What's that got to do with anything?"

"And where are you?"

"Sitting in my own goddamn kitchen. What's your point?"

"Similarly," Bernie said, "you were having a drink on the night in question. So where was that?"

Lord gave Bernie a long look. "'Night in question,'" he said. "You sound like a cop."

"But not the 'similarly' part," Duke said.

"Huh?" said Lord.

"That sounded more like an educated guy to me," Duke said.

Bernie raised his hand in the stop sign, also raised his voice just a little, and leaned closer to Lord, actually getting his face right in Lord's. "Where were you when the shrimp were stolen?"

"Easy, man," said Lord, leaning way back. "Think I haven't racked my whatchamacallit over this? The doc says I'm subject to blackouts. Happy now?"

"Only when you been drinking like a fish, fair to point that out," Duke added.

Bernie nodded like things were now making sense. "Where did you wake up the next morning?"

"I didn't," Lord said. "I woke up the next night."

"Where?"

"In the Robideaus's goddamn police station. Second cell on the left."

"How did you get there?"

"Bastards busted me, of course. Whaddya think?"

"Where?"

"Where what?"

"Where did the bust go down?"

"Who gives a shit?"

"I'm sorry?" Bernie said.

"Lord means the Robideaus coulda said it went down wherever they want," Duke said. "Lord being blacked out, and all."

"You're saying they framed you?" Bernie said.

"Square one, for Chrissake," said Lord. "Wet behind the ears? What's with Baron, thinkin' we could use someone like you to—"

"Lord?" said Duke.

Lord went silent, although I can't be sure about that because all I wanted to do was give the backs of Bernie's ears a quick lick or two, check out this supposed wetness. He hadn't just stepped out of the shower, but we had been out in the rain. Still, I myself was completely dry. I shifted closer to Bernie, waiting for the right moment.

"Someone like me to do what?" Bernie said.

"Um," Lord said.

"Nothin'," said Duke. "Lord was just runnin' his mouth. Tell 'im."

"I was just runnin' my mouth," Lord said.

Bernie drained his glass, glanced at me in a strange sort of way, almost like . . . like he wanted to see something real. What a thought! I couldn't understand it at all.

"Let's move on to this grandmother of theirs," Bernie said. "Alleged victim of the crime."

"What about her?" Lord said.

"Grannie Robideau's a Robideau," Duke said. "The Robideaus been enemies with the Boutettes goin' way back."

"Even further," said Lord.

"Meaning they're enemies of your brother Ralph."

"Wouldn't say that," Lord said.

"Why not?"

"Ralph's got no enemies," said Duke. "He's a loner, keeps his nose clean."

Keeps his nose clean? That had to be important. I checked the noses of everyone in the room. All clean, if you didn't count the long hairs sticking out of Lord's. I wasn't sure whether to count them or not. Had this problem ever come up before? Not in any case I could think of, and we've cleared a bunch. I licked my muzzle: totally clean. So where were we?

"What about these patents of his?" Bernie said. "Patent disputes are commonplace."

"Wouldn't know about that," Lord said.

"Ralph's a genius," Duke said.

"IQ like two fifty, two sixty."

"Way up there, anyways."

Bernie's eyes were very bright, like he was maybe about to laugh. Was something funny? Probably not, because instead of laughing, Bernie said, "What has he invented?"

"Gizmos," said Lord.

"Vannah mentioned that. Can you be more specific?"

Duke and Lord turned to each other. "What was that funny-looking thing, sorta thick?" Duke said.

"Had a special kind of steel, I know that," said Lord. "Came all the way from Germany."

"Japan."

"Germany."

"Japan."

Bernie held up his hand and the Germany-Japan back-and-forth came to an end. "How long has he been reported missing?"

"To who?" said Lord.

"The police," Bernie said. "You can file a missing persons notice after twenty-four hours in most jurisdictions."

"The cops?" Duke said. "You mean down in the parish?"

"Isn't that where he lived on the houseboat?"

"Yeah," said Lord. "But we didn't file no report."

"Why not?"

"Why not?" said Duke. "Because the cops in St. Roch is all Robideaus."

"And they're our enemies," Lord said.

"You covered that," Bernie said.

Duke sighed, a long, weary sound. "There you go," he said. "No matter what I do, I always end up going through these things twice."

"Hank Williams say that?" Lord said. "Still the best, now and forever."

Bernie drained his glass real quick, like he needed that drink bad. He gave his head a little . . . whoa! A little shake? Yes, he did. Wow.

"When was the last time either of you saw Ralph?" he said.

"Musta been before I got busted," Lord said. "Let me think."

While Lord was thinking, Duke said, "I seen him last week, maybe Thursday or so."

"And when did he disappear?"

"More like the Sunday or so."

"Where did you see him?"

"I paid Ralph a little visit over by his boat," Duke said.

"Yeah?" said Bernie. "You do that often?"

"Whenever he's runnin' short on cash," Lord said.

"Pot callin' the kettle," said Duke, losing me completely.

"Right back at ya."

"Times two."

Bernie held up his hand in the stop sign. "Does Ralph have lots of money?"

"He does all right," Duke said.

"But no one knows exactly," said Lord.

"Ralph playing things close the vest," Duke said.

"Kind of a loner," said Lord.

"Got that," Bernie said. "Where does his money come from?"

"Gizmos," Duke said. "Dint we mention that already? Fact is, he was workin' on one when I dropped by."

"What was it?"

"Metal contraption, about so big. Had two of them, now I think of it. The other one looked pretty much the same, but Ralph said it was a piece of crap."

"What was it for?" Bernie said.

"Huh?"

"The contraption—what's its purpose?"

"Search me," Duke said. "But Ralph was pretty pissed off about something. Cussin' and such, which ain't him at all."

Lord started laughing. "Meaning you came up empty."

Duke glared at him. "None of your damn business."

Lord kept laughing, slapped his knee. Bernie opened his mouth like he was about to say something, then changed his mind. We hit the road, hadn't gone a block before I leaned across and gave him a quick lick behind the nearest ear. Totally dry, just as I'd suspected.

Bernie laughed, gave me a pat. "You're in a friendly mood."

No, not that at all. But . . . yes, I was!

EIGHT

rackpot idea, quote unquote?" Bernie said.

We were back in the Porsche, crossing a bridge over a wide river, the widest river in my life by far, the water shining in the sun. And so much of it!

"Is that what we are?" Bernie went on. "Someone's crackpot idea, come to life?"

I couldn't help him. When the quote unquote thing starts up, he's on his own.

"Do those two birds actually think they can manipulate us?"

Uh-oh. Birds: not my favorite, as I may have mentioned already. I looked up and saw birds right away, more than two. Which two did Bernie mean? I wasn't sure, but then a big brown one with a huge beak dove down toward the water, and a few moments after that an even bigger brown one followed it. The first bird plunged right into the water, smack, without even trying to slow down, disappeared under the surface and came up with—what was that? A fish? And then the two birds were fighting over it. A mistake, because the fish wriggled free and fell back into the river. The two birds rose up as one, beating each other with their wings. Even from this high above, I could hear their squawking. We had nothing to fear from those two birds. Bernie was right again. I put a paw on his knee. He gave me a pat.

We drove over the bridge, were soon on a two-lane black-top in flat country, the wettest, greenest country I'd ever seen, some kind of creek or canal glistening through the trees almost the whole time.

"Bayou country, big guy," Bernie said. He sniffed the air. Whoa! How often did that happen? "I think I smell something." *Go on, Bernie, go on.* But he did not. There was lots to smell, of course, way too much to go into now, but sometimes in life one certain smell dominates all the others—take the time all the trash haulers in the Valley went on strike—and that was the case in bayou country. This was a rot domination zone, no question, rot falling down on and rising up through all the other smells out there. Quite pleasant: I liked it here.

"On the other hand," Bernie said and then paused.

On the other hand what? I couldn't remember the first hand. Once at a party, maybe that time some of the guys had a beer keg throwing competition, Bernie'd said that if people had a different number of hands they'd think different. But nobody had gotten it, whatever it was, and we'd had to leave pretty soon after. That keg bouncing down the street after us: what a sight! Especially under a full moon. But that wasn't the point. The point was . . . the thread, the thread. I was in danger of losing it, and then the danger passed, and it was gone. I was back to feeling tip-top, or even better.

"What if the whole family's in on it, even Ralph," Bernie continued after a nice relaxing silence, "and they're using us as a cat's paw against these Robideaus?"

Whoa! Stop right there! Or even before. Us? A cat's paw? Had

I ever heard anything worse in my whole life? Panting started up, big-time.

"Nah, no way," Bernie said, after a moment or two. "Too Byzantine."

I got the "no way" part. No way meant forget it, one of my specialties. The panting got itself under control. Meanwhile, the road had narrowed, the trees looming in closer and closer. Their leaves were dark green, but a kind of whitish fringe grew over everything, touching the ground in some places. I'd never seen anything like that whitish fringe. The smell was a bit like the smell of the sponge in the tub after one of Leda's long baths; back in the Leda days, of course. Bernie always took showers, and so did Suzie, so there were no more sponges at our place. I missed them: a damp sponge in your mouth is a nice feeling, as long as it's not too soapy. Here's another thing about the smell of the whitish fringe. It made my eyelids heavy.

Bernie's a real deep sleeper, can sleep through just about anything—like when that truck loaded with cymbals rolled over practically right in front of our house!—but I'm not like that. Even if part of me is sleeping deeply, there's another part that always knows what's what. For example, we'd slowed way down, the sound of the Porsche throttled down to just a mutter. I opened my eyes.

We were driving along a street in some little town. On one side stood some trailers up on blocks, a few houses, all a bit lopsided, and a store or two, green things sprouting in every open space. And what was this? Chickens on the loose? Plus some members of the nation within the nation—that's what Bernie calls me and my kind—resting in the shade.

"Ch—et?"

On the other side was one of those canals they seemed to have out the yingyang in these parts. A bayou? Was I getting this right? Don't count on it. Lining the near bank of the bayou was a long and narrow wooden boardwalk, with some piers extending out in the water. Boats, big and small, were tied to the piers. Across the bayou was a setup that looked pretty much the same—a little settlement with boats docked in front of it. Nothing seemed to be moving except for us and the chickens pecking at the dirt: not the air, not the water—a deep dark green, like no water I knew—not a branch or a flower. I sat up very straight, always best when coming into someplace new.

Bernie parked at the foot of one of the piers. "This is it, big guy," he said, wiping sweat off his brow with the back of his arm. "Boutette family pier is third from the end." We hopped out— me actually airborne, Bernie not—and walked out along the pier. Fish smells hung in the still air, and so did a scent that reminded me of frog or toad or snake, but more peppery, an odd kind of peppery mixed with poop. Other than that, this pier didn't seem to have much going for it. No boats, for example. All the other piers had boats tied to them, but not this one. So therefore? That was Bernie's department. I followed him to the end of the pier and got in a quick lick of the arm he'd used to wipe the sweat off his forehead.

Bernie gazed across the water for a bit, then looked up the bayou to where several little bayous seemed to flow into it, and finally down the bayou, shading his eyes from the sun. The bayou got wider in that direction, bent in a long curve, the water vanishing behind a wall of trees.

"Could hear a pin drop," he said.

Kind of a puzzler. Bernie was saying he was capable of hearing a pin hit the floor? Like one of those pins Suzie used for sticking notes on the wall of her cubicle back when she was with the *Valley Tribune*? Or did he mean a bowling pin? I'd gone with him to the Police Athletic League Bowling Night once, probably wouldn't be doing that again anytime soon. But I remembered the racket whenever the bowling ball blew those pins sky high. Bernie could hear that, no problem. I pointed my ears up. Not a peep from any type of pin I knew, but I did hear a low *throb-throb* coming from beyond the bend in the bayou.

Bernie turned and started walking back to the foot of the pier. I stayed where I was, eyes on that distant gleam of water where the bayou rounded the bend.

"Chet?" Bernie said. "Let's go, big—" He paused, gave me a close look. "Something up?" He came and stood beside me. We're partners, me and Bernie.

The nose of a boat came into view, and then the whole boat, small and metal, with a putt-putt motor at the back, the first *putt* always solid sounding, the second kind of sputtering. I had heard that kind of mismatch thing from the Porsche more than once; it always meant the tools would soon appear.

Sitting at the back with a relaxed grip on the motor's stick-out handle was a big, gray-haired woman wearing a halter top and shorts. And what was this? A patch over one eye? That always worried me. As she came closer, a similar sort of boat but black instead of silver started up from one of the piers on the far side and headed down the bayou. A woman was driving that black boat, too, an even bigger gray-haired woman, also in a halter top and shorts, but without an eye patch. As the boats passed each other, not too far apart, both women did that middle-finger raising thing. The name for this is giving the finger. We have ways of doing something similar in the nation within, but no time to get into that now. With humans, I'd seen bloody scenes come next plenty of times and got ready for anything. But the boats went their separate ways, the women not making eye contact even once.

The silver boat came *putt-putt*ing toward us. I'd actually never been up close to a boat. The little waves it made were beautiful, and so were their sounds, a bit like the wind in the trees but thicker and somehow more satisfying. The woman cut the engine and the boat glided in a long slow curve, coming to a stop right beside the pier and rocking gently in the water.

The woman rose, picking up a coiled rope. Bernie held out his hand to take it from her, but she ignored him and whipped the rope around a rusty metal bar kind of thing sticking up from the pier and locked it down with a tight knot. I'd seen that knot before—Bernie is great at knots and had taught Charlie a whole bunch—but the name didn't come to me. I was cool with that.

Some squarish cages lay in the bottom of the boat. The woman grabbed one and heaved it up on the dock.

"Help you with that?" Bernie said.

She paused, fixed her eye on him, and then on me: a big dark green eye, pretty much the same color as the bayou, and not at all friendly.

"You the detective?" she said.

"That's right," Bernie said.

"Then you might as well, long as I'm paying you anyways."

Which I didn't get. Wasn't Vannah paying us? This . . . this pirate woman! Yes, I'd made a connection—a connection coming from a time after Leda left when Bernie and I watched a lot of pirate movies—one of my very best! For a moment, I actually couldn't think of another. The moment passed. A welcome breeze sprang up in the still air, coming from somewhere behind me.

"Mrs. Boutette?" Bernie said.

"My friends call me Mami." The dark green eye got a bit colder. "Are we gonna be friends?"

"Don't see why not, Mami. I'm Bernie Little. And this is Chet."

"He plannin' to blow us all down with that tail of his?"

Bernie laughed. What was funny? Something about my tail? How could there be anything funn—I took a quick backward glance—not something that requires much head turning here in the nation within, by the way, and saw that my tail was in action, big-time. You might think it would be a snap to ramp it down to stillness in a matter of moments. You'd be wrong. No offense.

"How's my idiot son?" Mami was saying.

Bernie licked his lips. That's something I'm always on the lookout for with humans, but Bernie? We were in new territory. "Which of the, ah, um . . ." he began, and came to a halt.

Her dark green eye narrowed, seemed to get less green, more ice-cube colored. "I'm talkin' 'bout Baron, of course."

"Right, right," said Bernie. "Frenchie."

"Frenchie?"

"What we call him back home—just a friendly nickname."

"Friendly."

"He's a likable guy."

"If he's so likable, how come you put him behind bars?"

"That was business."

That bayou-colored eye of hers opened wider and warmed up. "You're an *homme serieux*."

"Huh?" Bernie said.

"Cajun talk," said Mami. Her eye moistened, like she might be on the verge of tears. That would have been a stunner. It didn't happen. "The truth is, Bernie, I've got three idiot sons. It's like Ralph soaked up all the IQ points meant for the others." She gazed over at the buildings on the other side of the bayou, and then into the trees beyond. From down in the boat, she reached up and grabbed Bernie's hand, squeezed it so hard it bore a red mark when she let go. "Find him for me, please."

"We'll do our best," Bernie said, flexing his hand. "Is there a Mr. Boutette in the picture?"

Mami felt in her pocket, took out a can of dip. "What picture would you be talkin' 'bout?" she said.

Or something like that. I'd known plenty of dip chewers—take our mechanic, Nixon Panero, for example—but never a female one. She popped off the can top with her thumbnail, a short, thick thumbnail, black at the edge, and offered the can to Bernie.

"Maybe later," he said.

Another stunner. What a case this was turning out to be, whatever it happened to be about! Had Bernie ever chewed dip before? Just once, when he was a kid, long before we got together, of course. He'd told Nixon that it had made him puke. Humans don't like puking. In the nation within we don't really like puking either, but it's no big deal. And then sometimes you find yourself scarfing up the very puke you just puked! What was that all about? Life is full of surprises. But forget all that, because just then I happened to catch a brightness in Bernie's eyes, sure sign that he was having a bit of fun.

"Ain't no Mr. Boutette, if that's what you're askin'," Mami said popping a thick dip in her cheek. "He's long gone."

"Where?" said Bernie.

"On the bottom." Mami waved one of her big strong hands down the bayou. "Fell off of a shrimper in a storm."

"I'm sorry."

"I'm not." With a grunt, Mami hoisted another cage up onto the dock. Bernie stacked it on the first one. That was when I noticed what was inside those cages: crabs! Lots and lots of crabs, some blue, some yellow, all wriggling around. I knew crabs from the tank at Big Al C.'s Place for Crabs, a joint we used to hit in South Pedroia—don't get me started on Big Al C., now breaking rocks in the hot sun—but I'd never seen them like this before, up close and—how would you put it? Kind of . . personal, that was it. The next thing I knew I had my front paws up against that top cage. All that wriggling and those little crab eyes! And the claws: What was with those wicked-looking claws? I only wanted to see better. Maybe I did end up seeing better and maybe I didn't, but there wasn't much time for any certainty, because just about right away both those cages somehow toppled off the pier and fell splash into the water, sinking out of sight.

Mami went bright red and turned on me, screaming in the loudest, screechiest voice I'd ever heard. The air around me shook with all these words I didn't know, but they sounded not good.

"Chet!" Bernie said. "In the car! Now!"

I was already halfway there, needed no encouragement from anybody. I knew one thing for sure: Mami was the scariest human I'd ever met.

NINE

A dented old pickup with painted crabs and shrimp on the side appeared and drove to the end of the pier. The driver, a wiry dude with a bushy white mustache but no other hair on his head got out. The wiry dude and Mami did some talking. He counted out some money. They did some more talking. He called her a bad name. She called him a bad name back, one Leda had used on Bernie, right before the end. The wiry dude counted out more money and jammed it into her hand. Then he and Mami loaded crabs into a big steel tub in the truck bed. The wiry dude drove off, trailing crab smell that showed no sign of drifting away any time soon even though the crabs themselves were gone. I felt nice and calm inside. Was it possible I'd messed up in some way? I didn't try to remember, just kept my eyes on Bernie. Any moment now he'd be calling me over. *Chet! C'mere, big guy!*

But that didn't happen. I waited, partway out of my seat, front paws on the edge of the door. Meanwhile, Bernie and Mami were talking—some distance off, true, but I could hear them perfectly well.

"Ralph keeps the Zodiac right here, tied to this very cleat,"

Mami said, pointing to the metal stick-up thing she'd roped her boat to. "He takes it places time to time, anchorages he's interested in, but not without tellin' somebody, and nobody got told. Night of the fifteenth she was floatin' right here. Morning of the sixteenth—gone."

"That a Saturday night?" Bernie said.

Mami nodded. "Relevant fact. I can see you have a head on your shoulders."

Hard to miss: that was my first thought. But maybe it had something to do with Mami only having the one eye. That was as far as I could take it, but not too shabby, in my opinion.

". . . Sunday mornings we get a lot of hung-over worshippers in the pews," Mami was saying. "And up at the pulpit, too—sorry to bust your bubble."

"That bubble got busted long ago," Bernie said.

Mami spat a thin brown tobacco chew stream down off the pier and into the water. "We're gonna get along good you and me, in what they call a like-minded way."

Bernie tilted his head to one side the way he does sometimes. What does it mean? I didn't know. But then came a surprise.

"What does that head tilt mean?" Mami said.

Wow! Mami and I were thinking along the same lines? Did I like that? Not one bit.

"Nothing," Bernie said. "It means nothing."

So now I knew. Today was shaping up nicely.

"Men," Mami said.

I waited for more. Bernie seemed to be waiting, too. But when no more came, he finally said, "And no one saw or heard from Ralph since?"

"Nope."

"Does he carry a phone on board?"

"Lotta good it does," Mami said. "Reception in these parts is like bees in a bottle."

Whatever that meant, I wanted no part of it. I'd had experiences with bees, unforgettable, even though I'd tried and tried.

"Did anyone check these places he liked to take the boat?"

"Do we all look stupid to you down here? Stands to reason we did that first thing."

Bernie gazed at her. Was he trying to see if she looked stupid? And what did stupid even look like? I had no idea. "Still," Bernie said, "that's where I'd like to start."

"Meanin' you want me to waste my time babysittin' you around the damn swamp?"

"Nope. I'll just need you to draw me a map."

Mami squinted at him till that one eye was just a slit of bayou green. "You can read a chart?"

"Yeah."

"Ex-military by any chance?"

"Correct," Bernie said. "And I'll be wanting to rent a boat, if you can point me right."

"Way ahead of you," Mami said.

Way ahead of Bernie? That I'd have to see.

Mami had a pickup of her own, even more banged-up than the one that had driven off with the crabs. It made a clanging noise and also a *scrape-scrape* that bothered my ears the whole time we followed her down the main street, inland on a dirt road that grew more and more rutted—trees and bushes right up against us, the spongy-smelling fringes sometimes trailing on our hood—and came to an end at another bayou. This bayou was very narrow, the tops of the trees on both sides almost meeting in the middle. There was a dock with a tall squarish boat—kind of like a trailer—tied up to the end. A small motorboat drifted behind the big one, connected by a seaweedy rope that sagged in the water.

We parked behind Mami's pickup and got out.

"Noticed the Stars and Bars bumper sticker on your truck," Bernie said.

"Got a problem with that?" said Mami.

"I do."

"My great-great-great fought with General Lee," Mami said. Up to that point, I'd been following along pretty well.

"So did mine," said Bernie. Now I was totally lost, but it didn't matter because at that moment I picked up that new smell again, the one that reminded me of frog or toad or snake, but more peppery, a strange poop-peppery mix. I sniffed my way down to the water's edge. There was snake, too—I'd been smelling snake constantly as soon as we'd entered bayou country—but this new one, so much more interesting, wasn't snake. It got stronger and stronger as I came to the water. I gazed down into the dark stillness. Tiny insects skittered around on the surface here and there. I suppose I could have licked them up, maybe if the air hadn't been so thick: I just wasn't that hungry. I took a nice drink instead, which turned out to be not the best water I'd ever tasted—too warm, too flat, too muddy, too salty. But no complaints. I realized how thirsty I was—crazy how that happens sometimes when you start to drink—and lapped up some more. And what was this? I tasted a—what's does Bernie say? Soupçon? That was it: a soupçon, which maybe means a bit of soup, chicken noodle being my favorite—surprising how often people leave soup in their bowls—but forget about that. The point is I tasted a soupçon of that interesting new smell they had in these parts. Hope that makes sense. It does where I come from.

"This is *Little Jazz*, Ralph's houseboat," Mami was saying.

"You best bunk down here. Nearest motel's a rat hole. I don't recommend it."

Made perfect sense. Shut-eye in a rat hole? I knew I wouldn't get much.

"And any explorin' you want to do, just take that there pirogue. Mix is fifty to one, and keep the goddamn prop offen the bottom. There's a chart on the console inside—red X's is where he likes to go." She tossed him a set of keys.

Bernie caught them—real easy, the way Bernie catches stuff—and said, "One more thing."

"What's that?" said Mami, pausing with her hand on the open door of the pickup.

"Why didn't you file a missing persons report?"

"Didn't you go over all that with Duke and Lord? 'Cording to my information, you did."

"Just confirming it," Bernie said. "The cops here are aligned with or possibly members of this other family, the Robideaus. Does that sum it up?"

Mami didn't reply. She got in the pickup, sitting sideways to us so we couldn't see her good eye, only the patch. That was scary, if I happened to be the type who gets scared, which I'm not.

"I'm going to take a wild guess," Bernie said.

There was a long silence. Then Mami said, "Go on if you're gonna."

"That fellow boater of yours back in town was Grannie Robideau," Bernie said.

Mami snapped her head around, glared at Bernie with her good eye. The patch-only angle suddenly seemed better to me. "She's no goddamn fellow of mine and you best watch your mouth, pretty boy."

Pretty boy? No one had ever called Bernie pretty before. Bernie's very good-looking, of course, certainly one the best-looking people in the whole Valley, but pretty? Pretty was all about Tulip and Autumn, for example, two very nice young women—and off-the-scale patters—who worked for our pal Livia Moon at her house of ill repute back in Pottsdale, and not about tough men like Bernie, and Bernie was a tough man, never forget that.

Bernie's face didn't change at all. He made no mention of the pretty boy thing. Instead, he said, "What's the story on the load of shrimp Lord stole from her?"

"Who told you that?"

"Lord himself, although not directly."

"What the hell does that mean?" Mami said.

"In fact, he ended up denying it, if I followed him correctly. But his denial was the kind guilty guys come up with, at least in my experience. So now that the cat's out of the bag, what went down?"

Now that what? I sniffed the air and detected not a trace of cat. Was that because the cat was in fact still in some sort of bag? Not likely. Bags don't stop me: I can smell every single item in a grocery bag. And what bag was he talking about? I trotted over to a tree and raised my leg. It was all I could think to do.

"I got nothin' to tell you," Mami said. "G'wan back to where you come from, far as I'm concerned. Blood is thicker than water."

Take it from someone who's tasted both: Mami was totally right about that. But how did she know? She had to be watched like a hawk. I'd watched plenty of hawks watching me out in the desert, knew how it was done.

"We're not going anywhere," Bernie said. "But we've worked a lot of cases, Chet and I, and one thing I can tell you is that the results are always better when there's trust between us and the client."

"Yeah?" said Mami, turning the key. "Then how about this'll be the exception that proves the rule?" She backed away from the dock in a fast, tight turn, then slammed to a stop, the pickup rocking back and forth. "Get one thing clear. Lord didn't grab those shrimp. A whole goddamn ton—you think he could pull off something like that? And where'd those shrimp end up—ask yourself that." Then Mami hit the gas and zoomed away on the rutted road, trailing dust that formed a golden cloud in the sunlight and slowly vanished. This was a lovely spot in its way.

Bernie looked at me. "I should have handled that better."

What a crazy idea! He'd handled whatever it was perfectly. We walked onto the dock, a floating dock that was kind of unsteady under our feet. At first I didn't like it and then I did.

"And proves was a way of saying tests at one time," he said. "So exception that proves the rule doesn't even mean what she thinks."

That zinged over my head, here and gone. We stepped up onto the deck of *Little Jazz*.

My very first ever time on a boat! I liked its old wooden smell from the get-go. We walked around the whole deck from back to front and back again, went down a few steps into a sort of living room, the floor covered with a strange shaggy sort of rug.

"Welcome to suburbia, circa 1963," said Bernie.

I didn't get any of that except for the welcoming part. Very nice of Bernie to say, but not necessary: we were partners, after all.

Bernie opened a low door, crouched down, and peered into a small dark space. "What's keeping this thing afloat is my question," he said.

Not mine. It hadn't even occurred to me. All I knew was that we were floating, no problem, and also that a pita chip was somewhere in the vicinity, the smell of a pita chip being just about impossible to miss, at least in my world. In a moment or two I'd found it behind a stool at the eating counter in the kitchen part of the boat. I downed it in one not-very-crunchy bite, totally satisfying. Freshness doesn't matter at all when it comes to pita chips; does it ever matter with any foods? None came immediately to mind.

Meanwhile, Bernie was sitting at the control console, examining some papers. "If I'm reading this chart right, one of Ralph's anchorages is less than a mile from here," he said. "How about we check it out in that pirogue and then see if we can hunt up some chow?"

All of that pretty confusing except for the very end. I loved when that happened. It was like wandering around in a strange place and then suddenly you're home. So were we home in some kind of way? Things were going well.

A ladder led down off *Little Jazz*'s back deck and onto a small platform at water level; the pirogue was tied to the platform. "Some things you need to know about boats," Bernie said, as we jumped down to the platform, me actually jumping, "beside the most important fact that they're a hole in the water into which you throw money."

Oh, no. What a terrible idea, worse than Hawaiian pants or even the tin futures play, which would have made us rich except for an earthquake in Bolivia, or maybe because the earthquake didn't happen. Was Bernie about to throw three K into the bayou? I didn't know what I'd do.

"First, there's all the lingo," he said. "Bow for front, stern for back, et cetera. Then, with small boats like this it's important to remember—" A whole lot of things, but I was too worried about the money to concentrate. I kept my eyes on Bernie's hands, as though . . . as though he was a perp! That was bad of me, but I couldn't stop.

Bernie showed no sign of reaching into his pocket. Instead, he grabbed the rope and pulled the pirogue up against the platform. Then he knelt down so our faces were close. That meant something important was coming.

"Okay, big guy, I know this is all new. What I want is for you to hop in the bow, right in front of this thwart—" He patted a sort of seat in the pirogue. "—and then sit nice and still. Can you do that?"

What a question! I was almost insulted. Except nothing like that could ever happen between me and Bernie. He patted the seat again and said, "Go," followed by "sit," and maybe something else. All I knew was that a moment later I was sitting in the bow of the pirogue, facing front, perfectly motionless.

Bernie smiled, a very nice sight. He had beautiful teeth for a human. "You look like a natural-born sailor."

Bernie got into the back of the pirogue, fiddled with a switch or two on the motor, pulled a cord, and *vroom vroom*! A nice *vroom vroom* with the deck of the little boat vibrating softly under my paws, but we weren't going anywhere. Bernie untied the line and pushed off.

And then we were gliding over the water, watery sounds bubbling and swishing all around me. How lovely! I'd had no idea being in a boat was so wonderful! Plus the bow was obviously the best place to be, just like the shotgun seat. I sat up even straighter, gazing straight ahead, missing nothing. Chet, the natural-born sailor: what a life!

TEN

We moved along the narrow bayou, cruising through patches of shade and patches of sunlight. A fish with a thick-lipped face that reminded me of Fritzie Bortz—funny how the mind works—jumped right out of the water, its scales like a bunch of tiny flashing mirrors. An empty beer can drifted by, and then a container of laundry detergent and a wicker chair. It was beautiful out on the bayou, no question about that, but I wasn't used to the damp, heavy heat, and I didn't seem to be getting used to it. All of a sudden it hit me: How about a swim? I couldn't think of a single reason why not; I didn't even try.

"Ch—et?"

I sat back down.

"There'll be time for a swim later."

Later? I tried to remember what that was about. The whole idea resisted me, retreating into a shady patch in my mind and staying there. Meanwhile, we were coming to a sort of fork in the road except we were on water. A dude named Yogi Berra—possibly a perp—had once told Bernie, if I'm remembering this right, and I should on account of how often Bernie's mentioned it, that when you come to a fork in the road take it, and that's what Bernie did. We know the ropes at the Little Detective Agency, although no one puts a rope on me, amigo.

The new waterway rounded a corner and opened up into a big round lake lined by green grasses and some tall trees, all that greenery reappearing on the surface of the water. And a boat—hey! our boat!—was doing that same doubled-up thing. Our boat but with one very rough-looking customer in the bow. The hair on the back of my neck rose right away, and I got ready to—

"Chet! For God's sake! How many times do we have to go through this?"

Go through what? While I tried to remember whatever I was supposed to remember, the rough customer stopped baring his enormous teeth and so did I. Why look for trouble? And what was this? His ears didn't match? And one of them had a tiny notch taken out of it, the kind of notch a whizzing bullet might have . . . At that moment, I remembered what I was supposed to remember. Then there was nothing to do but give myself a good shake, which was what I did.

"Chet! You're going to tip the goddamn boat!"

And then we'd have our swim? That sounded pretty good to—

"CHET!"

I went still.

Out in the middle of the lake rose a small island. Bernie glanced at the map. "This is it," he said. "Isle des Deux Amis. Kind of a long name for such a little spot. Means island of two friends, maybe."

Excellent name in my opinion. A few trees grew on Isle des Deux Amis and another one had fallen into the water and lay there partly underneath. Bernie steered around it, cut the motor, and we glided up to a low sandy bank and came to a stop with a gentle bump. Bernie held out a rope end, waved it around a bit. A waving rope end within snatching distance? Who could resist?

"Think you could hop out with it?" he said.

I didn't even have to think, which is usually when I'm at my best. I'd leaped onto the shore—more muddy than sandy, as it turned out—and trotted up to the nearest tree, marking it at once, the rope end still in my mouth.

Bernie stepped out of the boat and—oops—sank down in the mud to his ankles. He pulled his feet free with a couple of wet sucking plop sounds, not unpleasant, and then said a few things I'm sure he didn't really mean. He walked over, took the rope end, and tied it around the trunk of the tree.

"My best sneakers, big guy." They were? What about the other pair, the one without the paint spatters? "This whole god-damn state's drowning."

That sounded like a problem, and maybe scary, too, but right then I was more interested in the fact that another member of the nation within had already marked my tree, lower down—much lower down, in fact, meaning a little guy—not very recently, certainly not today or the day before. Other than that, all I learned about the little dude was that like me he was a fan of Slim Jims. Suppose he had one? Snatching it away from him would be a snap! Maybe not a nice thought. I tried to get rid of it, but it didn't want to leave.

"Time for a quick recon, Chet."

I'd been just about to come up with that on my own—I knew it! Quick recons were what we always did first thing in a new place, especially crime scenes. Uh-oh. Was this a crime scene? I got ready for anything.

We moved on to ground that was a little higher and found a sort of path lined with sawtooth grasses I'd never seen before and proved to myself how sharp they were right away. "No footprints," Bernie said. "If Ralph came here, you'd think there'd be footprints. Although with all the rain . . ."

He went quiet, but the thoughts kept on going in his mind: I could feel them, like birds flying in the night. One thing was for sure: no footprints. That didn't mean no humans had been here. In fact, there'd been two, around the same time as that little member of the nation within. Two human smells, both male and alike in lots of ways, but that was something you had to get past in this business. Funny thing about me: it didn't take a lot of effort. None at all, was the actual truth, if you must know. For example, one of these dudes had a garlicky thing going on and the other had overdone it with the same aftershave that Bernie used before Suzie made him stop, the one that comes in the square green bottle.

"I'm worried we're a bit like a fish out of water down here," Bernie said.

Whoa. A fish out of water? I love being in the water myself, but the fact is, I move much faster on land. And so would a fish, unless I was missing something. Therefore: nothing to worry about. We were going to crack this case—missing persons, if I remembered correctly—crack it wide open!

"Easy, big guy!"

What was this? I seemed to be up on my hind legs, front paws on Bernie's chest. Maybe not the right time. But before pushing off, I gave those stitches on his forehead a quick lick. They were right there in front of my face, after all; you'd have done the same.

Bernie looked down at me, wiping his forehead with the back of his hand in the nicest way. "Something—" His gaze rose beyond me, Bernie cutting himself off before saying "bothering you, big guy?" which I'd heard many, many times and now heard again, just inside my head. The answer was nothing was bothering me: nothing hardly ever did! We had good times, me and Bernie.

Bernie moved toward a tree stump, not the kind smoothly cut by a tree guy with a chainsaw—and it didn't have to be a tree guy: how about Mrs. Teitelbaum cutting down Mr. Teitelbaum's prize tangerine tree while he watched helplessly from his chopper, just taking off from the Teitelbaums's private helipad? The Teitelbaum divorce: a nightmare. But forget all that. The point was that this particular tree stump was the kind where the tree just split off and fell with help from nobody. There it was, lying almost completely hidden in the sawtooth grass. The stump itself was all soft and rotten, with small white mushrooms growing inside and some interesting bugs wriggling around in there. And what were those tiny glistening whitish things? Bug eggs of some kind? I couldn't help wondering how they'd ta—

"What have we here?" Bernie said. Caught on a piece of bark that stuck up from the edge of the stump was a pair of glasses. Bernie took surgical gloves from his pocket, put them on, and picked up the glasses: black-framed glasses that reminded me of some long-ago singer Bernie liked, the name not coming to me at the moment.

"Buddy Holly–style glasses," Bernie said. Wow! The very next moment and there it was! Was I cooking or what? "Who else wears glasses like this?"

I had no idea. Bernie reached into his pocket again, this time taking out a photo. We looked at it together. Was this the photo Vannah had given him? I remembered something about that. "Ralph Boutette," Bernie said, his voice quiet. Ralph had on glasses just like those in Bernie's hand. A ray of light shone down through the trees and caught the lenses, glaring on a fingerprint or two. Fingerprints are big in our business, which I'm sure you know. What you may not know is that sometimes they leave behind a smell, like now. Ralph Boutette's glasses gave off a very faint smell of garlic.

Bernie put the glasses in a baggie and tucked them away. Then we took a real close look at the stump and the area around it. After that, Bernie went down to the pirogue and brought back the paddle. We went over the whole island, Bernie using the paddle to hack away at the sawtooth grasses so we could see underneath. At first all that paddle hacking was a bit too exciting for me. And even not just at first! We spent what seemed like a long time, the sun, no hotter than back home but so much heavier, if that makes any sense, sliding down the sky, and sweat dripping off Bernie's face. Mosquitoes arrived. I'd only seen them once before, on a case we'd worked at a wilderness camp in the mountains, but not like this, in swarms. I hated their sound and when they went for my nose, but otherwise they didn't bother me. Bernie was another story: he smacked at them, yelled goddamn bastards a few times, ended up with bite bumps all over his arms and legs, plus bloody and sweaty little smears here and there. As for our search we came up with zilch.

Back in the pirogue, we rode away from the Isle des Deux Amis, the mosquitoes following us for a while and then giving up. Bernie cut the motor, dipped his hands in the water, washed off the bloody smears.

"Gonna need a transfusion," he said, losing me completely. I started panting. If Bernie needed something, it was my business to know.

"Hot, big guy?" he said. "You can take that swim now, if you like." He patted the water with his hand. I got the idea, perhaps in midair.

And then I was splashing right in. Ah! I went under, bobbed up, and started swimming. Swimming is just like trotting, except underwater. Anyone can do it. The pirogue drifted toward the far shore of this lake or whatever it was and I swam alongside, just my eyes and nose above the surface, my style when it comes to swimming.

"Looks like fun," Bernie said.

Bernie: right again! And even though I wouldn't have minded if this water'd been a lot colder, it was still plenty fine. *Come on in, Bernie, come on in!* But he did not. I swam along beside the boat to my heart's content, which was how I liked to operate. As we got closer to the far shore, a house appeared, a strange sort of house with the front part up on stilts right over the water. Sunlight glinted off a pickup parked in the nearby trees.

"That pickup look familiar to you?" Bernie said.

Or something like that. I make it my business to listen to Bernie and listen good, but in this case I was distracted by a smell, specifically that froggy snaky smell mixed up with peppery poop. It got stronger and stronger, seemed to be rising up from deep down in the lake.

"Sure looks familiar to me," Bernie said. "Back in the boat, big guy."

Did I have to?

"Chet! We're not on vacation here."

Uh-oh. Was I messing up? I immediately swam to the side of the pirogue, raised my paws up on the top edge, a total pro. Bernie helped me in. I gave myself a shake, but a real quick one, wasting no time at all. Then I sat up in the bow, perfectly still, eyes on that pickup, maybe important for some reason. I actually kind of remembered it, especially those painted crabs and shrimp on the side.

We rode up to the stilt house, and I saw that the front part was a deck. A sign was nailed to one of the stilts. Bernie read it: "Beware of Iko." A wiry dude with a bushy white mustache walked onto the deck and looked down at us. That mustache brought it all back: this was the dude who'd bought Mami's crabs. So there I was totally in the picture. What was next? Something good: I just had the feeling. Then I noticed the gun in his belt and wasn't quite as sure.

Bernie cut the motor, reached out, and got a grip on one of the stilts, holding us steady.

"Hey," he said, looking up at the wiry dude.

The wiry dude put his hand on the gun butt. Guns and hands: I watch them real close. "Lookin' for someone?" he said.

"That's exactly it," Bernie said. "And maybe you can help. I'm Bernie Little and this is Chet." Bernie took a quick glance at that gun. "Are you Iko?"

The wiry dude squinted down at Bernie. Then he laughed. "You're not from around here."

"True," said Bernie.

"Where you from?"

"Arizona."

Ha! We were from Arizona? I'd wondered about that.

"Got a moment or two to talk?" Bernie went on.

The wiry dude made a gesture with his hand. "This here's my camp."

"Very nice."

"Where I come for relaxin'. So if this is gonna be a relaxin' talk, then yeah. Otherwise no."

Bernie smiled. He has different smiles, which maybe I haven't mentioned before, some of them actually not even friendly. This particular smile was one he used on perps. It looked friendly unless you know Bernie. I know Bernie.

"Would fifty bucks help you relax?" Bernie said.

"Not as much as a C-note," said the wiry dude.

"Imagine a grand," Bernie said. "You'd be in a stupor."

The wiry dude laughed again, this time long and loud and to the point of hacking and even a bit of horking, but off the side of the deck, not in our direction.

ELEVEN

"I had me a dog once," said the wiry dude, whose name turned out to be Mack Larouche. We were sitting on the deck of his camp—Bernie and Mack in lawn chairs, me on the floor, which was actually nicer than any lawn chair I'd ever tried, those straps with the in-between spaces always so uncomfortable—and having drinks—beer for them, water for me; not the warm, thickish water from the bayou but something much tastier. Mack gazed out over the lake. "Come to a bad end."

"Sorry to hear that," Bernie said. "What was his name?"

Mack turned to Bernie. "Nobody's ever asked me that before."

Bernie said nothing. I've run across some other humans—not many—who are good at saying nothing, Cedric Booker, for example, our DA pal back in the Valley, and Suzie, too, come to think of it, but no one in Bernie's league. Excepting Suzie, come to think of it again. All of a sudden, I missed her. Bernie missed her, too: sometimes he spoke her name in his sleep.

"Dog was a she," Mack said. "I called her Lucinda."

"After Lucinda Williams?" Bernie said.

"How'd you know that?"

Bernie shrugged.

"You like that song of hers, 'Metal Firecracker'?" Mack said.

"One of my favorites," Bernie said.

By which he meant one of our favorites. Easy to slip up on something like that, and I forgave him even before it happened. But that wasn't the point. The point was "Metal Firecracker"! How often we'd zoomed across the desert in the Porsche with "Metal Firecracker" cranked up to the max or even more on the sound system. Then one afternoon Bernie had turned to me and shouted over the music, "We're in a metal firecracker ourselves, big guy, ever think of that?" And I hadn't, not one single time. I made up for that in the following days, big time.

"Me, too," Mack said. "She sang it for me one night."

"I knew she was from around here," Bernie said.

"Lake Charles ain't around here, not to my way of thinking. But that one night she was right where we are now, and that's for goddamn sure."

"You're saying Lucinda Williams sang 'Metal Firecracker' on this deck?"

Mack nodded. "This was at the height of my heroin addiction."

"Meaning it was a hallucination?"

"You never know."

"One of the drawbacks of heroin addiction," Bernie said.

"You're so right," Mack said. "But back then it was a plus. That's the heart of the matter."

"Meaning now you're clean?" Bernie said.

"Clean enough," said Mack. "Maybe not squeaky."

Bernie lowered his bottle, gave Mack one of his direct looks. "I'm paying for squeaky."

Mack gave him a direct look back. "Fair enough," he said, lowering his bottle, too. "Who are you looking for?"

"Any guesses?"

"Any guesses? I thought you were playing straight with me."

Bernie looked away for an instant and then his direct gaze on Mack was back in place, but had I ever seen him break off that gaze before? Not that I could remember. I gave it the old college try, although I wasn't sure what that meant exactly: every time we drove by Valley College, the kids—and I love college kids, don't get me wrong—were mostly playing Frisbee or smoking weed. Sometimes both at once, true, but that was about it.

"Ralph Boutette," Bernie was saying. "You know him?"

"Sure," Mack said. "I know everyone around here."

"Were you aware that he's missing?"

"Not exactly," said Mack, taking a nice big swig of his beer.

"What does that mean?"

"Heard talk, but I didn't take it seriously." Mack licked beer droplets off his mustache. He had a nice pink tongue, with plenty of size for a human. "Ralph's an odd duck—everyone knows that."

Whoa. Not me, amigo. I was just finding out now. I'd had experience with ducks, not good. They're a kind of bird, something I hadn't been clear on at first, and my history with birds is nothing but trouble. Bird beaks are surprisingly nasty, and ducks have them, too, as I came to learn and then learned again and maybe one more time after that. So my takeaway? If ducks were now in the case, we had problems.

"Tell me about this talk you heard," Bernie said.

Mack stroked his mustache. "Have to organize my mind, get it all in the right order."

"My guess is you're good at that," Bernie said. "No one ever took the SATs for you, did they, Mack?"

"Like Ralph did for all his goddamn brothers, plus every

dumbass kid who could scare up twenty bucks?" Mack had a good laugh. "How'd you know about that?"

"Came up in the course of things," Bernie said. "Word was that otherwise Ralph's stuck to the straight and narrow all his life."

"Far as I know—the point I was makin', in fact, over at Rooster Red's."

"What's that?"

"Joint just the other side of the St. Roch line." He handed Bernie a card. "Good for one free drink—happen to have an interest in the place."

Bernie tucked the card away. "There was talk of Ralph going missing?"

Mack nodded. "Some of the boys were saying Ralph got himself mixed up in some serious shit, and I told them that just wasn't him. He's just wandered off somewheres, Ralph being Ralph."

"What serious shit are we talking about?"

Bernie cocked his head a little, the way he did when he wanted to listen real close. I listened real close, too. Getting mixed up in serious shit happened to me once, even to the point of rolling in it. What had gotten into me? That was what Bernie kept asking when he hosed me down.

"It's kind of complicated," Mack said, "and I don't think it has anythin' to do with, um, other developments or what have—"

"Talking about the shrimp heist?" Bernie said, cutting him off. Bernie did that sometimes, just another one of our techniques at the Little Detective Agency. We've got a bunch: the last one is pretty much always me grabbing the perp by the pant leg. I noticed that Mack was wearing shorts. No problem. I'd come up against that before, found other ways. "Gotta think outside the box," Bernie says, and I'm totally with him on that: I'd been in boxes once or twice—if a crate wasn't a box, then what was? Never again.

"Not sure you could call it a heist," Mack said.

"What would you call it?"

"More of a mystery. A ton of shrimp came into the town dock on a Saturday night and Sunday morning it was gone."

"Were they your shrimp?"

"Woulda been—I was set to buy 'em first thing Monday morning."

"So who took the hit?"

"That's what's not too clear, at least to me."

"Wasn't it Grannie Robideau?" Bernie said. "I don't get all this uncertainty. Lord Boutette stole Grannie's shrimp. Isn't that the story?"

"That's a story, anyways," said Mack.

"It must have convinced the authorities," Bernie said. "Lord's under arrest and awaiting trial."

"I heard," Mack said.

"Let's go back to the scuttlebutt at Rooster Red's," Bernie said. "Want to hear my guess?"

Mack shrugged.

"Indulge me," Bernie said. "My guess is there's a theory going round that Ralph, despite this lifetime of just about perfect straight-arrowness, barring the SAT caper, was in on the shrimp heist, and now he's on the run, or hiding out somewhere."

There was a long pause. Then Mack said, "You're kinda quick to understand how things work in these parts."

"But you're not buying it," Bernie said. "How come?"

"Makes no difference what I think."

"No?" said Bernie. He rose, walked to the end of Mack's deck, stared out at Isle des Deux Amis, very small in the distance. Then he turned to Mack, rubbing his hands together and looking sort of refreshed, like he'd just splashed cold water on his face, which he actually did sometimes. And then some on me! The fun we had! But that's not the point. The point is this refreshed look thing was all about the technique Bernie called trying a new tack, for reasons not clear to me, my only experience with tacks being when I found one on the office floor and decided to give it a little chew. That single tack was more than enough; I didn't have the slightest interest in a new one.

"I'm curious about this feud," Bernie went on. "Boutettes and Robideaus—what's behind it?"

Mack shook his head. "Goes back before my time."

"To when?"

"The Civil War."

"They were on opposite sides?"

"No, no, nothin' like that. Our side, the both of them. Know about the Zouaves?"

"They wore colorful uniforms?"

Mack nodded. "That was the problem. The Boutette and Robideau dudes of the time got into a dispute over who owned this one particular jacket with lots of red embroidery. Led to a duel, and there's been bad blood ever since."

"Christ," Bernie said.

"Uh-huh," said Mack. "Another coldie?"

"If you're having one."

"Hell, I'm having a dozen—it's my day off."

A dozen: not a small number, as I recalled. I'd seen dudes down a dozen beers plenty of times, never pretty. Mack went inside. Bernie turned to me.

"'Our side'—you catch that?" he said.

Actually not. Mack was on our side? Nice to hear. This case was confusing. But the money was good. Hey! Good money and it had also smelled of shrimp: I'd caught the smell when Vannah handed it over. And hadn't Bernie and Mack just been going on and on about shrimp? So therefore? At the Little Detective Agency, in case I haven't brought this up already, so therefores were Bernie's department. I'd taken this particular whatever it was as far as I could. Not too shabby.

Mack came out with two beers, handed one to Bernie.

"What do you know about Isle des Deux Amis?" Bernie said.

"It's that there island." Mack pointed at it with his chin. I liked when humans used their chins for pointers. I can point, too, no worries about that, but I use my whole body.

"When was the last time you were on it?"

"Me? Actually on it? Been years."

"Ever see other people there?"

"Nope. Nothin' to attract anybody."

"With the exception of Ralph," Bernie said.

"Huh?"

"Isn't it one of his favorite anchorages?"

Mack looked down at his feet. Bare feet: very dirty, the ends of the nails all black; in short, really interesting.

"Mack?" Bernie said. "Look at me."

Mack slowly looked up, sort of met Bernie's gaze.

"What are you hiding?"

Mack tilted back the bottle, took a long swig. It made him look a little tougher. I'd seen that kind of toughness, the bottled kind, disappear real fast.

"Nothin'," he said. "And now, all the same to you, I've got work to do."

"It's Sunday," Bernie said, "your day off. Those shrimp disappeared on a Sunday, and so did Ralph." Bernie took out the baggie with the Buddy Holly–type glasses inside and held it up so Mack could see. Mack's eyes locked on that baggie. "Ralph was anchored off Isle des Deux Amis that Sunday morning," Bernie said. "You were right here. So you saw him. Now I just need to know what you saw and we'll be out of your hair."

Of which Mack had none, except for that bushy mustache. I felt a bit pukey.

"I got no memories of that day," Mack said.

"How is that possible?"

Mack didn't take his eyes off the glasses. His voice went quiet. "Truth is I backslid that day, drug-wise." He looked up, took out the fifty Bernie'd given him. "Want this back?"

Bernie shook his head. "You may be needing it."

Sweat beads popped up on Mack's forehead. You saw a lot of human sweat in bayou country. And very little back home in the Valley. I came close to giving that some thought.

TWELVE

See the way St. Roch is divided in half by the bayou?" Bernie said. "Boutettes on one side, Robideaus on the other—it's almost too damn convenient."

We were in the Porsche, Bernie at the wheel, me riding shotgun, which was always our setup except for once after a long night at Pony Up, a dive bar in South Pedroia we no longer visit, and with the engine off, the car hadn't been moving anyway. And then all of a sudden, with me in the driver's seat and Bernie sort of—let's say napping in the front seat—it was! Moving! And fast! A story for another time.

Right now we were crossing a bridge over the bayou. A narrow one-lane bridge where we'd had to wait on a red light while a battered old van came clanking across from the other side: didn't seem all that convenient to me, but if Bernie said so, then it was. I'd never been on a more convenient bridge! And the view was beautiful: sunset over the bayou, the water fiery red, the trees and buildings black against a purple sky. Bernie says I can't be trusted when it comes to colors, so forget the red and purple parts. But not the black. I'm very good at black.

We drove over the bridge, followed the bayou for a bit, lined with docks just like the other side, the air fishier than any air I'd ever smelled, then turned up a street and parked in front of a low building with a blue light hanging over the door. Blue lights meant the law. We're on the same side as the law, me and Bernie, except for a whole confusing bunch of other times. There's even a lawman or two wearing an orange jumpsuit on our account. They look so different that way!

Bernie opened the door under the blue light—bugs buzzed around it, big-time—and we entered the building. I've been in many cop offices, most of them messy with half-full paper cups all over the place, and also plenty of leftovers lying around, often within easy reach. Leftovers: one of the great human inventions, and leftovers within easy reach were even better.

The St. Roch setup was the other kind of cop office, the kind you hardly ever saw, neat and tidy, like Leda and Malcolm's place in High Chaparral Estates, which I'd only been in once, and very briefly. No paper cups here, no leftovers, no files stacked to the ceiling, no dust. Although there was mold growing down in the basement, growing wildly: that had been obvious the moment I'd stepped in the room.

Two lawmen sat at side-by-side desks. They weren't wearing orange jumpsuits yet, in fact they had on crisp, unwrinkled uniforms and kind of reminded me of FBI types Bernie and I have come across—clean-shaven, short-haired, watchful. What else? They smelled like brothers. Other than that, I had zilch so far.

The lawmen looked up at us. They both had ginger-ale-colored eyes and curly ginger-ale-colored hair, although one had lots of gray mixed in. That meant he was older: we have the same thing in the nation within. Take my old buddy Spike who hangs out at Nixon Panero's yard, his face practically white now, but still a fine scrapper, with a snarl that makes you want to back away pronto, which I never do, goes without mentioning. If there was time, I could now add something about how come I know about ginger ale—which happens to be Charlie's favorite drink at the moment, although he's not allowed to have any at their place in High Chaparral Estates, and it's possible he's officially not supposed to at our place either—but there isn't.

The older lawman smiled in a friendly way and said, "Help you?"

"Sheriff Robideau?" Bernie said.

"Guilty as charged," the lawman said, raising his hands like he was turning himself in. Whoa! We'd closed the case already? Could I even remember a quicker result? Maybe the time that Stylin' Sammy Minsk was still in the middle of hiring us to find his wife's missing diamond ring when it fell out of a hole in his pocket right in front of my eyes. I grabbed him by the pant leg without even having to move, and the fraud squad from the insurance agency sent us a nice check, which Bernie put in his chest pocket, things going downhill from there.

"Bernie Little," said Bernie. "And this is Chet." They didn't even look at me. My tail, which had started up in a normal meet-and-greet sort of way, ramped it down, although not all at once. Bernie stepped forward and laid our card on the sheriff's desk, the new card designed by Suzie, the one with the flower.

The sheriff gazed at the card, meanwhile . . . tracing the outline of the flower with his fingertip? I couldn't be sure from my angle. "Little Detective Agency," he said.

"Correct," said Bernie.

"Out of where?" said the deputy. The sheriff handed him the card. The deputy examined it, and yes, traced the outline of the flower with his fingertip, no question about it. "Long way from home," he said.

"It's about Ralph Boutette," Bernie said. Then came a pause, a space in time that went on too long to feel right. Sometimes after a few drinks, Bernie starts talking about the big bang. "See what it means, big guy? Space and time are the same thing—not just two sides of the same coin, but the coin itself." No coin or money of any kind ever appeared after these talks; and also no big bang ever happened, which suited me just fine. Fourth of July? Not my cup of tea. Tea isn't my cup of tea either, in case you haven't figured that out already. Water's my drink, pure and simple, and Thanksgiving's my favorite holiday. Can't beat it for leftovers—to bring up leftovers again, and how can that be bad?—just scattered around all over the place, and everyone collapsed in front of football on TV. Dark meat's best, but I don't complain about white. It's fun listening to all the burping while I hunt around. Human burping is actually one of the best things they do, although I'm not sure they know that.

No burping was happening at the moment, too bad because I now wanted to hear some pretty bad. The sheriff and his deputy were watching Bernie, their eyes giving nothing away. Were they thinking about space and time? That was as far as I could take it.

"What about Ralph Boutette?" the sheriff said at last.

Right. Ralph Boutette. Just like that, I was back in the picture.

"We're looking for him," Bernie said. Totally true, and it couldn't have been fresher in my mind.

"Why?" said the sheriff.

"Not sure I understand your question." Bernie and I? Peas in a pod on this one. I've had pea experience, with pods and without. They aren't high on my list, as maybe I mentioned already, not so much on account of the taste, which I don't mind, but because of the way they get all mushy and stick to the roof of your mouth. Must have happened to you.

"No mystery," the sheriff said. "Mr. Boutette is a local resident. We don't know you, and looking out for our people is job one."

"Nice to hear," Bernie said. "But if a missing persons report has been filed on Ralph, it would be a matter of public record."

"And you're the public?" the sheriff said. Bernie didn't answer. The sheriff turned to his deputy. "Got an MP on Ralph?"

"Not as of four p.m. today. Want me to check the log?"

"I do."

Deputy Sheriff Robideau tapped at his keyboard. These brothers were very polite lawmen, spoke in quiet, nonthreatening voices, but they were kind of nervous at the moment, human nervousness being hard to hide from me. It has a real sharp scent, as you may or may not know, that cuts through other smells the way sour milk does, for example, or a pot on the stove after the water's boiled away but the heat's still on, something that goes down from time to time at our place on Mesquite Road.

Deputy Robideau looked up, shook his head. "Negative."

Sheriff Robideau turned to Bernie. "You know something we don't, Mr. Little?" Of course he did! A whole bunch of things! He was Bernie!

"Wouldn't put it like that," Bernie said. And that was Bernie, too, not rubbing it in. "But his family can't seem to locate him and they're worried."

The deputy laughed.

"What's funny?" Bernie said.

"Them being worried about him," Deputy Robideau said.

"I'm not getting it," Bernie said.

"Because they all know goddamn well—" the deputy began, but the sheriff cut him off.

"Scooter?" he said. "I'm pretty sure this gentleman didn't come here for a whole lot of small-town gossip."

Gossip: a new one on me, but from the look on his face, I knew that Bernie wouldn't have minded hearing some, whatever it happened to be.

"You're the boss, Chip," said Scooter Robideau, his lips barely moving.

The sheriff—Chip was it? Chip and Scooter? Just like some members of the nation within I knew!—turned back to Bernie. "The Boutettes are worried about Ralph."

"Correct."

"And they've hired you."

Bernie opened his mouth to answer, but Scooter piped up again. "Why'd they pick someone from so far away?"

The sheriff smiled, or it might have been that teeth-gritting thing. "Actually my second question, Scoot." Scooter's eyes went kind of blank. "Question one," the sheriff went on, "is what explanation, if any, did the Boutettes give you regarding Ralph and his whereabouts?"

"You'd have to ask them," Bernie said.

The sheriff kept smiling or gritting away. "Oh, I intend to."

"You do?" said Scooter.

The sheriff's smile faded. "But I don't expect much help from that quarter."

"Why is that?" Bernie said.

"Put it this way," said the sheriff. "If you do find Ralph, failure to inform this office might be risky."

"How's that?"

"Not saying for sure. This is a friendly talk, after all—we're known for our hospitality in these parts, Mr. Little. But keeping us out of the loop could place you right on the edge of negligent activity."

"What kind of negligent activity?" Bernie said.

"The kind that might resemble aiding and abetting," said the sheriff. "Depending on where you're coming from."

"Meaning you think Ralph was in on the shrimp heist," Bernie said, almost before the sheriff finished talking.

The sheriff sat back. "You're quick on the uptake."

The sheriff was right about that. Normally I have good feelings for any admirer of Bernie, but they weren't there at the moment.

"Not quick enough," Bernie was saying, "to know for sure if I'm being threatened."

"Threatened? My goodness."

"Just on the chance that any negligent activity amounted to a crime in someone's eyes," Bernie said. "If you see where I'm coming from."

"Who said anything about a crime?" the sheriff said.

"Fella's got crime on the brain," Scooter said.

That made the sheriff smile again. He was a very pleasant lawman, if a little on the nervous side. Nobody was perfect, as you hear all the time, excepting one person I could think of, no need to name him, I'm sure.

That unnamed person was smiling, too. We were all getting along great, except maybe for the nervousness part. Not that Bernie was nervous, not a bit, although he can get nervous, just about always around a certain kind of woman. I wasn't nervous either. When was the last time? At the vet's, most likely; can't think of anything else that makes me nervous, and—uh-oh, all of a sudden I was thinking about the vet! Nothing but going to the vet could fit in my mind! I needed to gnaw on something real bad, this nearby wooden leg of Scooter's desk, for example. I tried not to shift over in that direction, but I have the kind of body that knows how to shift on its own.

"An occupational hazard," Bernie said.

The sheriff laughed. "Isn't that the truth?"

"What is?" said Scooter.

The lines around the sheriff's eyes deepened a little bit. That was all it took to make him look annoyed. "Crime on the brain," he said. "What else?"

Scooter had the same sort of lines around his eyes, although not so prominent. Everything about Scooter was more prominent in Chip. Now he looked annoyed, too. What was going on? They were brothers. Just then I had a real strange memory, the farthest back memory of my whole life, a memory of lying in a whole big mess of puppies! The memory faded away, just when I was about to make . . . what would you call it? A connection?

Maybe it would come to me another time. You could always hope. And hey! I always did! I forgot all about gnawing the leg of Scooter's chair, remembered, then forgot again, once and for all. Just like that, I was back to feeling tip-top.

"How about explaining why you suspect Ralph?" Bernie said. "Is there any actual evidence?"

The sheriff leaned forward, looked Bernie in the eye, tapped his fingertip on the desk, just the once but very firmly. "Don't like that phrase, 'actual evidence.' Not the way you said it."

Bernie made no reply.

"I suppose," said the sheriff, sitting back a bit now, "the Boutettes told you they can't get justice in this town."

"Can they?" Bernie said.

The sheriff took a deep breath and let it out real slow through his nose. That made a sound I like a lot—wind through the trees only a lot smaller—but the point is that when humans do that, it means something's going on in their mind, exactly what was a mystery.

"They've got it into their messed-up heads that we're mortal enemies going back to the Civil War," the sheriff said.

"A Zouave uniform dispute, I believe," Bernie said.

"You're kidding," the sheriff said. "They went into that?"

"The Zouave thing I heard elsewhere."

"Mind telling us where? Just out of curiosity."

Bernie hesitated. Didn't see that very often. I could feel him thinking. "Mack Larouche," he said. "The shrimp dealer."

"There's a surprise," Scooter said.

"But it could have been anybody," the sheriff said. "The whole parish is crazy."

"Batshit crazy," Scooter said, hanging me up right there. The night a bat flew into the house, back in the Leda days, and Bernie chasing after it with a broom, swatting and swatting the air! Had I ever been more excited in my life? Those screams of Leda's: I can still hear them. Had the bat left any poop behind? Would I have missed something like that? Does the bear shit in the woods? That was too much. I lost the thread completely.

". . . but," the sheriff was saying some time later, "this so-called feud is a figment of their imagination. Or totally one-sided. We—meaning the Robideaus—are long past it. Even if we weren't, I'm running an up-to-date, by-the-book operation here. There's no room for any of that nonsense."

"Good to hear," Bernie said. "But I witnessed a little scene between the two grannies that didn't look too friendly."

"Excluding them, I should've added," the sheriff said. "They're beyond hope. But here's how I know Ralph was in on the heist. One—Lord Boutette's not smart enough to conceive, plan, or carry out anything like that. He can barely conceive, plan, and carry out taking a piss. Two—Ralph's taken off."

"But Ralph's known for being on the straight and narrow," Bernie said.

Or something of the sort. What was that piss thing again?

Was anything in life easier? I'd have to rethink Lord from the ground up.

"True," the sheriff was saying. "But he's a Boutette first and always. Family is number one."

"And what about you?" Bernie said. "Robideaus first and always?"

The sheriff made that single fingertap again. "The law is first and always," he said. "At the moment, we only want to pull Ralph in for questioning. And in that spirit, Scooter's going to start canvassing the town, and he's also going to file an MP ASAP—"

"I am?" said Scooter.

"—with a five grand reward, the maximum our budget perm—"

"I thought it was—" Scooter began.

"Scooter?"

"Yup."

"ASAP meaning now."

Scooter rose, scraping his chair in a way that hurt my ears, opened a door at the back of the room, reached around the corner, grabbed a set of keys off a hook, and closed the door. Then he went out the front and headed for a cruiser. But I wasn't really watching that. Instead, my attention was on that closed door at the back of the room. The door had only been open for a moment, but I'd glimpsed another room behind it, and in that room a dude was sitting at a desk, wearing headphones and glancing up in a startled way. A sort of familiar dude in a dark suit. Familiar from where?

I glanced at Bernie. He was listening to the sheriff, maybe had missed that back room scene.

"You'll have our complete cooperation," the sheriff said.

Bernie nodded.

"In exchange for yours."

"Understood."

A sort of familiar dude in a dark suit. Wearing headphones, which was why . . . why he'd taken off his small-brim cowboy hat, which had been hanging on the wall behind him! The dude from Donnegan's who'd offered us a high-dollar gig, the details gone from my mind, if they'd ever been there: Cale Rugh.

Bernie and the sheriff looked my way.

"What's he barking about?" the sheriff said.

"No idea," Bernie said.

"Nice looking dog. Think he'd like a treat?"

"Safe bet."

But this wasn't about a treat! This was about Cale Rugh, sitting in the back room with headphones on, and that startled look on his face. Something was wrong. *Bernie! Open that door! Check out the back room!* I kept barking. The sheriff gave me a Milk-Bone, the very biggest size. I stopped barking.

"Wanted a treat, all right," said the sheriff.

"Looks that way," said Bernie.

Or something like that. The Milk-Bone had pretty much my whole attention. Did that make them right about me? What a thought! It broke into many, many pieces and zipped on out of my mind.

THIRTEEN

Notice how the Robideau brothers are kind of educated and smooth—even a bit unregional—and the Boutette brothers are not?" Bernie said as we drove back across the bridge. "How did that happen?"

No clue. I felt a Milk-Bone crumb on my muzzle—I'm pretty good at feeling things on my muzzle—and made short work of it.

"Are families the key?" Bernie continued, or maybe we were on to something else. "Not just in this case, but in everything?" Everything: wow. Not so easy to think of everything at once, but that was Bernie. "How about mine for starters?" he went on.

Bernie's family? This was interesting. Starting with for starters, there was his mom, a piece of work who sometimes comes to visit—take last Thanksgiving—bringing her own gin and calling Bernie kiddo. "Never feed a dog at the table," she says. "He'll get into bad habits." But at the table she sneaks tasty morsels to me behind her back, so maybe I didn't get what she meant; plus the bad habits thing is a new one on me. Then there's Charlie, of course, and also Leda, back in the pre-divorce days. Who else? I waited to hear.

Bernie turned off the bridge, drove by the dock on the Bou-tette side of the bayou, his eyes on something far away. "My great-grandfather, Ephraim Little, graduated from Princeton. My grandfather went there for two weeks and then hopped a steamer out of Newark. My dad didn't even get through high school. Then the downward escalator stops, sort of, and I end up at West Point—but a total fluke and only because of my high school base-ball coach. What does that all add up to?"

No clue there either, and if escalators were involved, I wanted no part of any of this. I'd been on an escalator once. Never again. I'm the type who likes to get up and down stairs on my own. Meanwhile, huge dark clouds were taking over the sky, making the houses and the trailers and the bayou and the trees all look small. I kept my eyes on those clouds.

"And what about Charlie?" Bernie said. "Where's he headed?"

Charlie? He was a great kid and I loved him. Other than that, I had zilch.

Bernie pulled up in front of a trailer raised up on blocks. The sign in front was shaped like a member of the nation within. This was a vet's clinic: the smells can't be missed.

"Chet?" Bernie looked down at me. "What are you doing on the floor?"

I was on the floor? Maybe so, but why the vet? Did a bullet once take a little notch out of one of my ears? I knew something about that, but if so it was long ago. I was feeling tip-top, hadn't been shot at in ages.

Bernie laughed. Something was funny? "C'mon, big guy. This has nothing to do with you. Are we working a case here or what?"

We were working a case at the vet? I remembered nothing about that, but if Bernie said so then . . . then I didn't have to re-member. Hey! With Bernie around, maybe I didn't have to bother remembering anything at all! My mind could be free just to . . . just to . . .

At that moment the phone buzzed.

"Hey," said Bernie.

Captain Stine's voice came over the speakers, harsh and hoarse, like he partied every night, although in fact, according to Bernie, he never partied, not even back in his college days.

"How're you doing?" he said.

"Fine," Bernie said.

"Still in one piece?"

"Why wouldn't I be?"

"No particular reason," Stine said. "Spent much time in the Lone Star state?"

"Not recently," Bernie said. "I was based at Fort Hood way back when."

"Make any enemies while you were there?"

"Spill it."

"I was enjoying working up to this at my own pace," Stine said.

"Have your fun elsewhere," Bernie said.

Stine laughed. He had the kind of laugh that sounded like it needed oil, if that made any sense, which it didn't, but too late now. "And here I thought we were buddies," Stine said.

Bernie said nothing, one of his best techniques, if that hasn't come up already.

Stine stopped laughing. "We got an ID on the Quieros dude who tried to take you out. Angel Melendez, Guatemalan national with no visa or green card, living in Houston, second ward."

"Never heard of him."

"And the Quieros?"

"We've been through that already."

"Maybe you offended one of them without knowing it," Stine said. "They're very touchy, what with all that machismo shit they have to carry around twenty-four seven."

What a horrible job those guys had, whoever they were. I couldn't help feeling bad for them.

"Nothing like that happened," Bernie said.

"Nothing like you offending someone happened?" said Stine. "Did I hear that right? Must be a bad connection."

"What do you want to do?" Bernie said. "Score easy points off me or solve the case?"

"Right back at ya," said Stine.

Click.

Bernie looked at me. "Know what I think?" I waited to hear, ears cocked way up high. "It was a car theft job gone wrong, with a second dude around somewhere, maybe getting scared off when I came outside."

Second dude? Could I have missed that?

Bernie smiled at me. "I'd bet the house you sniffed out a second dude that night, could clear this all up in a second."

Bet the house? But I hadn't smelled a second dude, not a whiff. I barked at Bernie, a bark of the sharp and loud attention-getting kind. Losing the house was out of the question.

Bernie laughed. "I'm right, huh?" I barked again. He laughed some more. I barked some more. He gave me a pat. "That's enough, big guy. Let's get to work." I tried to hit the brakes on the barking thing, maybe didn't quite get it done. "Ch—et?"

We hopped out of the car. I gave myself a good shake, not the long kind that goes from head to tail and back again—no time for that if we were on the job—but enough to clear my mind. The feeling of a clear mind? One of my favorites. And it's a feeling I get just about every day! We climbed a couple of cement block steps and entered the vet's trailer.

There was a small room in front, the rest of the trailer walled off. Behind those walls all sorts of barking started up right away, plus some meowing. The person at the desk was the kind Bernie calls a no-nonsense woman—I knew that from the expression on her face: a square-shaped face that had been in lots of weather, a face you often saw on no-nonsense women. She looked at me, then Bernie, back at me, then raised her voice.

"Knock it off."

The barking and meowing stopped at once. That was when I noticed the bird in the woman's hands, a black-and-white bird with some orange here and there, although it was hard to be sure about the colors on account of the bird being covered practically from beak to tail with some oily stuff. It had small eyes the same color as the oily stuff, but they weren't fierce the way birds' eyes usually are. Instead, they looked dull and even . . . not happy. Not that birds ever seemed happy to me, but this particular bird was actually sad, no question about it, and even though birds are way down on my list, I got a sudden urge to give it a lick. How crazy was that! Especially with the bird being covered in all that gloop, which I didn't want anywhere near my tongue.

"You the vet?" Bernie said.

"Uh-huh," said the woman.

"I'm Bernie Little, and this is Chet."

Her eyes shifted toward me. "Something wrong with him? We're closed right now—I forgot to put up the sign."

"Nothing wrong with Chet," Bernie said. "Is that a tern?"

"Black skimmer," said the vet, dabbing at a folded wing with a cotton ball.

"Was there an oil spill?" Bernie said.

The vet's lips, already thin, got thinner. "Not that I'm aware of." She picked up a fresh cotton ball, dipped it into some liquid, wiped off a blob of gloop. The vet had big strong hands, but her grip on the bird was kind of loose. *Take off, bird. Fly away.* I tried to make the bird get a move on with my mind, if that makes any sense. Not to the bird: it didn't even twitch.

"Is it going to be okay?" Bernie said.

The vet had dark eyes, almost as dark as the bird's, and now they turned fierce in a very birdlike way. "Almost certainly not. And if you're not here for an emergency, we're closed for business right now, like I said."

"I don't know for a fact that it's an emergency," Bernie said. He laid our card on her desk. Her glance moved over to it.

"You're a detective?"

"Hired by the Boutette family to find Ralph."

She looked quickly up at Bernie. "Did something happen to Ralph?"

"He's missing."

The vet opened her mouth to say something, but Bernie spoke first.

"I know, I know—he's a loner, kind of eccentric, goes off on his own. Everybody around here's in a big hurry to mention all that. But I've been doing this for a long time. Ralph Boutette is missing."

"What do you—" the vet began, but at that moment two kids came in, one after the other and each of them holding a bird covered in gloop.

"Doctor Ory?" said the bigger kid. "We were fishin' and we found these."

"Are they dead?" the smaller kid said.

The bigger kid turned on her. "Can't be dead. Their eyes are open."

I love kids, but maybe there are things they don't know. For example, I'm pretty sure from some of the cases we've worked that you can be dead with your eyes open; and these two birds were. The smell starts up right away and I could sniff it out, even with all that gloopiness in the air.

Dr. Ory rose, holding out her bird toward Bernie.

"Um," said Bernie. "I'm not . . ." But he took the black skimmer in his cupped hands, real careful, like it was one of those Christmas tree ornaments that break so easily, even just from getting brushed by your tail on a run around the tree. Around and around and around and . . . Meanwhile, Dr. Ory had gone over to the kids and given their birds a quick look. She took a couple of baggies from her pocket and put a bird in each, sealing up the baggies tight.

"But their eyes are open," the bigger kid said.

The smaller kid started to cry. I went over and sat beside her, and was still way taller. I crouched down a bit: it was all I could think of to do. She turned my way and her eyes got big. The crying stopped, at least the sound part, if not the tears.

"Where did you find them?" Dr. Ory said.

The bigger kid's lower lip trembled. "At the place where we go fishin'."

"By the old tour dock?"

The kid nodded, getting his lower lip under control.

"You did good, kids," she said. "Wash up over at the sink and go on home."

The kids did what she'd told them. After they'd gone, she turned to Bernie, hands out for the black skimmer. Bernie shook his head; his eyes had that hard look now. When I see that I get my paws under me, all set for just about anything.

Doctor Ory put the black skimmer in a baggie. "Afraid I'll have to cut this short," she said.

"Heading over to the old tour dock?" Bernie said.

Doctor Ory glanced at Bernie in a new kind of way. "Yes, as a matter of fact."

"We're coming," Bernie said. There was a pause. When humans don't like an idea, they get a look on their faces like they've just tasted something not too good. Dr. Ory got that look now. "Unless you've got some objection," Bernie added.

"Suit yourself," said Doctor Ory.

FOURTEEN

Dr. Ory drove a very small but new-looking car that made hardly any sound at all. A car with no *vroom vroom*? Not my kind of ride, baby. We followed her down the street that bordered the bayou, around a bend and out of town. The clouds got darker and so did the bayou. It disappeared behind a wall of growing things—so much green around here, not so easy to get used to—and then slipped back into view again, kind of like a very long and wide silvery snake; a thought I wished I hadn't had. Dr. Ory pulled up to an old falling-down shack. We parked beside her.

"They used to take swamp tours out of here," she said over her shoulder, walking down toward the bayou. "Business went under a few hurricanes ago."

"A Boutette-owned business, by any chance?" Bernie said.

Dr. Ory paused, then kept going. "Their timing could be better."

"Was Ralph involved in the business?"

"I doubt it—Ralph's an inventor."

"So I've heard," Bernie said as we came to the remains of a dock, just a few rotting planks hanging over the water. "I haven't been able to get a line on what he actually invents."

Dr. Ory gazed down into the water. It wasn't as still as it had looked from a distance but lapped at the bayou bank in tiny waves and made sucking sounds at whatever was holding things up down under us. "This is the farthest upland point reached by the tide," she said. "A good place to find things washing in from the Gulf."

"Like dead birds," Bernie said.

Dr. Ory nodded. We all scanned the water, except for me, since I already knew there were no dead things out there at the moment. I smelled rot to beat the band, whatever that might mean—would I ever forget that night at Blackheart's Desert Roadhouse where the fans beat up some way-past-it old band because they refused to play their one hit? And in the fight it turned out the singer's long hair was actually a wig and he was bald underneath? That was when we took off, and took off fast. But where was I? Rot? Yes, I smelled rot and . . . and also there was that strange scent again, froggy, toady, snaky, with the peppery poopiness mixed in.

"Don't see anything," Dr. Ory said.

"I've got binoculars in the car," Bernie said, and went to fetch them.

That left me alone with Dr. Ory on the dock. Why hadn't I gone with Bernie, like I normally would—especially when there was fetching involved? I had no idea. There was of course the fact that she had a biscuit in the front pocket of her jeans, but aside from that, I had no idea.

Dr. Ory turned to me. "Hey, Chet," she said. "One hell of a looker, aren't you?"

Dr. Ory: a gem. And if not a gem—not in Suzie's class, for example—I liked her just fine.

She smiled, the strange sort of wavery smile you see from humans who don't do a lot of it. "That's some tail wag you've got there."

My tail was—? Yes, no doubt about it. I tried to tame it down a bit, but my tail sort of has a mind of its own, as I'd learned in the past and was now learning again in the now, where I actually don't end up doing my best learning. When did I do my best learning? I tried to think.

"A real champ, I can see that," Dr. Ory. How nice of her! Any chance that a real champ would be getting a biscuit any time soon? She stopped smiling. "It's your buddy I'm iffy about."

What was this? She was iffy about Bernie? How could that be? My tail went still, actually began to droop before I took command.

Bernie returned with the binoculars. He held them to his eyes, scanned the bayou. "Nope," he said. "No birds." Then he went still. "But there's a boat coming out of the swamp up there."

"Let me see," said Dr. Ory.

Bernie handed her the binoculars. She peered down the bayou. Me, too. I saw a bright green boat in the distance, with a single small figure standing in the—what was the word Bernie had taught me? Bow? Kind of like—bow wow! I knew I would never forget again.

"What the hell's he doing out there?" Dr. Ory said.

"Who?" said Bernie.

"Somebody from Green Oil. That's their shade of green—it's on all their crap." She started jumping up and down, calling and waving. No way anyone on the boat could hear her—I could barely pick up the sound of the green boat's engine myself—but the small figure seemed to turn our way. Then the green boat started moving in our direction.

"Do they have platforms out in the Gulf?" Bernie said.

Dr. Ory nodded. "The newest one's not twenty miles from here."

The green boat—a bigger boat than I'd thought, with a steering wheel console set up in the middle and a covered sort of cabin in the bow—slowed down as it approached, came to a stop, gently rocking, about one long leap from the dock. The driver was one of those dudes with gray hair—cut real short in his case—who otherwise didn't look old at all. He wore a bright green T-shirt with short sleeves that made it easy to see his big arm muscles, and also a pair of wraparound shades, the kind where you see yourself in them. I saw myself, plus Bernie and Dr. Ory. I don't like shades to begin with, and those mirrored ones are the worst.

"What were you doing out there?" Dr. Ory said, her face set in a hard look.

"Hey, you're the vet," the man said, no hardness at all in his voice. "I came by and introduced myself a few months back. Wes Derrick, VP Environmental Security."

"I remember," said Dr. Ory.

Wes Derrick turned to Bernie and smiled in a good-pally way. Bernie didn't say anything.

"This is Bernie," Dr. Ory said.

"Nice meeting you, Bernie," said Wes. "That your dog?"

"We're more like partners," Bernie said. Wes seemed to give Bernie an extra-long look. Hard to tell, what with those shades, and why would he be doing that? Bernie had told him the truth, pure and simple. Dr. Ory was also watching Bernie, but in a different way.

"Good-looking pooch," Wes said at last. "What's his name?"

"Chet."

Wes smiled. "Nice name."

He was right about that. Chet: It was me and I was it! Wow. What a thought! And now we were all getting along great. Was a ride in this bright-green boat a possibility? I didn't see why not.

"Sometimes I wish I had a dog," Wes said.

Kind of strange: didn't he already have one? It sure smelled that way. In fact, I came very close to thinking it was a dog I knew, impossible since I was new here, had no buddies yet.

"Probably doable," Bernie was saying. "What's environmental security?"

"Job one, far as I'm concerned," Wes said. "It's all about making one hundred and ten percent sure that Green Oil is the very best global citizen around. Which is how come I'm out here now, matter of fact, in answer to your question, ma'am. We got a report of a possible AAW, and I check each and every one of those suckers out."

"What's AAW?" Bernie said.

"Adversely affected wildlife. In this case, we had an incoming about kids maybe finding a bird of some sort in not the best shape."

"Two bridled terns, both female," said Dr. Ory. "Dead from exposure to toxic oils and tars. Plus I found another bird myself—black skimmer, male—now also dead."

"Can't tell you how sorry I am to hear that," Wes said. "And the fact that it appears to be an isolated incident with no underlying company involvement doesn't make it any easier."

"What are you talking about?" Dr. Ory said.

"Break it down for you," Wes said. "Isolated incident means just the three AAWs." He motioned down the bayou. "I've checked the whole stretch from Point Grief on up to right here and found zip. No more AAWs, no slicks, no tar balls, zip. No underlying company involvement means our monitoring systems out on the platforms are reporting negative across the board. Not one single solitary pumped ounce has gotten away from us."

"What about that new platform?" Dr. Ory said.

"Number nine?" said Wes. "Same as all the others, reporting negative." The bright green boat rose a bit, then settled back down. Ripples appeared on the surface and slowly vanished. Wes seemed to be watching them, although I couldn't be sure on account of his shades. "Any reason you're asking about number nine in particular? It's not even operational yet."

"Why is it so close?" Dr. Ory said.

Wes took off his shades, just like I'd been wanting him to. He had soft brown eyes. I'd been expecting something else, not sure why. Funny how the mind works.

"Don't know what to tell you, ma'am. That's where the oil is. But the fact of number nine being the newest also makes it state of the art in terms of safety and all those good things." He glanced at his watch. "Anything else I can help you with? I'm a touch overdue."

"What do you think happened to the three birds?" Bernie said.

"Can't say for sure," Wes said. "But it's the kind of thing that probably happened routinely long before there was an oil business, and will long after we're getting all our power from cold fusion or whatever's around the corner."

"Not following you," Bernie said.

Wes turned his soft brown gaze on Bernie. "Not local, are you?"

"True."

"From out west somewhere?"

"Right again."

"I'm pretty good with accents, comes from a life spent in the oil patch. If you were from these parts, Bernie, you might know we get natural oil seeps out in the swamp sometimes. Not much of a stretch to imagine a bird or two diving down for a fish and getting all mucked up."

"So this was a natural event?" Bernie said.

"Sums it up," said Wes. "But, ma'am, you turn up anymore victims, you give me a call, anytime, night or day." He pressed a button and the engine started up, rumbling real low. The bright green boat slid up to the dock. "Here's my card," Wes said, handing it to Dr. Ory. He backed the boat away and started to turn it down the bayou. "Enjoy your visit, Bernie." Wes waved and drove off, not real fast but with nice and steady power. I couldn't take my eyes off the waves the boat made, spreading so evenly across the bayou. Boats: I was loving everything about them.

Bernie and Dr. Ory seemed to be watching the waves, too, both of them real quiet. It was beautiful on the bayou. Maybe I could even get used to the air, so thick and heavy.

"How about I buy you a drink?" Bernie said.

"I could use one."

I've been in a lot of bars, comes with the territory, and seen bar-type things happen you wouldn't believe so I won't bother running through them. Rooster Red's in St. Roch wasn't the best or the worst. Hey! It wasn't even the first Rooster Red's I'd been in! That was in Dry Wells, a desert town about a day's ride from the Valley, just the one visit and it had ended with—but I wasn't going to mention things that you wouldn't believe, so forget it. I learned it's not so easy to get a toilet seat off from around the neck of one of those real-thick-necked bikers: let's leave it at that.

"What I actually wanted to talk to you about," Bernie said, "was Napoleon."

"Ralph's dog?" said Dr. Ory, putting down her beer. Bernie was drinking beer, too. Water for me, of course. We had a nice corner table in the back of the room, with a fan blowing in our faces and a view through a big window of rusted-out cars and a pile of old bricks. There's all kinds of beauty in life.

"I assumed you'd be his vet," Bernie said.

"That's right."

"Tell me about him."

Dr. Ory blinked. "Tell you about Napoleon?"

"Yeah."

She shrugged. "He's a typical four-year-old pug in good health except for some early-stage arthritis in his right hip."

"What's he like?"

"You're asking me about Napoleon's . . . personality?"

"Yeah."

She gave Bernie a look. "You're an unusual sort of detective."

"Do you know many?" Bernie said.

"Actually you're the first."

"We're all like this."

Dr. Ory laughed, then took a sip of beer. It left her with a beery mustache she didn't seem to notice. "The fact is, Napoleon's very well named. He's dictatorial, crabby, likes everything just so. Ralph feeds him on ground filet mignon and nothing but."

Ground filet mignon? At that moment I understood the case through and through. We had to find Ralph and find him fast.

"I'm guessing they have a close relationship," Bernie said.

Dr. Ory nodded. "Ralph's one of those men who's awkward around people, but animals are a different story." She paused. "Do you know the type?"

"Negative," Bernie said. He drained his glass and raised it high for the waitress to see. Sometimes Bernie gets thirsty in a real big hurry. I'm the same way.

Throat clearing is an interesting thing. In humans it means they're about to start something over; for us in the nation within it means we've got something caught in there. Dr. Ory cleared her throat now and said, "What do you think's happened to Ralph?"

"Two narratives at the moment," Bernie said. "Narrative one is all about his eccentricity—loner off by himself, all that. Narrative two is—"

The waitress came with a fresh beer for Bernie. She had a long ponytail, not as long as tails I'd seen on some actual ponies, but I always liked seeing any kind of tail on a human. "Just letting you know we've got an all-you-can-eat fried shrimp special, ten ninety-five including sides," she said.

"Not for me," Dr. Ory said.

"We're not eating," Bernie said, then checked the waitress's nametag and added, "uh, thanks, Fleurette."

That was Bernie: so polite. Maybe there were some dudes around who weren't comfortable with other people, but no way was he one of them.

"Narrative two," he went on when Fleurette went away, "is more complicated, involving a shrimp heist and the Boutette-Robideau rivalry."

"Shrimp heist?"

"You didn't hear about it?"

"I've learned to tune out anything to do with their stupid feud."

Bernie nodded like that made sense. "A ton of shrimp was allegedly stolen from Grannie Robideau by Lord Boutette, who's since been arrested for the crime. The Robideaus think Ralph was involved and he's on the run."

"What a crazy story."

"You don't buy it?"

"Not saying that," said Dr. Ory. "Anywhere else, involving any other participants, I wouldn't believe it for a second."

"But?"

Dr. Ory sighed. "But here, with them, anything's possible. Who ended up with the shrimp?"

"Good question," Bernie said.

Or something like that, but I got distracted by a side door opening and the deputy sheriff, Scooter Robideau, stepping inside. He looked our way and stepped right back out.

"Chet!" Bernie said. "What's all that noise about?"

Dr. Ory laughed. "He smells grub," she said, just as the kitchen door swung open and Fleurette came out with a huge tray of fried shrimp.

But that wasn't it at all! Until it was. That shrimp smelled too good to resist, at least to me. And then to Bernie and Dr. Ory as well! They changed their minds about the shrimp! Chet the Jet catches a break!

FIFTEEN

We bought a nice big supply of chow and put it away in *Little Jazz's* galley, which turned out to be the kitchen—Bernie doing most of the putting away and me helping as best I could—and then sat on the deck and watched the sun go down.

"If we light this little coil," he said, "the mosquitoes won't bother us."

He lit the little coil. The mosquitoes stopped bothering me even though they were still bothering me. Meanwhile, the sun disappeared, and the tops of the trees went black at the same time the sky behind them was on fire, and so was the bayou all around us. After a while, the sky blackened and blurred in with the trees, the water holding on to the daytime a little longer. Then all we had for light was the orange glow of the coil. I watched mosquitoes dive down onto it and vanish with a sizzle.

"Maybe you're wondering why I didn't show Ralph's glasses to the sheriff," Bernie said.

Me? No. And even with him now bringing it up, I still didn't feel like wondering about it. Was that bad of me? The truth was, I felt like listening to those mosquitoes sizzle away, a brand-new kind of fun for me, and brand-new kinds of fun were the best, although the old familiar kinds of fun were pretty good, too. Even just as good, so forget all this.

"Comes from being outsiders here," Bernie said. "Can we trust the sheriff? Even a little? And the Boutettes—haven't they got a right to know about the glasses? But do we let down our hair for them? En masse or just one? And if just one, which? Mami? Duke? Lord? We're in a madhouse."

Uh-oh. That didn't sound good. Weren't we on a houseboat? I felt it rise and fall very slightly, creaking in a very pleasant way against the dock. And what was this about our hair? I'd been shaved once, something about the heat. Never again, Boutettes or no Boutettes.

All of a sudden, my eyelids got heavy. I started to have a thought about madhouses and houseboats maybe being the same thing.

"But here's a starting point," Bernie said first thing the next morning, a cup of coffee in his hand, steam rising into the still air. "I didn't show Ralph's glasses to the sheriff or to the Boutettes, but I did show them to Mack. Does that mean that deep down in my unconscious mind he's the one I actually trust?"

Bernie's unconscious mind? That was new. And it had a deep down part, meaning we were probably dealing with something pretty big. So where was he keeping it?

"What are you sniffing at, big guy? I need a shower?" And then Bernie did something amazing: he raised his arms, one after the other, and sniffed his pits! That Bernie!

"I don't smell anything," he said.

Of course not, but at least he'd tried. You had to love Bernie.

"How about we get started," Bernie said, "and grab something to eat along the way?"

After that, there was a bit of commotion, and then Bernie

said, "Okay, okay." He poured kibble in my bowl, had himself a nice muffin, and hardly a moment or two later we were on the move in the pirogue, Bernie driving, me standing tall in the bow, no time lost. Breakfast is the most important meal of the day: you hear humans say that all the time.

Back in the boat and slicing through the water, waves starting right up out of nothing on both sides of the bow. What a sight! What a feeling! I forgot my problems pretty quick, not hard since I had none at the moment. Hey! Were we making those waves ourselves? I wondered about that all the way to the fork in the bayou. We went the same way as before and were soon on the lake. Bernie slowed down as we came to Isle des Deux Amis and steered us completely around it.

We gazed at the island. A big black bird on a branch of the tallest tree gazed back at us.

"Know what we'd do if we were playing by the book, big guy?" he said. Shoot the black bird right out of the tree? That was my only idea. "Let the sheriff in on Ralph's glasses and get him out here with a work crew and a backhoe."

Bernie powered down to nothing and we came to a stop, rocking gently in the water. His eyes got a distant look. He rubbed his chin, something that hardly ever happened with Bernie. It meant he was doing his hardest thinking. I could feel it, as though he was trying to lift a huge weight, like that time at the gym when he'd bet a couple of muscleheads that—but let's not go there.

"At least I've come up with a solid reason for not playing this one by the book," he said after a while. He gave me a smile. "It's on account of you, Chet."

On account of me? What had I done? That little fuss about breakfast? All at once, I felt a bit pukey. My tail got ready to sag, not possible since I was sitting on it, although it tried anyway.

"Remember when we searched the place?" he said, gesturing at Isle des Deux Amis. "You'd have found a body if there was one. So that's that." He hit the throttle and we took off across the lake. I stood up, giving my tail a chance to raise itself high, which it did at once. We were a team, me and Bernie, had dug up a body or two in our career, me doing most of the actual digging. Not to take anything away from Bernie when it comes to digging—he's not at all bad for a human. But can humans get their legs involved in digging the way we do in the nation within? You know the answer. Not the point. The point is, I know what I'm doing in the sniffing-out-bodies department, one of my best things. Once I even smelled one in a freezer. Was the perp surprised or what?

"Have to do better than that," Bernie had told him after he'd checked the freezer.

"But when will I get the chance?" the perp had said as Bernie snapped the cuffs on him. "I'm a cinch to get life without parole."

That had made Bernie laugh. "See, Chet," he'd said, "there's some good in everybody." Which I'd already known, but it was nice to hear.

"Meaning you'll let me go?" the perp had asked.

Making Bernie laugh even harder. The fun we had in this business! A bright yellow butterfly fluttered by the pirogue. I snapped at it for absolutely no reason, snapped and missed, which was always the way with butterflies.

And very soon after that, we were tying up at Mack's dock, Bernie tying the actual knot, but I'd jumped onto the dock with the free end of the rope in my mouth, just trying to help.

"Good boy—you remembered."

Remembered what? My mind was blank on that one. We walked around the deck, checked things out.

"Pickup's not around," Bernie said. "Meaning he's probably not here." Bernie took out his credit card. "Just as well." He moved toward the glass slider at the back of Mack's house. Bernie was real good at slipping locks with that credit card, but for some reason the sight of the card brought to mind that horrible night when the maître d' at the Ritz had cut our credit card in half, not because we were breaking into rooms—no way, not that night—but because he said it was no good. No good—that maître d' had never even seen us before, didn't have a clue as to how nifty Bernie was with that card. And after that how come Bernie hadn't popped him in the mouth? It's always fun to see dudes with a combover get popped in the mouth, on account of how what they've got left for hair goes flying straight up and just like that they're bald. Our night at the Ritz was a complete mystery to me.

Bernie got busy with the card, then paused and glanced at the sign nailed to one of the stilts. "Iko's gotta be his dog." Bernie peered through the glass. "Don't see one."

Because there was no dog on the scene, except for me, of course, which I'd known from sniff one. But it wasn't only that: any member of the nation within would've been barking his head off by now.

"Hey," Bernie said. "It's not even locked." He slid the door open, stuck his head inside, and peered around some. Or maybe not. I was already inside Mack's crib and couldn't be sure about what was happening behind me.

Mack's downstairs was one big space with a living room part at the front and a kitchen in back. Bare wooden floor and lots of empty beer cans around: it reminded me of a mountain cabin we'd been in on a case involving a wilderness camp and a missing kid, except that the walls of that cabin had been bare, and these walls seemed to have . . . ? Was it possible? The heads of animals sticking right through them? Open-eyed animals—a deer, a bear, a mountain lion, and a big-horned sort of goatish creature I wasn't familiar with. Oh, yes, I'm familiar with mountain lions and bears; don't get me started. The point was these open-eyed beings didn't give off the scent of the living or the dead. If anything they smelled like Bernie's suit—he has just the one, and I don't see the problem with the checked-pattern, no matter what anyone says—when it comes back from the dry cleaner's. That was a smell I didn't particularly like, but I'd never hated it until now.

I felt Bernie's hand on the top of my head, just resting there for a moment, and then gone. My mind cleared in the nicest way. We got to work.

Casing the joint is one of our best techniques at the Little Detective Agency. I sniffed around under the furniture—snapping up a fried chicken ball before I'd hardly begun. One of the many nice things about fried chicken balls is that they're a kind of a ball, and balls roll when they get dropped. I've had good luck with fried chicken balls in my career—also pineapple chicken balls and sweet and sour chicken balls, too important not to mention.

Meanwhile, Bernie was opening a set of drawers. He always starts with the bottom one and works up. I'm not sure why, just know it's the right way. I finished up with my part, finding no guns, no ammo, no dope, no blood, none of the sort of stuff we looked for, and went over to Bernie. He was going through a drawer—an old pair of sweatpants, a bunch of papers, and—

"What's this, big guy?"

He held up a metal thing, kind of like a piece of pipe but very thick and very short, with a big sort of nut at one end. Bernie peered into the open end. "Looks like it's been heated up." He sniffed at it. "But I don't smell anything." No? Even though his nose was practically touching the thing? Bernie's nose is small when it comes to noses in general, but for a human it's right up there. So what's it for? He tried to work the nutlike thing off the pipe part, but it was stuck. He peered at it again. "Heavy-duty threads, but they're warped," he said, way too hard to understand and by me in a flash. Bernie started to put the pipe thing back in the drawer, then paused and tucked it into his belt instead. I'd been hoping it would go back in the drawer. Its smell reminded me of the birds in Dr. Ory's office.

We went into the kitchen. Bernie opened the fridge. There was a tub of fried chicken inside, plus a few cases of beer. Another fried chicken ball struck me as a very good idea at that moment, but it didn't happen. Casing a joint builds your appetite real fast: I'd noticed that in the past and now noticed it again.

We climbed the stairs to the top floor, Bernie leading and then me, although I ended up getting there first. Not much to see: a bedroom with an unmade bed and the bedside fan still on, clothes on the floor, a closet, a big mirror on the wall—Hey! With Bernie in it! And a real tough-looking member of the nation within. I got ready to . . . Me? Had I been through this before?—and also there was—

I ran to the closet and barked.

Bernie smiled and came over.

"Found the shrimp, didn't you, Chet?"

Shrimp? What was he talking about? Normally in this setup we take positions on either side of the door, Bernie draws the .38 Special, and the door gets opened real quick and real careful. None of that happened now. Why not? Something about shrimp? There were no shrimp!

I barked again.

"Good boy," Bernie said, and opened the door in a free and easy way, like it was our own closet back home on Mesquite Road.

No shrimp. Just Vannah Boutette, no news there, and the fact that she wasn't wearing anything was probably not a shocker either. The only surprise was the gun in her hand, and me being surprised by that could only mean it hadn't been fired in a long, long time, or never. She pointed the gun at Bernie.

SIXTEEN

"Oh," Vannah said. "It's you."

Bull's-eye: it was us. I was glad to hear her say that: getting somebody mixed up with somebody else can send things off the rails pretty fast when guns are around. Vannah's gun was kind of small, with a pretty pink grip, but I'd seen what even small guns could do. The question was why didn't she seem to be lowering it? Wasn't Vannah the client? I had a real clear memory of her handing over three grand in greenbacks, the very best kind, in my opinion, three grand now in Bernie's front pants pocket, nice and safe. I could still pick up the faint scent of shrimp those bills were giving off.

"Correct," Bernie said. "So how about pointing that popgun in some other direction?"

Vannah smiled. Some humans, but not many, know how to smile in a dangerous way. Vannah turned out to be one of them, although Bernie might have missed that. His gaze, which normally in a situation like this would have been on her face, with a glance or two down at the gun, seemed to be wandering a bit.

"How come men think they're only the ones with balls?" she said.

Had I heard that right? How could I not have, what with my hearing being the way it is and the fact that she was only a step or two away? This was the most confusing moment of my life.

"Um," Bernie said. Maybe he was confused, too. We're a lot alike in some ways, me and Bernie. "Maybe we could discuss that under more peaceable conditions."

The gun stayed the way it was, pointed at Bernie's chest. "Am I making you nervous?" Vannah said.

"Not that so much," Bernie said. "More like angry."

Uh-oh. Bernie was angry? That meant one thing and one thing only: I was angry, too! It came over me so suddenly, like a hot red flood, although maybe not the red part, Bernie being of the opinion that I can't be trusted when it comes to colors. The next thing I knew that little popgun was clattering across the floor, Bernie had a tight grip on my collar—the brown one, black only for dress-up—and Vannah was holding her wrist and no longer smiling, dangerously or in any other way.

"What the hell? He bit me!"

Bernie peered at Vannah's wrist. "More like an accidental tooth scrape, I'd say."

"Why'd you go and let him do that?"

"Begs the question," Bernie said.

"Huh?"

Which was always what we got when Bernie raised the begging-the-question thing.

"Doesn't matter," Bernie said. "Why were you hiding in the closet?"

"Because I heard you sneaking around downstairs, why else?" Vannah said.

When Bernie's not buying something, he has this quick head

shake, a simple one-two. There it was. "How do you explain your reaction when you saw it was us?"

Vannah shrugged. Bernie's gaze dipped down, but for just an instant; he dipped it back up pretty quick, as quick as I'd ever seen him in this kind of setup, the naked woman setup happening surprisingly often in our business. He bent down, picked up the gun, broke it open.

"It's not even loaded," he said.

"Must mean we're friends," Vannah said.

Bernie tossed her the gun. She caught it in one hand, real easy, then pointed it again at Bernie. "Bang," she said.

"Put it away, for Christ sake," Bernie said.

"Where?" said Vannah.

"Get some clothes on," Bernie said.

"Now I am making you nervous—don't deny it."

Bernie said nothing. Vannah came out of the closet, went over to the bed, put on jeans and a T-shirt that were tangled up in the sheets.

"You've got something going with Mack?" Bernie said.

"What a disgusting suggestion," Vannah said. "I'm totally faithful to Frenchie, except when it comes to work, and Frenchie's totally cool with that, especially in this putrid economy."

"There was an uptick in the latest jobs report," Bernie said.

"I don't believe any of that shit," Vannah said, giving her hair a shake. "But what you're missing is that Mack is my brother."

"Ah," Bernie said.

"What does that mean?"

I was with Vannah on that. I waited to hear.

"Wish I'd known, that's all," Bernie said. "Ah" meant he wished he'd known something? At last I knew! I got a very good feeling about the case.

"Why?"

"Context is everything in this business." Wow! A new one on me. Maybe it was one of Bernie's jokes. I'd always thought the business was about grabbing perps by the pant leg. "It might have helped me do a better job on our first go-around out here."

"Did you scare him?"

"Why do you ask that?"

"Because he was expecting me for breakfast."

"Do you usually eat in the nude?"

Vannah laughed. "I sleep in the nude, even for short naps— which was what I was doing while I waited for Mack to show. How about you?"

"How about me what?"

"Sleep in the nude."

"Um," said Bernie, followed by "er," and then "I don't, uh, have a hard and fast rule about it."

"Hard and fast, huh?" said Vannah, which I didn't get but for some reason that led to a long silence, finally broken by Bernie.

"I don't see how I could have scared Mack," he said. "Doesn't he know I'm working for you?"

"Not easy to know what he knows and doesn't know," Vannah said. "Mack has his own reality. There's a lot of that in these parts, in case you haven't noticed."

"I'd like to find out more about his reality," Bernie said. "Where do I look?"

"I don't know," Vannah said. "The fact is . . ." She paused, then gave Bernie a look, hard and direct. "Can I trust you?" she said.

"You're the client," Bernie said. "This won't work if there's no trust between us."

"That's a careful answer."

"It's the only one you're getting."

Vannah turned away, facing the wall with her back to us. Human fear has a sharp kind of cheesy smell that just can't be missed. It was coming off her in waves. I felt not too good about her wrist.

"I need time to think this over," she said.

"Take a month or two," Bernie said.

She turned. "You really think—" Then she had a good look at Bernie's face, and her own face went red, or at least pink, which I'm pretty sure of, a pinkness that started on her neck and rose up like a jar getting filled. "How come Frenchie didn't tell me you were a prick?"

"Maybe he likes me," Bernie said.

"That wouldn't mean anything," Vannah said. "He's got lousy judgment when it comes to people."

Bernie eyed her and said nothing, but his gaze seemed to be speaking, if that makes any sense. I even thought I came close to hearing what it meant.

"A prick for sure," Vannah said.

For some reason that word coming up again so soon made me think of a long-ago night down Mexico way, a huge round moon, and a member of the nation within named Lola. Funny how the mind works, but I didn't worry about that, just enjoyed the memory. It was one of my very favorites.

". . . emotions and personalities are immaterial," Bernie was saying when I tuned back in. "You've got to make a decision."

"I'm a woman—have you noticed?" Vannah said. "Emotions are at my core. Why do you think I'm here?"

"Good question," Bernie said. "I thought you were back in the Valley."

"It's a free country," Vannah said. I was totally with her on that—it was one of my strongest beliefs. "But the truth is I was worried about Mack. It doesn't take much to tip him back into that world."

"The drug world?"

Vannah nodded. "He's not answering his phone."

Bernie went to the window and gazed out. "Does Ralph have a drug habit?"

"No way," Vannah said. "He's as straight as they come. Which is what makes their friendship so improbable."

Bernie turned quickly. "Whose friendship?"

"Mack and Ralph's," Vannah said. "Best friends, really—in Ralph's case I'd say Mack's his only real friend in the world."

"Are they gay?" Bernie said.

"I wouldn't know," Vannah said.

"I have more faith in you than that."

She gave him a sharp glance. "Especially about matters of sex?"

"I didn't say it."

Vannah was still for a moment or two. I thought she was about to get real mad, but instead she laughed. "I've made my decision: I'm trusting you. For now."

"Great," said Bernie. "Let's kick things off with a true answer to the Mack and Ralph question."

The Mack and Ralph question? All of a sudden, I was a little lost. I licked my muzzle, encountering a nice surprising leftover flake from the fried chicken, and felt back on track, but totally.

"I really don't know," Vannah said. "This is still a very old-fashioned place in some ways. But if I had to guess, I'd say Ralph was one of those asexual people you hear about sometimes."

"And Mack?"

"Mack is more complicated. He's been married twice, for starters."

"But?"

"Yeah," Vannah said. "But."

Then came a long silence. I could feel both of their minds at work. My own mind was work-free at the moment, just sort of feeling their thoughts, which was more than good enough for me.

"Do you think they're together somewhere?" Vannah said.

Bernie didn't answer right away. His thoughts, whatever they were, got darker. "It's one possibility," he said, "especially if the Robideaus are right about Ralph."

"I'm not following you," Vannah said, which made two of us.

"They think he was in on the shrimp heist."

"How stupid are they?"

"Why is that stupid?"

Vannah just shook her head.

"If you know what happened to the shrimp, Vannah, now's the time to tell me."

"Lord hijacked them, period."

"Maybe," Bernie said. "Where are they now?"

"The shrimp?"

"Yeah. What happened to them?"

Vannah raised her hands, palms up. She had nicely shaped hands, not big, but they looked strong and soft at the same time, in fact reminded me of the hands of Tulip and Autumn from Livia Moon's. I made up my mind about Vannah on the spot: she was a keeper. Too bad about her wrist, but it really was just a scrape: there was hardly any blood at all, except for a tiny pool on the floor. I licked it up and that was that.

"Should we try to trace them?" she said.

"The shrimp?" Bernie said. "That would have been my next move."

"But?"

"Ever heard of the Quieros?"

"Is that the taco joint?"

Bernie smiled at her, a very nice smile that reminded me of some of the smiles he sent Suzie's way. I missed her.

"What's funny?" Vannah said.

"Nothing," said Bernie. He took the strange pipelike thing out from under his belt and showed it to her.

"What's that?" she said.

"I was hoping you'd tell me."

"Some kind of plumbing?"

"Could be."

"What's it got to do with anything?"

"Probably nothing." Bernie tucked it back in his belt. Then he rubbed his hands together. I loved when he did that: it meant we were gearing up. "All I need from you now is the name of Mack's drug contact."

"You don't want to get involved with those people," Vannah said.

"I'm actually in the mood for it."

Her eyebrows—like a lot of women, Vannah didn't have much going on when it came to eyebrows, certainly nothing to match Bernie's, so lovely and thick, with a language all their own—rose. "You're a doper?"

"Lose the *R*," Bernie said.

For some reason, Vannah thought that was pretty funny.

We rode up to the city, Bernie at the wheel and me in the shotgun seat, Vannah staying behind in case Mack returned, or maybe for some reason having to do with the fried chicken. I hadn't been clear on that, but Bernie and I had both had some and she hadn't, so I couldn't really blame her.

We took the bridge high over the river. "Mighty Mississip, big guy," said Bernie, and if he was talking about the river he was right about the mightiness, like an enormous living thing on the move, actually kind of snakelike, a thought I'd tried not to have, but there it was again. But a few moments later, my mind forgot whatever had disturbed it, and was now nice and clear. Way to go, big guy! Chet the Jet!

We got off at a ramp and not long after that entered a crummy neighborhood. I knew crummy neighborhoods from back in the Valley, and this one was as crummy as the crummiest. That didn't mean the people in them were crummy—we had some good buddies in Vista City, for example, like Ronny and Vonny Von Runge, great old-timey musicians who sometimes let Bernie sit in on ukulele, and probably would again, as soon as they got out of Central State Correctional, their plan to dress up as toll takers on the new turnpike we have in the Valley and get rich in a day having fallen apart for some reason I couldn't remember.

We drove down a rutted street lined with boarded-up houses and came to one that wasn't. Bernie pulled over, checked a scrap of paper Vannah had given him, then took the .38 Special out of the glove box and stuck it in his pocket. I loved the .38 Special, hadn't seen it in way too long. And Bernie was a crack shot, could hit spinning dimes right out of the air. Maybe that would be happening real soon.

"All set?"

What a question! Bernie caught up to me at the front door, a very big and solid-looking door for such a small boxy house.

"Nice and easy, big guy," Bernie said. I sat beside him, which was what nice and easy meant. He knocked on the door.

A little eyeball slot in the door opened right away and a dark eyeball looked out. A deep, raspy voice came through a speaker. "Don't know you."

"Bernie Little," Bernie said. "And this is Chet. We're friends of Mack Larouche, down in St. Roch."

"Still don't know you."

"We can get past that just by you opening the door," Bernie said.

"Tryna be funny?"

"We're just trying to see Cleotis. Anything beyond that's gravy."

Gravy was a possibility? I smelled none but inched closer to the door anyway, something I can do in a sitting position, no problem.

"Cleotis don't talk to nobody he don't know."

"We have a mutual friend."

"You said that already. And you look like a cop."

"I'm not a cop."

"You look like a cop."

"How about I flash my non-cop badge?"

"Huh?"

Then another voice came through the speaker, but from farther away. "Let him in."

Big heavy bolts got slid aside, one, two, more. The door swung open. A real big guy stood before us, a sawed-off shotgun in one hand, pointed at the floor. He gave us an unfriendly look, at the same time speaking over his shoulder.

"He's got this real big mother of a dog."

"So?" The second voice again, coming from through the partly open kitchen door at the back. "Do your goddamn job. Pat him down."

"Chet won't like that," Bernie called toward the kitchen.

Wouldn't like what, exactly? I was still back at the mother thing, my mind refusing to get around it. "And I'm not armed," Bernie added.

"Pat him the fuck down."

"You heard the man," said the big guy. "Get over by the wall."

"It's really not nece—" Bernie began, but then the big guy planted his big free hand in the middle of the Bernie's chest and shoved him against the wall, so hard Bernie's feet left the floor. Bernie hated that kind of thing. It brought out a side of him I hardly ever saw, but I saw it now, saw it in the way he bounced off the wall, spun around, and chopped the big guy in the throat with the side of his hand, saw it in his wild eyes.

The big guy went down fast, clutching his neck, doing some moaning and writhing, and also sort of looking surprised, way too late. Bernie swept up the sawed-off, pointed it at the kitchen door. A dude in a bandanna charged through it, drawing a gun from his belt.

"Drop it," Bernie said.

The dude wasn't nearly as big as the other guy, had a face that reminded me of Prof at Valley College back home, our go-to buddy when it comes to tracking money that perps don't want tracked. Prof was a smart man and had smart eyes. This dude was sort of like that, but younger, thinner, and maybe a little darker. He dropped the gun.

"Cleotis?" Bernie said.

The dude nodded.

Bernie lowered the shotgun. His eyes went back to normal. "What's with you drug dealers?" he said. "Why does there always have to be this drama?"

"We're all prisoners of one culture or another," Cleotis said.

SEVENTEEN

I stood right beside the big dude, still lying on the floor, although he'd amped down the noise a bit. Actually, it was more like I was standing over him instead of beside, specifically at the head end.

"Sweet Jesus," he said, "goddamn animal's gonna bite my face off."

Or something like that. The big dude wasn't so easy to understand now, his voice having come all over raspy.

"His name is Chet," Bernie said. "Not goddamn animal."

"What the fuck are you talking about?" the big dude said.

"So an apology would be nice," Bernie said.

"You want him to apologize to the dog?" said Cleotis.

"A general apology will do."

"Will it make him stop with the goddamn snarling?"

"Give it a try."

Someone was snarling? News to me, but now that the idea was out there, I thought I did detect a little snarling, perhaps from some distance away.

"Herman?" Cleotis said.

"Yeah?" said the raspy dude.

"What's the holdup? Apologize."

"Fuckin' hell. I'm sorry as shit."

"Apology accepted," Bernie said.

"Didn't stop the snarling," Cleotis said.

Cleotis was right about that. I could hear it now for sure, loud and clear.

"Ch—et?" Bernie said, in this special way he has of saying my name.

The snarling stopped. It got nice and quiet in Cleotis's crib, even peaceful. When things turn peaceful, you pick up little details you might have been missing. For example, I noticed that my mouth was open kind of wide, and it was even possible that I was drooling on Herman's head. Not a lot, but most humans have a thing about being drooled on. I like it when humans like me. It's as simple as that. I got my mouth closed nice and tight and backed off a step or two. We were guests, don't forget. I took a nice deep breath, smelled pot, coke, and smack, not usually found all in one place. The learning never stops in this business.

This was a shotgun house. I was very familiar with the type, totally comfortable. We sat in the kitchen, Cleotis and Bernie—with the sawed-off across his knees—at the table, me at the window where I could keep my eye on a real big black bird perched on a clothesline. As for Herman, he'd gone upstairs for a little lie-down.

Cleotis examined our card, looking at the front, the back, the front again.

"Are you the kind of PI who sells folks out to the cops?" he said.

"Sell?" Bernie said. "Never. I give sometimes, but hardly ever and certainly not here. I've been hired to find a missing person, and as soon as we find him we're gone."

"Talking about Mack the shrimp guy from down in St. Roch?" Cleotis said.

"Not originally, but now he's missing, too."

"Sounds complicated," Cleotis said. He shook a cigarette out of a pack lying on the table and lit up. "Smoke?" he said.

Bernie gazed at the cigarette pack. Oh, no. I'd seen that gaze before. And he was trying so hard to quit, once and for all. That was what he always said: *Once and for all.* What did it mean? I wasn't sure. Now he said, "One can't hurt." I knew the meaning of that: he'd soon be lighting up—like now, with Cleotis holding a lit match across the table in a friendly sort of way, although his eyes, so smart, got a quick here-and-gone look that didn't seem friendly at all—inhaling nice and deep, blowing out a slow stream of smoke, and saying "Ah."

"Care to sample anything else while you're here?" Cleotis said.

"Huh?" said Bernie, giving him a close look. "What makes you ask that?"

Cleotis's eyes got vague and cloudy. He shrugged.

Bernie was still for a moment. Then he reached over to the ashtray and mashed the cigarette out. He and Cleotis stared at each other. Cleotis's eyes got a little vaguer.

"The man we were looking for originally is Ralph Boutette, also from St. Roch," he said.

"Never heard of him."

"According to our information, he and Mack Larouche are best friends."

"I wouldn't know."

"But you know Mack."

"I do."

"In what context?"

Cleotis smiled. He had very nice teeth, maybe the biggest and whitest I'd ever seen on a human. "In what context, man? In the context of I deal smack and he's a customer."

"When was the last time you saw him?"

"Three weeks ago this coming Friday at nine p.m. He was here for about ten minutes, spent five hundred and fifty bucks."

"You're very precise," Bernie said.

"This is a business," Cleotis said. "I keep records."

"In your head?"

"It's that kind of business."

Bernie gave him a look. "Someone like you—"

"Don't even say it," Cleotis said, the vagueness gone from his eyes now; in fact, they were a little too bright, in my opinion.

Bernie nodded. "How was Mack when you saw him?"

"His usual self."

"Meaning?"

"Smelly," said Cleotis.

That caught my attention. Smells hardly ever got mentioned in our interviews. Was this an interview? I thought so, and if it was, then the case would soon be cleared, on account of Bernie's interviewing technique. I bring other things to the table.

"Smelly?" Bernie said. He'd noticed, too. No way to sneak something like that past Bernie.

"Mack stinks of shrimp," he said. "An occupational hazard. Even his money stinks."

His money stinks? That came so close to reminding me of something. I don't like that not-quite-remembering feeling at all, but it usually goes away pretty soon—like right now!—and then . . . and then . . .

"Why does Mack come all this way to feed his habit?" Bernie said. "No sources closer to home?"

"Good question," Cleotis said. "Are all PIs as smart as you?"

Bernie gave him a hard look.

"Not pulling your chain," Cleotis said.

Don't even think about it, amigo. Chain up Bernie? You'll have to go through me first.

"You're obviously a sharp guy," Cleotis went on. "And this dog of yours is aces, no doubt about that. He wouldn't be for sale, by any chance?"

"Correct," said Bernie.

Cleotis picked up our card, gave it another glance. "Maybe you don't realize you're in one strange corner of the country right now. My advice? Go on back home. When dudes start disappearing in ones and twos in these parts, there's never a clear-cut result."

"We'll have to prove that to ourselves," Bernie said. "And this may be a strange corner of the country, but you're not walled off. Ever heard of the Quieros?"

Cleotis had one of those smooth, unlined faces. Lines appeared on it now. "Heard of them, yeah, but they're not around here."

"Yet," Bernie said. He rose. "Where should I start looking for Mack?"

"He'll turn up," Cleotis said.

"Alive?" said Bernie.

"I've seen it happen."

"Does he keep a place up here in the city—an apartment, maybe?"

"Wouldn't know about that," Cleotis said.

Bernie made this little *click-click* mouth sound that means we're out of here. We left the kitchen, went to the front door.

Bernie leaned the sawed-off against the wall and we walked outside, hopped in the Porsche, and drove off, nice and slow, in no particular hurry. We don't scare easy, me and Bernie.

We turned down the first street we came to, turned down the next one, and then the next, and hey! We were circling the block, just another one of our techniques at the Little Detective Agency. We've got a bunch. Perps and gangbangers: heads up.

We parked by a big pile of trash around the corner from Cleotis's. "Shutters all closed on his side windows, big guy. Meaning we can see them but they can't see us." He gave me a pat. We sat. That was what this was called: we were sitting on Cleotis's house.

After a while it started to rain. Raining again? What was with this place? Bernie closed the roof. Rain pitter-pattered down on it, dialed up to pounding, then went back to pitter-pattering again, a very soothing sound. I took my eye off Cleotis's crib for a moment to see if Bernie was enjoying the pitter-patter, too. His head was slumped forward and his eyes were closed. No surprise there: sitting on dudes often made Bernie sleepy. I turned back toward Cleotis's house. Water ran steadily from the drainpipes into a gutter and down to the street, a very pleasant sight. The rain pitter-pattered on and on.

And what had we here? A car pulling up in front of the house? Yes, a small white car with a mashed-in headlight on one side, the windshield wipers going back and forth, back and forth in a way that was hard not to watch. But I made myself not watch them as a woman in a baseball cap got out of the car and hurried to Cleotis's front door, her flip-flopped feet splashing through puddles in the yard. She knocked on the door. It opened and she went inside, but not before I'd noticed one other thing about her, namely a long ponytail hanging down from above the back strap of her cap. That ponytail got me to thinking. I thought for a bit, then shut it down and just watched those wipers going back and forth, then cranked up the thinking again, then shut it down and went back to watching the wipers, then—

Bernie straightened up real suddenly. "What are you barking about?"

Whew! I'd been trapped in a real bad circular thing there. And leave it to Bernie: he'd busted me out of it. Things were much quieter, any barking that might or might not have been going on now silenced. Bernie glanced toward Cleotis's house, saw the car.

"Customer in a hurry," he said. "How do we know? The engine's running."

Bernie: the smartest human in the room. Did a car count as a room? I'd hardly started to wonder about that when Cleotis's door opened and the ponytail woman came out. Bernie went still.

"Fleurette?" he said. "The waitress from Rooster Red's?"

I knew I'd remember! Sometimes all I need is a little time.

"Good boy, Chet. Good, good boy."

My tail did what wagging it could, not easy in the shotgun seat. Fleurette hurried to her car, jumped in, and took off right in our direction. She went by us without a glance, one of those drivers who lean over the wheel, holding on tight. We followed.

Bernie's the best wheelman in the Valley, in case you don't know that. He could follow from close behind, way behind, from many lanes over, even from in front, all without being spotted by the target, the trickiest part of following, which was how come we kept an eye out for Fleurette checking her rearview mirror. But she didn't, not even once, so we followed mostly from close behind—into a nicer part of town, the rain stopping all at once, steam rising off the pavement.

"The scales are starting to fall from my eyes, big guy," Bernie said.

Oh, no! Had this ever happened before? Not that I recalled.

Did it hurt? I glued my own eyes to Bernie's, saw nothing new. All I knew was that scales—take the one Bernie keeps under the bed with the dustballs, for example—are pretty big and hard to miss. I saw no scales, not falling from Bernie's eyes, not on his lap, not on the floor. But if Bernie said scales were falling from his eyes, then that was that. All I could do was wait and see what happened next, not my usual approach. What was my usual approach? Make it happen! Which is why they call me Chet the Jet, although only Charlie actually calls me that. And me.

What happened next was Fleurette turning onto a street lined on both sides with nice-looking old buildings and—whoa! Lots and lots of drunks? Yes: there's no hiding drunks from me, drunken humans being different from nondrunken ones in so many easily spottable ways. These particular drunks were wandering around with big plastic cups in hand, most of them—even the very fattest and wobbliest—dressed in shorts and T-shirts.

"Welcome to Bourbon Street, Chet," Bernie said. "Keep an eye out for my wallet—I lost it here twenty years ago."

Twenty years sounded like a long time, but I might have been wrong about that, numbers maybe not showing me at my best. As for Bernie's wallet—a nice old leather wallet with a smell all its own—I knew for a fact that he had it in one of his front pants pockets. Just the same, I kept my eye out for wallets, and what did I see almost first thing? A skinny skateboarding kid zooming down the street and lifting a wallet right out of some drunk's back pocket in a single smooth and easy motion. I loved kids! The drunk took a huge swig from his plastic cup and pointed out a neon naked woman sign to a buddy drunk. They both got a big kick out of it.

Fleurette made a few turns, ended up on a quieter block. She parked in front of a building with a coffee cup sign hanging over the door and went inside. Bernie pulled in right behind her real quick. We jumped out—me actually jumping, and through the open window, what with the top down, not so easy for a hundred-plus pounder—and hurried into the coffee shop. Why were we hurrying? I only knew why I was hurrying: it was on account of Bernie hurrying. Sometimes he gets this look on his face meaning there's no time to lose. He had it now.

The coffee shop was small and dark and pretty much empty, one customer gazing into a steaming mug over at a corner table and nobody behind the counter. Fleurette was already at the back, opening a door and starting up a flight of stairs, her ponytail swinging through a shaft of light.

She'd closed the door behind her, but it wasn't locked. Bernie opened it real slow. No sign of Fleurette on the stairs, rough and wooden stairs leading to a dimly lit landing above. Bernie turned to me, finger across his lips, meaning we were in quiet mode. Great idea! We hadn't been in quiet mode for way too long. We started up the stairs, Bernie first and me following, but I was in the lead by the time we got to the top, all of that commotion taking place in quiet mode. We were pros, me and Bernie.

We stepped into a narrow corridor lit by one hanging bulb, with a door on each side and another at the end, all of them closed. I followed Fleurette's scent—typical young female with an extra touch of shrimpiness—down to the end door. Bernie put his ear to it. Did he hear that sound from inside, one of those quick human breath intakes, maybe called a gasp? He showed no sign of it. Instead he drew the .38 Special, turned the knob, and threw the door open.

Fleurette, standing by a bed, which was pretty much the only furniture in the room, wheeled around toward us, her eyes wide and her face all out of shape. Bernie pocketed the gun right away.

We moved toward the bed. Mack lay on it, wearing nothing but a T-shirt with a leaping fish on the front. I saw again what a wiry dude he was, not much flesh on him at all. A needle was sticking out of one of his skinny arms.

"Oh, my God," Fleurette said, both hands over her mouth, something women did but never men. "Is he—"

Bernie put his finger on Mack's neck, but I already knew the answer, actually wasn't even thinking much about it. Instead, my mind had suddenly taken me by surprise, lighting up a memory from my puppy days, long before I got together with Bernie. I had hardly any memories from that time, not easy days living with gangbangers in an abandoned house in South Pedroia. Raul, the only gangbanger who had no interest in swatting or kicking at me or my kind, had ended up this way, on a bare mattress bed just like Mack. I even remembered the T-shirt he'd been wearing, decorated with a picture of an AK instead of a fish. Funny how the mind works.

EIGHTEEN

O h, no," Fleurette said. "No, no, no." She backed away from
the bed, hands pressing her face like she was holding it together. She looked at Bernie, then at me, and Bernie again. All
kinds of changes went on behind her eyes. She spun on her heel—
one of the cooler human moves, in my opinion—and strode toward the door, like she was out of here and that was that: probably
not in the cards, on account of how we do things at the Little
Detective Agency when dead bodies are in the picture.

Sure enough, Bernie blocked her way. She tried to cut around
him, but I got there first. Blocking someone's way was a fun game
I liked to play from time to time, or actually just about any time.

"Who are you?" Fleurette said, backing up. "Let me go. You
have no right."

"Have to do better than that," Bernie said.

Her eyes narrowed in that squinting look humans sometimes show you, never a pleasant sight—undoing the whole heel-
spinning thing in a way I couldn't even begin to understand, so
I didn't waste a moment on it—and said, "I've seen you before,
right? At Rooster Red's?"

"Nice try," Bernie said.

"What do you mean?" Fleurette said. "Now I remember distinctly—you had a beer with Dr. Ory just the other day."

"True as far as it goes," Bernie said.

"I don't understand," said Fleurette. "And you're starting to scare me."

Bernie glanced over his shoulder at Mack, lying on the mattress, the needle still sticking out of his arm. I wished Bernie would take it out. "You weren't scared already, Fleurette?"

"I was. I am. I'm scared out of my mind."

"You'll have to get past that," Bernie said. "There's not much time."

"For what?"

"Let's start with Cleotis."

"Cleotis? I don't know any—"

Bernie's voice didn't get louder, but it changed in a way that made it seem bigger and way harder to ignore—not that I'd ever think of ignoring Bernie—and got the fur on the back of my neck to stand up a bit. A furry thing like that happening, all from just the sound of him. That was us. We're a good team, me and Bernie, as a lot of perps could tell you. What he actually said I sort of missed. It might have been: "Start with what he told you about me." Or something like that.

Fleurette shook her head, so hard that her ponytail kept swinging after her head had gone still. I came very close to asking myself if the same . . . something or other. "He—he didn't mention you," Fleurette said. "I don't even know your name."

Bernie gave her a long look. "Bernie Little," he said. "And this is Chet."

She shot me a sidelong glance. "Normally I like dogs."

"That'll work perfectly with Chet," Bernie said. He handed

Fleurette our card. "We've been hired to find Ralph Boutette. Any idea where he is?"

"Ralph Boutette? Is he lost? I don't understand."

"How well do you know him?"

"Ralph? Enough to say hello to on the street, but I can't even remember the last time I saw him. He's not a customer at the restaurant. Ralph's a bit of a loner, in case you haven't—"

Bernie held up his hand in the stop sign. "Tired of hearing that," he said. "And there's no time—I told you already. You've got maybe two minutes to be smart. I can't stall any longer."

"Stall?"

"The cops."

Fleurette put her hands over her chest. "You're calling the cops?"

"No way around it. I'm obligated to report unnatural deaths."

"Unnatural?"

"He didn't die of old age."

Fleurette turned to the bed. "Poor Mack. I didn't know he was in to mainlining."

"No?" Bernie said. "He wasn't exactly shy about discussing his addiction with me the very first time we met."

"I'm not talking about his addiction," Fleurette said. "I'm talking about mainlining. Mack hates—hated—needles. He was a snorter."

Bernie's voice went quiet. "How do you know?"

Fleurette looked away. "I, uh, heard."

"Do you work for Cleotis?"

She said nothing.

"Look at me," Bernie said.

Fleurette turned to him real slow, like it took all the strength she had. Her eyes met Bernie's for a moment, then moved down slightly, to maybe his nose. Bernie has a very nice nose, not small for a human and with a tiny sort of bend, hardly noticeable at all, that he says he'll get fixed when he's sure he won't be in anymore fistfights. Which I hope is never! He's so good with his fists, as lots of perps could tell you; a pleasure to watch, although just watching at times like that isn't my best thing.

"It's not really what you'd call working for him," she said. "I run an errand or two, that's all."

"Running dope, you mean," Bernie said.

"Judge me all you want," said Fleurette. "I've got an autistic kid at home—two of them if you count my husband."

"You can explain that to the cops," Bernie said, taking out his phone.

"Oh, no, please," she said. Her face twisted up in a way I don't like seeing even in bad guys. Was Fleurette a bad guy? I didn't think so. "Please let me go."

"Why should I?" Bernie said, his voice real hard, so maybe I was wrong about Fleurette.

"They'll put me in prison." She started to cry, tears running down her face, one or two dripping to the floor. "What will happen to my kid?"

"I'll try to cut you a break," Bernie said. "But you've got to tell me everything."

"Everything about what?"

"Start with why you're here."

"Why I'm here?" Her mouth opened, closed, opened again, but no sound came out.

"Cleotis sent you is the answer," Bernie said.

She stayed motionless for a moment or two. Then she nodded. Bernie: a great interviewer, which I may have mentioned before, but why not again?

"What did he want you to do?" he said.

"Cleotis doesn't like getting talked about behind his back."

"You'll have to weigh that little quirk of his against your kid's future."

"Oh, Christ," Fleurette said, wiping her tears on the back of her arm. "How come everything happens to me?"

"You're doing better than Mack," Bernie said. "For now."

Fleurette backed away. "Are you threatening me?"

"The situation is threatening you," Bernie said. "We're your only chance to push back a little."

"Who's we?" Fleurette said.

"Chet and I, of course."

Fleurette looked at me. It so happened that I'd moved over to where a few of her tears had fallen, and was at that very moment licking them off the bare floor. Hadn't tasted human tears since . . . since I couldn't remember when! How do you like that? Fleurette's were warm and salty, with just the very slightest hint of pot smoke.

She blew out a long breath, seemed to get smaller.

"Cleotis told me to get right over here and move Mack somewhere else."

"Why?"

"He didn't say—I swear to you."

"Where did he tell you to move him?"

"He said Mack would know. My job was to get him out of here and fast."

"Cleotis was helping Mack hide out?"

"I think so."

Bernie glanced around. "Who owns this place?"

"I don't know."

"What about the shrimp?"

Fleurette blinked. "Shrimp?"

"The shrimp that got stolen from Grannie Robideau."

"I don't know anything about that."

"No?" Bernie said. "Someone the spitting image of you has been serving those stolen shrimp by the trayful over at Rooster Red's."

"How—" she said, her face, kind of pale to begin with, paling some more. When human faces get that way, fainting often comes next. I got ready—to do what I wasn't exactly sure. But how could it hurt to be ready?

No fainting happened. Fleurette took a deep breath—I could hear her sucking in air—and said, "How do you know that?"

"Actually knowing would be giving me too much credit," Bernie said. "More like a hunch until you confirmed it."

Fleurette gave Bernie a hard look. "Why are men such jerks?"

"No time to get to the bottom of that now," Bernie said. "Did Mack own Rooster Red's?"

Fleurette went on giving Bernie the hard look for a bit, finally nodded. "His dad built the place."

"Is his dad still around?"

"Died a long time ago."

"How?"

"They said his liver gave out."

"What about his mother?"

"Same thing, except later," Fleurette said. "Mack was pretty much alone in the world, except for his friendship with Ralph."

"And Vannah, of course."

"Vannah?"

"Vannah Boutette—his sister."

"Vannah's not close to anybody," Fleurette said. "Where'd you get that idea?"

"Doesn't matter," Bernie said. Which was nice to hear, all this back-and-forth being not so easy to follow. And now I had the green light to not even try! Bernie always comes through. "Who stole the shrimp?"

"Lord Boutette? That's what everybody says."

"Was Ralph in on it?"

"Ralph? Sure doesn't sound like him."

"Did Mack do a lot of that—buying stolen goods?"

"Maybe a little."

"How much did he pay for the shrimp?"

"I didn't see them come in," Fleurette said. "Actually I sort of did, but it was still dark. I was working the early shift, so it was maybe five in the morning."

"Sunday morning."

"Right. Usually I open up, but Mack was already there. I could hear him talking in the kitchen. The lights weren't on so I just sort of waited out back."

"Why?"

Fleurette shrugged. "The lights not being on, and all. It was just kind of . . . I don't want to say creepy."

"Who was he talking to?"

"Some man. I didn't recognize the voice."

"So it wasn't Lord Boutette?"

"No."

"What were they talking about?"

"I couldn't tell. The ventilating fan—the big one over the back door—was running. It's pretty noisy. Then after a minute or two, the other man came out. I don't think he saw me—I was in the shadows, kind of behind my car."

"What did he look like?"

"Like I said, it was pretty dark."

"Could it have been Ralph?"

"This guy was a lot taller."

"What else?"

"Nothing, really."

"What did he do?"

"Walked around to the front of the building. I heard a car start up and drive away, but I didn't see any headlight beams."

"Describe his walk."

"Huh?"

"Posture, gait, anything you noticed."

"Like I said, it was—"

"Don't tell me it was dark, Fleurette. Just try to remember."

Fleurette closed her eyes, a very interesting human thing. Why do they do that? Did something change inside them? Did something change inside me when I closed my eyes? I thought about closing them but decided against it. We were on the job.

Her eyes opened. "I do remember one thing," she said. "He walked like a cowboy."

"Yeah?"

"Not the kind of walk that comes from riding horses. I'm talking about the kind that comes from wearing cowboy boots, if that makes sense."

"It does to me," Bernie said, which had to mean we were cooking. When cases started to make sense to Bernie it was just about time for me to grab the perp by the pant leg. Fleurette was wearing shorts, but not the real short kind, nothing I couldn't handle.

". . . and then?" Bernie was saying, meaning we weren't quite at the pant leg moment.

"Mack came outside. It was starting to get a little lighter and I could see he was counting money. I sort of pretended I'd just driven up." She shook her head. "I'm not sure why I did that. Just a feeling. We said good morning, he drove off, and I went in. Later, when the oyster guy came, I opened the big cooler. It was empty the night before and now it was full of shrimp."

"Mack was counting money?" Bernie said.

"A fat wad, if you want the truth."

"I do," Bernie said, his eyes real watchful.

"I've told you the truth," said Fleurette.

Bernie nodded, but just a little. "You've got our card," he said. "Don't be afraid to use it."

"I can go?"

"Drive safe."

I kept an eye on those short pant legs until she was out the door.

NINETEEN

Just like us in the nation within, humans come in different colors, and also just like us the particular color ends up being not the most interesting thing about them, or even close, in my opinion, although I'm not at my best with colors, so don't pay attention to any of this. The point is that the cops who swarmed into the room above the coffee shop not long after Fleurette had gone were all different in color, going from very light to very dark. The darkest cop wore the fanciest uniform, fancy uniforms being a little detail you watch for in this business. They all took in the sights in the same order: Mack lying on the bed, Bernie standing nearby, me sitting at his feet. Then they all turned to the fancy-uniform cop, the way humans do when waiting to find out what happens next. The fancy-uniform cop was peering at Bernie.

"Bernie?" he said. "Can't be you."

"Why not?" Bernie said.

"Son of a bitch," said the fancy-uniform cop. Then he took Bernie in his arms and swept him right off the floor, a total first in my experience. "Son of a bitch," the cop said again, actually waving Bernie around in the air a bit. The eyes of all the cops got very big.

"Put me down, Henry," Bernie said.

"Is that an order, Captain?" said this Henry dude.

"More like a suggestion," Bernie said.

Henry set Bernie back down on his feet but didn't quite let him go, instead started pounding him on the back. Bernie did the same to him.

"Son of bitch," Henry said. "I can't believe this."

"Everybody has to be somewhere," Bernie said.

Henry glanced at the other cops. "Catch that, gentlemen? 'Everybody has to be somewhere.' Bernie Little here's always the smartest guy in the room, and don't you forget it." From that moment on, I knew Henry and I had a lot in common, were going to get along great. I wasn't too sure about the other cops, most of them now eyeing Bernie in a pinched-face sort of way.

"Cram the cynicism, ladies and gentlemen," Henry said. "Without Bernie Little there'd be no more me, and I know how broken up y'all'd be if that happened."

The cops sort of shuffled around, gazing this way and that. None of them looked broken up to me.

"Saved my life, this pig-headed hard-ass," Henry said. "Mine and a whole shitload of others, that goddamn day."

The cops started seeing Bernie afresh, although I couldn't be sure, my mind at that moment knocked off the tracks by the pig-headed thing. I've had an encounter with a pig or two in my time—none pleasant, and one actually a bit painful, pigs turning out to be surprisingly aggressive when cornered—but the point was, I'd seen pig heads extremely up close, and they weren't at all like Bernie's: just for starters, Bernie had nothing you could call a snout. Then there was shitload, also a problem. I could never hear that word without thinking back to the Portapotty trailer-truck fiasco at Spaghetti Junction, the place where all the Valley freeways meet. Right in front of our eyes! And even closer, our windshield wipers nowhere near up to the job! A horrible memory, and if a repeat was on the schedule, we were looking at a bad day, not that any day could actually be called bad.

"Was this in Iraq, Lieutenant?" said one of the cops.

"Damn straight," said Henry.

"What went down?" said the cop.

"Hell on earth," Henry said, finally letting go of Bernie. "We were trapped in this goddamn—"

Bernie made a little back-and-forth wave with his finger.

"Huh?" Henry said. "Don't want me to talk about it?"

"Well, um," said Bernie. "Everyone did their job and there's nothing really to, uh . . ." He gazed down at his sneakers, still kind of dirty from getting stuck in the mud on Isle des Deux Amis.

"Haven't changed a bit," Henry said. He took Bernie's chin in his hand, and for one crazy instant, I thought he was going to kiss him. He gave Bernie's head a little shake instead. "How's life?"

"I'm a private investigator out west these days," Bernie said, rubbing his chin. "This is Chet."

"Looks like a champ," said Henry, gazing down at me. "That tail wag's off the charts. I'd bet he's taken out a lot of wineglasses."

"You'd win," Bernie said.

Everybody laughed, at what I didn't know.

"What brings you to our godforsaken corner of the planet?" Henry said.

Bernie turned toward the bed, and then all the cops, like a flock of birds, did the same.

"That was you, calling it in?" Henry said.

Bernie nodded.

"What's the story?"

"We found him just the way you see."

"Who is we?"

"Chet and I."

Henry nodded, then went to the bed and pressed his finger on Mack's neck, just as Bernie had done. "OD," he said. "Textbook."

"Looks that way," Bernie said.

There was a slight pause. "You know him?" Henry said.

"Name's Mack Larouche," Bernie said. "He was a seafood wholesaler and bar owner in St. Roch."

"And your interest in him?" Henry said.

"Maybe we could step into the hall," Bernie said.

Henry turned to the cop in the next-fanciest uniform. "Get an ambulance down here. Find out what the barista downstairs has to say. The rest of you clear out."

The cops cleared out. The second-fanciest one got on her phone. The rest of us—me, Bernie, Henry—stepped into the empty hall, me arriving first after only a slight confusion.

Henry—a real big dude, in case I haven't made that clear—gazed down at Bernie, not something many dudes can do. "Private eyes working in my territory make me nervous," he said. Kind of a puzzler: nervous humans give off a sharp scent you can't miss, and I wasn't detecting the least whiff coming off Henry.

"Don't blame you," Bernie said. "I'd be the same. But this turned out to be a detour. We've been hired by some people in St. Roch to find a missing family member."

Henry jabbed his thumb at the closed door to Mack's room. "Not him?"

Bernie shook his head. "His best buddy."

"Get a decent retainer?"

"What's that supposed to mean?"

"Case doesn't look too promising from this angle, is all," Henry said. "Missing guy have a name?"

"Ralph Boutette."

"Doesn't ring a bell." Humans often said that, whether bells were ringing or not. At the moment, I heard only two: a church bell in the distance, and one of those tinkly bicycle bells only a few streets away. There was also a mouse in the wall, but that went without mentioning. "Who's your client?" Henry said.

"Sorry, Henry," said Bernie.

Henry's eyes didn't look quite as friendly now. "Hoping the deceased would lead you to Boutette?"

"That was the idea."

"How'd you track him here?"

"On a tip."

"From his supplier?"

"No," Bernie said.

"Because if you can ID the dealer, I need to know," Henry said. "Otherwise no harm no foul, no reason for further NOPD involvement. You and I can go down something nice and cold and rehash old times."

"Sounds great," said Bernie. "Have to take a rain check." Rain check: that had confused me so many times back home in the Valley, but now in this place made complete sense. A breakthrough: I loved that feeling! Was I now on the way to understanding every single thing in the whole wide world? I couldn't think of even one tiny reason why not. Chet the Jet!

"Sure thing," Henry said. "But you haven't answered the question—can you ID the scumbag who sold that little dude in there his last fix or not?"

Bernie looked Henry in the eye and said nothing. Henry stared back at him so long I started to get nervous myself. He shook his head.

"Hope you know what you're doing, Bernie. Lot of crazy muthas down there on the bayou."

"I'm learning that," Bernie said.

They shook hands and we started walking toward the stairs.

"Better learn quick," Henry called after us. "I'm talking about crazy swamp muthas who still write their own rules." He raised his voice; it followed us onto the stairs, sort of blowing down our backs. "Where bodies get lost real, real easy. Easier than not— hear me, you pig-headed son of a bitch?"

Downstairs the second-fanciest cop was leaning on the bar in a tired sort of way and writing in her notebook, no one else around. She glanced over at us.

"Wish I had a dog sometimes," she said.

"Plenty of rescues available."

"But it's a big responsibility."

"I've never actually thought about that," Bernie said.

The cop looked surprised. Maybe she didn't know we were alike in some ways, me and Bernie: some things never cross our minds.

"The captain sure seems sold on you," she said.

"His judgment is sound in other ways," Bernie told her. She laughed. "Find out anything from the barista?"

"Nada," the cop said.

"Who owns this place?"

"It's in receivership. She thought the whole upstairs was closed off, had no clue anyone was living up there, got pretty upset. I sent her home." The cop took another look at me. "What's his name, again?"

"Chet."

"Short for Chester?"

Whoa. Not the first time someone had run that one by us. What was wrong with plain old Chet, pure and simple?

We got in the car, roof up, no rain. "A lot to think about, big guy," Bernie said.

Really? I hadn't realized that, searched my mind for a thought. After a while I found one, a happy thought about snacks and how nice it would be if a snack or two came into my life real soon.

"But I'd say Mack's fear of needles would be number one, meaning a follow-up with Cleotis in on the agenda. How about we swing by Duke's little club on the way, maybe check out his menu?"

Menu? Something about a menu? How could you complain in this life?

We were parking in front of the Fishhead's sign when out the door strolled Duke, carrying something wrapped in foil. Not just something, but steak tips cooked teriyaki style. Smelling right through aluminum foil? It can be done. And what was this? He had a smudge or two of what looked like teriyaki sauce on his goatee? I took that for a good sign, no telling why.

He saw us, took a quick step forward like he was going to zoom off down the street, then stopped and backed toward the door. We hopped out, moved toward him, the two of us spread out a bit, just one of our techniques. Duke looked at Bernie, then me, and back to Bernie. Which right there was why this particular technique was so much fun: Duke couldn't look at both of us at the same time! Meaning that while his eyes were on Bernie, I could grab him by the pant leg before he could say Jackie Robinson, Bernie's favorite ballplayer, although not something I'd ever heard a perp actually say.

"Ch—et?" Bernie said.

At that moment, I found that somehow I'd gotten close to Duke's ankle and also that my mouth was open pretty wide. Funny how you can be in one spot and then another, so fast. What happens in between? A total blank! Maybe not you, speed-wise; no offense. But when Bernie says my name like that it means whoa, so even though my teeth had this feeling of wanting to press down on something real, real bad, a hard to describe feeling that just won't go away until—

"CHET!"

I backed off, even got my mouth closed, maybe not totally.

"What the hell's with him?" Duke said.

"Nothing," Bernie said. "What's with you?"

"Uh, same," said Duke. "Nothin' much, keep on keepin' on, like that."

"You don't seem happy to see us."

A sort of smile made a wavery appearance on Duke's face. "No, no, I'm real happy, couldn't be happier. Just a bit pressed for time, is all."

Bernie gestured at the foil package. "Grub for your brother?"

"Yup."

"Which one?"

"Huh?"

"Which brother."

"Lord, of course," Duke said. He shot Bernie a quick glance. "What're you gettin' at?"

Bernie didn't answer right away. Duke watched him, his smile wavering away to nothing.

"Tell you what," Bernie said. "We'll help you."

"Help me what?" Duke said.

"With your delivery."

"Don't need no help."

"It'll be our pleasure," Bernie said. "But first there's something I want you to see." He stepped over to the Porsche, reached under the seat, took out the thick pipe-like gizmo we'd found in Mack's drawer at the stilt house. "Look familiar?"

Duke eyed it and nodded. "The contraption I told you about, the one I seen on my last visit to Ralph's."

"You mentioned he showed you two, very similar."

"Yeah, but one was a piece of crap."

"This one?"

"Beats me."

"Take your time."

"Huh?"

Bernie handed him the gizmo. "Give it some attention."

"Think it's important?" Duke said.

"I wouldn't be subjecting my—" Bernie cut himself off. "That's what I'm trying to find out."

"Okeydoke," Duke said, turning the gizmo in his hands, peering inside. "Nope."

"Nope what?" Bernie said.

"Nope, I can't say which one," Duke said. "Hey! But where'd you get it anyways?"

"Turned up in the course of the investigation," Bernie said, taking back the gizmo. "What else did Ralph say that day?"

"Besides being pissed that one was crap?"

"Yeah."

Duke wrinkled up his forehead, thought for a bit. "Talked about the weather, 'member that distinctly. Ralph said it was gonna clear up, but I said it weren't, not with the wind outta the east, and he said it weren't outta the east at all, but outta—"

Bernie did the stop sign thing. "Did he say anything more

about the two pieces of equipment, such as their purpose, for example?"

"Don't need to shout," Duke said. "I hear pretty good, especially the left ear. Right's another story, all those years standing next to the drummer, back when I played bass in a Lynyrd Skynyrd cover ba—" He caught a look in Bernie's eye. "Nope. Nothin' about their purpose, nothin' about nothin'."

"Tell me about his friendship with Mack."

"They're buddies."

"Why?"

"Why they're buddies?"

"Right."

"You askin' me to explain, like, friendship between two people?"

"Exactly."

Duke wrinkled up his forehead.

TWENTY

"Maybe you'll think better if we walk and talk," Bernie said.

"Walk where?" said Duke.

"To Lord's place," Bernie said. "Kill two birds with one stone."

Even though I'd heard that one more times without result than I can count—which happened to be two, no better number in my opinion—I couldn't stop myself from taking a quick scan of the sky. No birds: there never were when the two birds with one stone thing came around. *Not going to happen, big guy.* Too bad. Bernie has a great arm, pitched for Army, as I may have mentioned, and I had no doubt about his ability to bring down one bird. But two at once? I couldn't wait, even though I knew from experience that I was going to have to.

"What's he barkin' about?" Duke said.

Barking? Yes, I heard it, too, for sure. I glanced around, spotted no members of the nation within.

"Probably just wants to get rolling," Bernie said.

That again? No! What I wanted was for Bernie to pick up a rock and fling . . . But then all of a sudden I did sort of want to get rolling. The barking stopped. We started down the street.

"Well looka that," Duke said. "It's like you know what's going on in his mind."

"We've been together a long time," Bernie said.

"Yeah? In dog years or human years?" Duke laughed.

What was funny? I didn't get that one at all, and neither did Bernie. "Not a meaningful distinction," he said.

"Huh?" said Duke.

"Especially if you're living in the now."

"Living in the now?" Duke rubbed his goatee, the way bearded-type dudes do when they're digging down deep in their minds. He discovered the teriyaki smear, gazed at his fingertips, a little confused, and then licked it off. Exactly what I would have done in his place. Maybe Duke was all right.

"Isn't that what life is all about down here?" Bernie was saying. "Living in the now?"

"You shittin' me, man?" Duke said. "We's all about livin' in the past."

Humans say lots of things I don't get. That one was the most ungettable I'd heard so far. I didn't waste any time on it, instead inched closer to Duke, walking right beside him in my most companionable style. In my judgment, the grip he had on that foil-wrapped package was kind of loose, even careless.

Duke knocked on the door of Lord's little green and yellow house. No answer. He knocked again.

"Your goddamn grub's here—open up."

The door stayed closed. I heard no sound from within, except for a running toilet, which happens all the time with toilets, even ours, and is one sound Bernie can hear real, real well. "There's only one aquifer, big guy. When it's gone, it's gone." He'd bought a new toilet and installed it himself, the plumber only coming at the very end, and the mopping up hadn't even taken the whole afternoon. Plus the fun we'd had! As for toilets in general: way too big a subject to go into now.

"Ain't even his normal nap time." Duke knocked again much harder. "Goddamn!" He made an impatient gesture and the foil wrapped package slipped from his—but no. Somehow he got a grip on it at the last instant. While all that was going on, Bernie reached out and turned the doorknob. The door opened.

"What the hell is wrong with him?" Duke said. "Who leaves doors unlocked in this town?"

We went inside.

"Lord? Lord?" Duke called. He put his hands around his mouth in a shape like the opening of a trumpet—love when humans do that!—and tried again.

No answer. Plenty of Lord scent around—not one of those everyday showerers, no doubt about that—although not as fresh as I would have expected, plus . . . what was this? Aftershave? Yes, the same square green bottle aftershave that Bernie used to like before Suzie put a stop to it. I'd picked up this aftershave scent somewhere else, and not too long ago. On Lord? Nope. I'm pretty good at remembering who smells like what, hard to explain why, just one of the things I bring to the table at the Little Detective Agency. But as for where I'd picked up this particular scent before, the answer refused to come forward in my mind, instead flitted about at the very edge. Does that ever happen to you? A very frustrating feeling. All of a sudden I wanted to lift my leg—just a notion, of course—against this hat stand Lord had in his front hall. You'd probably get some different sort of notion.

"Chet?" Bernie said. "What are you thinking?"

Whoa! I seemed to be right beside the hat stand and my leg was—not up all way, but certainly rising. How had that happened? I lowered my leg pronto, gave myself a good shake, clearing my mind of any bad notions—in fact, clearing it of everything—and followed Bernie and Duke into the kitchen, tail up, head up, a total pro.

They stopped in an abrupt sort of way, just inside the room. I squeezed in between them.

"Tell me I'm seein' things," Duke said.

Why would he want Bernie to do that? Of course, he was seeing things—weren't we all? I myself was seeing the old-fashioned stove with the claw feet—no bacon under it today, which I'd known from outside in the hall—the kitchen table where Bernie and the two brothers had polished off a bottle of bourbon, and on the table a sort of ripped apart black thing that might actually have been—

"Son of a bitch tore off the tether," Duke said.

Bernie nodded.

"What happens now?" Duke said.

"Jail time," Bernie said. "Soon as they run him down."

"What was the one you said was worse than a moron?"

"Cretin," Bernie said, "but they're not scientific terms and probably no longer socially acceptable."

"Socially acceptable?" said Duke. "What's that sposta mean?"

"I'm actually not sure," Bernie said, moving to the table. He picked up a sheet of paper lying under the remains of Lord's ankle monitor, held it so Duke could see.

"He left a note?" Duke said.

"Is this his handwriting?"

"How the hell would I know?"

"You're his brother."

"So? Think he was a novelist or something? Never wrote a word in his life, far as I know."

"What about in school?"

"Ralph did all the assignments—thought we'd been over this."

He grabbed the note and started reading. "'Dear Duke, Thanks for bringing over the supper—steak teriyaki, right?—but I'm up to here with this shit. I stole the damn shrimp, I confess. Meaning with my record I'd be doing time. Well, I ain't going to do no more time and that's that. I'm taking off for parts unknown and don't come looking for me. I'll be back when the dust settles. Tell Mami I love her. Your bro, Lord Royal Boutette.'"

"His middle name is Royal?" Bernie said.

"All of us got Royal for a middle name. 'Cepting Ralph, of course."

"What's his?"

"Can't see what that's got to do with anything."

"Never know in this business."

Duke gazed at Bernie for a moment or so. Did he see that brightness in Bernie's eyes, always a sign that he was enjoying himself? I sure did.

"Albert," Duke said. "Ralph Albert Boutette."

Bernie nodded. "What I'd like you to do now is read the note over—"

"'Dear Duke, Thanks for—'"

"—silently, and try to figure out whether it sounds like Lord."

"Sounds like him and silently at the same time?"

"Take a swing at it."

Duke shrugged, raised the note. His eyes went back and forth, back and forth, and his lips started moving although no sound came out. Charlie's lips did the same thing when he read: it looked way better on him.

"Hell, I don't know," Duke said. "Like what does Lord sound like, anyhow?"

"You're his brother."

"Why do you keep hammerin' me on that? You sayin' he sounds like me?"

"I'm saying you've known him your whole life," Bernie said, "meaning you must have a feel for how he expresses himself."

"Lord? He can't express himself for shit."

"Do you see that absence in the note?"

"Absence?"

"Is he expressing himself in his usual shitty way?"

Duke took another look. "Even shittier."

"How so?"

"How so? You think it's a smart idea, cuttin' off his goddamn ankle bracelet and takin' off like this?"

"Good question," Bernie said. "But not the one in front of us at the moment."

"No? How come?"

"Another good question," Bernie said. "You should be doing my job."

Duke laughed. He turned out to be one of those human laughers who open their mouth so wide you can see that strange pink thing hanging down at the back, a sight I don't like, no telling why. "Then I could pay myself 'steada you," he said.

Bernie went still. When he spoke his voice was extra-calm. I always listen for that extra-calm voice of his. What often happens next isn't calm at all.

"Are you paying me, Duke?"

"Uh, how do you mean?"

"Vannah gave us a three-grand cash retainer," Bernie said, "but if you—"

"Three grand? That thievin'—" Duke cut himself off, looked around in a confused sort of way, and happened to notice he was still holding the foil-wrapped steak teriyaki. He put them down on the tab—no, not the table. At the last second he maybe realized that would involve shoving the remains of the ankle monitor aside, so instead he laid the package on the nearest chair, which happened to be the chair right beside me. I'm having a very good life.

"Vannah did a little skimming?" Bernie said.

Duke licked his lips. "Not followin' you."

"Where did that retainer come from?"

"Can't say as I know."

"If you had to guess."

"I'm a real bad guesser," Duke said. "If I guessed the sun would rise tomorrow it wouldn't."

What was that? Something pretty scary. I tried to concentrate real hard, not so easy when at the same time you're kind of pawing a foil-wrapped package toward the edge of a chair until it . . . until it slips off and falls to the floor, landing very gently and making just the faintest crinkly metallic sound, almost certainly unhearable by human ears. I nosed it over to a cozy space between the stove and the fridge and hunkered down.

Then came more talk about the retainer, but they didn't mention its shrimpy smell, and after a while Bernie circled back to the note, which had to be the way to go. Bernie's a great interviewer, as lots of dudes breaking rocks in the hot sun could tell you.

"Forgetting the meaning of the note for the time being," he was saying, "and focusing just on the style, is it typical of Lord?"

"What's style?" Duke said.

Bernie took the note. "Here, for example, where he writes 'Tell Mami I love her.' Is that him?"

"Why the hell not? We love each other in this family."

Bernie—my Bernie, down under the interviewing Bernie, if that makes any sense, and if not, forget it—shot him a real quick glance, here and gone.

Duke leaned closer to Bernie, jabbed at the note. "But this right here—"

"'Your bro, Lord Royal Boutette?'"

"Yeah. That ain't him."

Bernie—Bernie blinked? A total first. Was this case turning out to be a tough one? It didn't feel the slightest bit tough to me. I polished off the last of the steak teriyaki, conveniently prepared in bite-size chunks, although I'm not fussy about things like that.

"Are you telling me his middle name isn't Royal after all?" Bernie said.

"No way, Jose," Duke said. "I'm talkin' about this bro shit. Boutettes don't go in for no bro shit."

"Lord wouldn't use the word *bro*?"

"What I just said. We don't talk no jive talk."

Bernie's face got a little harder. What was wrong? Weren't we getting places with the note? My feeling, maybe crazy: All we had to do now was ID this Jose dude and we could head for home.

And maybe Bernie was thinking the same thing, because he glanced around, found me in my little spot, and said, "Okay, Chet, let's—" Then came a pause, Bernie's gaze perhaps taking in the crumpled and torn remnants of the tin foil, although perhaps not. He cleared his throat. "Ah, hit the road. Time to split, big guy."

"Just a goddamn second," Duke said. Uh-oh. But his eyes were on Bernie, not me. "What does it mean, the style, all that?"

"Leave the note on the table," Bernie said. "The cops'll want to see it. And Duke?"

"Yeah?"

"Watch your back."

"That a threat?" Duke said, jutting out his chin, a very goat-like look, and not just because of the goatee, although I'm sure that helped.

"Not from me," Bernie said.

TWENTY-ONE

"Could it be," Bernie said as we walked to the car, "all just one big—"

One big what? I wanted to know, but Bernie had come to a stop in front of a store with cigar boxes in the window.

"How about we pop in here for a sec?"

We popped into the store and Bernie—oh, no—bought a pack of cigarettes. A whole pack: something he hadn't done since I couldn't remember when, certainly not today or yesterday. Back outside he broke the pack open and lit up.

"Ah," he said, smoke drifting slowly from his nose, as he turned into smoking Bernie, a more relaxed dude than regular Bernie. "What is it about smoking that makes you think better?"

I had no clue, but then came maybe the most amazing thought of my life so far: If smoking really made you think better, then he'd know the answer to the question! Wow! I thought that? No way, Jose! Uh-oh: Jose? Again? Hadn't that just come up? Did I know any Joses? Did I even want to right now? No, what I wanted to do right now was think that amazing thought I'd just had all over again. But . . . but it was gone!

"What're you panting about?" Bernie said. "Thirsty, big guy?"
Thirsty? No! What I wanted was to . . . to . . .

We came to the car. Bernie dug under my seat for the water
bowl—not my big kitchen water bowl from back home, but the
smaller fold-up one for road trips. He filled it with a water bottle
from the drink holder and set it on the sidewalk for me. I lapped
up every drop.

Bernie laughed. "Knew you were," he said, giving me a nice
pat. "Gotta hydrate like crazy down here."

Not sure what that was about, but doing things like crazy
couldn't be bad. Hydrate, was that it? Something to look forward to!

Bernie leaned against the car in a real relaxed kind of way.
"Suppose," he said, sucking in more smoke, the cigarette end
glowing bright, "things aren't what they seem and it turns out
we've got a red herring on our hands."

Red herring? That came up in some of our cases, usually the
worst. Wasn't this case going smoothly so far? I didn't see any
problems. And the truth was I had yet to catch sight of a single
red herring in my whole career, or even smell one from a distance.
I eyed Bernie's hands, strong hands and beautifully shaped, in
case that hasn't come up already: a cigarette in one, nothing in the
other, meaning no red herring on the scene.

"A goddamn monster of a red herring," Bernie said.

Which would be a snap to spot, and can you imagine the
smell? So where was it?

"Maybe we've got to go back to square one."

That was bad. The last time we'd gone back to square one?
The Portapotty case.

Bernie went over to a trash can and dropped his cigarette butt
inside.

"Let's roll," he said.

We hopped into the car, me actually hopping but Bernie getting in nice and smoothly, the way smoking Bernie did. I sat up straight and tall, on high alert, the only way to go if we were in for a rerun of the Portapotty case. As we drove away, an old man in a torn T-shirt stepped out of the shadows, took Bernie's cigarette butt out of the trash, and started smoking what was left.

We walked up to Cleotis's crib. Was this square one? Bernie knocked on that big and heavy front door. We waited for the little eyeball slot to open up, which it did not. I listened for the sound of anyone moving around inside, heard none. Bernie knocked again, harder. He called through the door.

"Cleotis, open up."

The door remained closed.

"Got a follow-up question or two, won't take more than a minute."

Silence from inside.

"Easy questions, Cleotis, and then you can get right back to the grindstone."

I knew grindstones—Nixon Panero had one, for example, at his auto body shop—"Stay clear of them sparks," Nixon said, which I'd already been doing, believe me—but I hadn't spotted Cleotis's on our first visit, would be on the lookout this time. I was all set. What was the holdup?

Bernie has this real quiet voice he sometimes uses for talking to himself. I heard it now. "Maybe they've all gone off to yoga class."

That hadn't even crossed my mind! I'd been to yoga once myself, and only very briefly, on an evening when we'd gone to pick up Suzie and her class hadn't quite finished. Until that moment, yoga had been a complete mystery to me, and then to see that it was all about humans stretching just like me, head way down and butt way up: how exciting was that! A bit too exciting, as it turned out, my memory of the exact endgame kind of fuzzy—although endgames in general are sometimes the most fun of all. But the point was that if yoga was next on our schedule, I was good to go.

Bernie raised his fist to knock one more time, knock good and hard—I could tell from the way his knuckles went yellowish—when a motorcycle came down the street. We turned to look, saw a huge bike rolling along real slow, the engine going *THROB THROB THROB* in a way that was low and booming at the same time. The rider glanced our way and pulled over, sticking out his foot to balance the bike. He wore a black helmet with a dark visor that covered his face clear down to his mouth. He jutted his chin in our direction and said something hard to hear, on account of that *THROB THROB THROB*. We went over to him.

"What's up?" Bernie said.

The biker's mouth opened. His upfront teeth, the two on top, were gold. You see that from time to time in this business. Once we spent practically a whole afternoon searching for a gold tooth that had fallen in a gutter after a little dustup between Bernie and a gangbanger. The gangbanger had been so grateful after we'd found it, although no handshaking went on what with him being cuffed by that time.

"Yeah, whassup for sure," said the biker. "Whassup wit' you, señor?"

Bernie gave him a look and so did I. A short but real muscular dude, almost as wide as he was tall: the kind Bernie says is built like a fire hydrant. That saying of his had led to a bit of confusion on my part in the past and right then I told myself I wasn't going there today even if this was the most fire hydranty dude on earth.

"You live in the neighborhood?" Bernie said.

The biker turned his head, maybe glancing around; hard to tell, with that dark visor hiding his eyes. "This shithole?" he said.

"Not your kind of thing?" Bernie said.

"No, is not," the biker said. He flashed that golden smile. "And you? You from the hood?"

"Not this particular hood," Bernie said. "Just visiting."

"Visiting Cleotis?"

"You know him?"

"Sure thing," said the biker. "How about you?"

"Wouldn't be visiting otherwise."

"Yeah? You friends?"

"More like acquaintances."

"Acquaintances? I do not know this word."

"Conocidos."

"Ah, conocidos," the biker said. "Cleotis had many, many conocidos round here. They gonna miss him."

"Why is that?" Bernie said.

"You are maybe not a close conocido, eh? Cleotis he moved away."

"I just saw him this morning."

The biker shrugged.

"Why did he leave?" Bernie said.

"Business, right? Go where is the business—the American dream, man."

"Heard of it," Bernie said. "Is that what brings you here?"

The biker laughed. "I am a dreamer, too."

"Don't look like a dreamer," Bernie said. "But it's hard to tell with that visor over your face."

The laughter stopped.

"I'm Bernie Little and this is Chet."

The visor turned my way. Was there room for me to jam a

paw in between it and his face? All of a sudden I wanted to give that a try, bad of me, I know. "Big dog," the biker said.

"And friendly with everybody. Just about. What's your name?"

"My name?"

"I just told you ours."

The biker was still for a moment. Then he nodded. "Pyro."

"Your name is Pyro?"

"Si."

Bernie held out his hand. "Nice meeting you, Pyro."

Pyro just sat for a few moments, leaving Bernie's hand hanging there. Then, real slow, he extended his own hand, wider than Bernie's but not as long, and also not beautiful like Bernie's. Pyro had one of the thickest wrists I'd ever seen on a man, although it was mostly hidden under the sleeve of his shirt.

They gripped each other's hands. Bernie shot a sharp glance at Pyro's wrist, but there wasn't much of it to see. One quick up-and-down pump and then Pyro was all done with the greeting part of our little encounter and tried to withdraw his hand. Bernie didn't let him.

"Hey, man, what the hell?" Pyro said, sounding a bit angry. Inside he was real angry: that gives off a smell I don't miss, but no time to go into it now, because at the same time I was picking up another scent off him, namely the scent of that aftershave that comes in the square green bottle.

"Just being friendly in the American way," Bernie said. "What's your best guess on where Cleotis went to pursue his dream?"

Pyro's mouth opened, closed, opened again. "Houston," he said, his voice quieter than it had been but the anger inside him had flowed into it, if that made any sense, and set it throbbing, kind of like his bike but in a human way. "Everybody goes to Houston."

Bernie released his hand. Pyro wiped it on his jeans, then gripped the handlebar.

"More opportunity in Houston," Bernie said. "What with the oil business and all."

Pyro turned to him, seemed to be giving Bernie a long look from under that visor. Then he hit the throttle and the *THROB THROB THROB* rose to a roar that shook the air—I felt it—and he zoomed off down the street, the front wheel rising right up over the broken pavement. We watched him go.

"I had a bike once myself," Bernie said.

I was just finding that out now? But what great news! Was there anything to stop us from getting another one? Today?

"Easy, big guy. Down."

"I didn't handle that very well," Bernie said as we crossed the bridge over the river. "But how do you get a guy to roll up his sleeve?"

What was this? The truth was I'd been caught up in watching all that water on the move and hadn't been paying the closest attention even though I always pay the closest attention to Bernie. How do you get a guy to roll up his sleeve? Was that the question? You could grab the end of the sleeve with your teeth and roll it back for him. Other than that, I had no suggestions. I wondered what guy Bernie might be talking about for a while and then went back to watching the river flow. I could have watched it forever, but my eyelids got heavy. That had happened to me many times although never quite like this. I felt like I was flowing along with the mighty Mississip, even part of it. Made no sense, I know.

It was dark by the time we got to the rutted road that led to the dock where *Little Jazz* was tied up. The Porsche's headlights were like drills drilling light into the darkness, something Bernie had said late one night out in the desert and which I'd never forgotten even though I didn't understand it the least little bit. Not that I didn't know what a drill was—we had one in the tool box back home; the last time it had come out the shock from Bernie drilling into some wire or other had knocked him flat, but he'd been up in no time with hardly any help from me and our power returned the very next day.

Back to our headlights drilling into the darkness, trees and bushes lighting up and then vanishing, some of them trailing those mossy fringes. We came around the last turn and the dock appeared, with the houseboat next to it, and the bayou beyond. A cloud drifted across the sky, uncovering the moon, and suddenly there were tiny moons rippling all over the water. I was just starting to enjoy the sight when I felt Bernie tense up beside me. He stopped the car real quick, cut the lights, and leaned forward, peering at the houseboat. I did the same.

Little Jazz looked like a piece of squarish darkness cut out of the rest of the night. Everything was still, except for all those rippling moons. Then a faint yellow glow flashed for a moment through one of little round windows at the front of the cabin. I thought: *.38 Special.*

Bernie took the .38 Special out of the glove box and stuck it in his belt, and also the flashlight, which hadn't occurred to me, not needing it personally. He put his finger across his lips, our signal for not making a sound. We got out of the car and moved silently toward the dock, me completely silent and Bernie just about.

TWENTY-TWO

The light reappeared in the little round window in the front—bow! I remembered!—of *Little Jazz*, a wavering sort of glow, like someone was moving around inside. We stepped onto the dock. It made a little creaking noise under Bernie's foot, that actually didn't sound that little to me, but there was no reaction on his face, so not a problem. And we had the .38—fact one as Bernie liked to say and I liked to hear. It was in his hand now, always nice to see, so much better than in the belt.

Side by side, we walked onto the deck of the boat about half-way between the bow and whatever the back was called; it would come to me. The moonlight made seeing pretty easy, at least for me, but I was more concerned with smells at that moment, of which there were lots, of course, but two caught my attention right away. One—the strange toady, snaky, even lizardy smell, but with that odd poopy peppery add-on—seemed to be coming up from under the boat, kind of weird. The other was the smell of a man, a man I was pretty sure I'd smelled before. The door leading to the house part of the boat—living room, kitchen, bedroom, lined up like shotgun cribs I'd been in—hung open. Being first through doorways is one of my little things, but Bernie was right behind me.

We could see right through the living room and into the kitchen where a man in a sleeveless T-shirt was kneeling with his back to us by the cabinet under the sink. He seemed to be rooting around in there with one hand, his other holding a flashlight. All I could really see of him was his butt and his heavy round upper arms. No biggie. I already knew who he was: Wes Derrick, the environmental guy with the soft voice and the soft brown gaze.

Bernie raised the .38 Special. "Freeze," he said, not loudly, just real clear. The fur on the back of my neck stood straight up, and I almost missed something, maybe something I should have been on to already, namely the smell of a second man, also known to me, but no time for that now, because he was close behind us—oh, no! not the old hiding-in-the-shadow-of-an-open-door trick!—which wasn't good at all and—

Cale Rugh burst out of the shadows and whacked Bernie across the back of his head. Bernie slumped to the floor like he'd fallen asleep all of a sudden. The next instant I was in midair, hitting Cale throat high—but no! Somehow he'd stepped aside—a real quick fighter unlike most humans except for Bernie and a few others I'd come across—his arm whipping through a beam of moonlight, a long-barreled gun in his hand. He hit me with it, not quite as square as he wanted: I was on the move, too, amigo. Just as I rounded on him, the flashlight beam swung over and lit his face, all twisted up.

He shielded his eyes. "Get that goddamn light off me for—"

Too late for you, buddy boy. I leaped again and this time I got him good, leading with my teeth and finding his gun arm. Cale went down under me, the gun clattering across the floor and him screaming, "Wes! Wes! He's gonna kill me."

Which hadn't been my intention—messing him up for what he'd done to Bernie was all I'd had in mind—but killing him sounded like an even better id—No. No it did not. I was mad, yes, but I didn't want to do that. Instead, I got my paws on his chest, lowered my face to his, just to show him who was who. Then he'd surrender, we'd cuff him, and—

"Wes! The gun! Shoot him!"

I heard Wes scrambling around behind us.

"Don't like to shoot a dog," Wes said.

"KILL HIM!"

Wes grunted like maybe he was . . . picking something up. I started to twist around in his direction. He had the gun all right, but by the barrel, not the grip, meaning he wasn't going to shoot, although he might have been planning to use it as a—

The moonlight found his soft brown eyes. He brought the gun butt down on my head.

I fell into a strange dreamy state where I wasn't quite asleep and could hear pretty well although I couldn't move, or maybe just didn't feel like it. The most important thing I heard was Bernie breathing, nice and regular, not far from where I lay. Cale and Wes were close by, too. Soon we'd be jumping up and doing what had to be done, me and Bernie.

"What now?" Wes was saying.

"I should put a bullet in Little's head," said Cale. "Deserves it—he brought this all on himself."

"Not sure I'm getting that."

"By turning down big bucks when he didn't even have a clue there was anything ulterior going down. Makes him one of those holier-than-thous. They're the ones that cause all the collateral damage—Mack being a case in point."

"Mack the shrimp dealer?" Wes said. "Did something happen to him?"

There was a pause. "Not that I know of."

And a longer pause. "Are you hiding things from me?"

"Grow up, Wes."

Then came a long silence. My head started to throb a bit. I thought about getting up, maybe in a while.

"What are we going to do?" Wes said.

"That's better," said Cale. "No *I* in team. Now's when your boating expertise comes in."

"Wouldn't call myself an expert."

"Know enough to cause an unfortunate fuel line accident?"

"I guess so, but why?" Wes said. "No way he could ID us from what went on here. Why don't we just tie him up or something?"

"Or we could make him sit in the corner," Cale said. "Christ almighty. You think we can let him keep roaming around?"

"Guess not."

"Then we're on the same page," Cale said. "But it has to look like an accident, no matter how half-assed. Bernie here's connected."

"To the mob?"

Cale laughed, a squeaky sound like something was rusty inside. "To some people we wouldn't want showing up—military guys, a DA or two, some cops."

"The Robideaus?"

"Hell no. The Robideaus are who we're counting on to do the half-assed investigation of the half-assed accident you're going to get cracking on."

"What about searching the place?" Wes said. "The whole point of the exercise."

"Just do your job and no one'll ever find it," said Cale. "Even if the goddamn thing is here, which I'm not so sure about."

"You're telling me that now?"

"I'm starting to have doubts about you, Wes."

Wes moved away. Then came a quiet time where I might have actually fallen asleep. Anyway: a blank. A smell brought me back to life, specifically the smell of gasoline, real sharp in the nose, almost stinging.

I opened my eyes, saw Bernie lying beside me, chest rising and falling in an easy rhythm. I could feel my own chest doing the same; we're a lot alike, me and Bernie. A happy thought, and I lost myself in it until the gasoline smell brought me out of it. Shifting my head a bit, I looked back through the kitchen and living room parts of *Little Jazz* to the stern—stern! It came to me!

Wes and Cale stood there in the light of the moon, Wes holding one end of a long tube that ran down through a hatch in the floorboards, and Cale reaching into his pocket. He took out a lighter. They were up to no good, what kind of no good I didn't know and it really didn't matter, what with me hating them so much, especially Cale.

Cale took the end of the tube from Wes. "I drop this on the deck and the gas spills out?"

"Correct," said Wes.

"Good job. Get in the boat and crank 'er up."

Wes climbed over the stern and out of sight. A motor made that coughing sound a starting motor makes. I found that I was on my feet and not feeling too bad, the throbbing in my head ramped down to something I wouldn't even call pain. Meanwhile, Cale was letting go of the rubber tube. It fell to the deck like a wriggling snake and liquid splashed out, silvery in the moonlight, a few drops landing on his cowboy boots.

"Damn," he said, quick-stepping back, too late. He flicked open the lighter and a short flame rose up from it. Cale made some sort of adjustment and the flame grew longer. Then he lowered the lighter and got ready to fling it, sideways-style, like a Frisbee. He didn't see me coming at all.

And even if he had, it wouldn't have mattered: that's how mad I was by then. *THUMP!* Like a big bass drum! Then everything went flying, the lighter rising the highest, spinning like a sparkler on the Fourth of July—not my favorite holiday, by the way—plus Cale and me also spinning—not quite as high, but enough to clear the stern of *Little Jazz*. We came crashing into a boat tied to the platform at the back—not the pirogue but a bigger boat that floated beside it, a green-painted boat with Wes at the motor. Wes's eyes got huge; the lighter sizzled as it hit the water; and then we threw down, trust me.

We had shouting, we had screaming, we had the taste of blood in my mouth. Wes fell against the motor and all of a sudden we took off backward, zooming away from *Little Jazz* and down the bayou. Wes kicked out at me. Way too slow: I got his ankle between my jaws.

"Do something, for Christ sake," he screamed. "He's biting my leg off."

I felt Cale's hand on my collar, pulling, yanking, jerking. I went stiff, all my muscles straining the other way, one of my best moves. Meanwhile, lights were appearing on shore, one, two, more.

"The net!" Wes shouted. "The net!"

"What goddamn net?"

"In the bow!"

Cale's hand left my collar. I squeezed Wes's ankle good and tight. He screamed again. The motor was screaming, too. I felt my very wildest. These two perps—and that was what they were, all right—were going to pay, and pay big time for—

What was this? Something fell over me with a soft thud, almost the sound a blanket would make. I don't like blankets on me and this was the same kind of feeling. I let go of Wes's ankle, tried to twist around, but I was all tangled up, tangled in . . . in a big fishnet! Cale loomed over me, tugging at this and that, and then Wes was up and tugging from the other direction. I snapped my jaws, got fishnet in my mouth, bit at it and bit at it, thrashed my body around with all my strength, but the net closed around me tighter and tighter until I couldn't move a muscle more than a twitch or two.

They rolled me up in a ball and shoved me against the side of the boat. All I could do was bark. I barked, but not loud, on account of hardly being able to open my mouth, the net pressing in so tight.

The scream of the engine died down, the boat coming to rest and rocking on the water. High above a cloud, silver at the edges and black in the middle, glided over the moon and the night went dark.

"I'm bleeding like a pig," Wes said.

"Don't want to hear about it," said Cale. "Let's go."

"Back to the houseboat?"

"What are you talking about?"

"Don't you want to finish what we started? The fuel line thing?"

"With every hillbilly in the swamp waking up? I thought you were supposed to be smart. Head for the rig."

"The rig?" Wes said.

"Something wrong with your hearing?"

"But what about him?"

"Him?"

"The dog."

Cale gazed down at me, his eyes in shadow, just two dark holes. "Snack time for Iko," he said. "Drive."

Iko? Had I heard that name somewhere? Was it important? *Bernie!*

I heard the engine crank up and felt the boat swing around but couldn't turn to see what Wes was doing in the stern, what with being so tangled up. The bow rose up and we sped across the water. Down on the deck, unable to see over the sides, I saw only the starless, moonless sky and Cale, picking up his hat from under one of the seats. It was all crushed up and dirty; I felt good about that. Cale flung it over the side, then stood in the bow, his back to me and his thin hair streaming in the wind. I barked just in case he was forgetting what I had in store for him, but couldn't rouse up much sound at all, and now I'd somehow got my whole muzzle stuck in one of the net openings.

Time passed, how much I didn't know, with nothing to hear but the throb of the engine, nothing to see but Cale's back and the night sky. After a while, a jagged hole appeared in the clouds and the moon poked through. Bernie had explained all about the moon to Charlie. It had once been part of the earth! Bernie knew just about everything. He'd know what to do right now, for example. Something quick and blazing with the .38 Special would have been my guess.

Cale raised his hand, made the slow-down motion. The boat slewed around to a stop. The engine went silent, and then there was nothing to hear but the water's peaceful lapping sounds around us.

Cale and Wes loomed up over me. Cale was closest, so I lunged at him, forgetting all about the net around me. How crazy was that? The truth was I couldn't move. How could anyone forget a thing like that? I tried to snap at Cale through the gap in the netting, got nowhere with that either.

"You take that end," Cale said.

They both stooped, both grunted, and next thing I knew they had me in the air, Wes on one end of the rolled-up net and Cale on the other.

"On three," Cale said. They started swinging me. "One. Two. Three."

And then I was airborne, sailing over the water for what seemed like a long time, my body all twisted up in the net. Three was not a number I had any use for: that was my only thought.

TWENTY-THREE

Everything is different underwater: the sights, so blurry; the sounds, actually kind of clear; the smells, not nearly so strong as above water and coming to me in a different way, impossible to describe; and the feel, which is the best part.

But not now. Now it was all bad. I was spinning slowly in blackness and also going down. I didn't want to go down, wanted more than anything to go up. Up was the only place not so completely black. *Swim, big guy! You're a good swimmer. Swim!* Bernie's voice, so clear he could have been right beside me. The truth was he was even closer than that. I swam toward the place of incomplete blackness.

Swimming is a lot like trotting, except in the water, so I'm good at it, no question. But not now. Now I could hardly get anywhere, and all because of the net. The net wanted me to go down. I wanted to go up. *Gotta want it, big guy.* I wanted it! I wanted it! I wanted it more than the net wanted it the other way, if that makes any sense, probably not. I swam my hardest, my legs making the water go *whoosh whoosh*. Was I getting somewhere? Yes, the incomplete blackness seemed closer. The net was still all around me, tangling me up, but looser down here than on the boat, the water lifting and shifting the cords of the net, almost the way the breeze ruffles a picnic blanket, say you and Bernie and Suzie and Charlie were on an outing. Oh, how nice that would be!

I churned my legs, one paw poking through the net and then another, rose up and up. But maybe not fast enough, because now my chest felt like it was getting pressed by something heavy. Air! I needed air and I needed it right away! All I had to do was open my mouth and take in a big, big gulp—

No, Chet! Hold on and swim, just swim!

But what about the feeling in my throat, a feeling that I had to breathe this very moment?

Hold on!

I churned and churned, all this crushing going on against my chest, my eyes stretching like they were getting pressed right out of my head—not that, please!—and then suddenly there was a loud splash, and I felt air.

Air! So wonderful! I'd never given a thought to the wonderfulness of air and wasn't about to start now. My nose was stuck in one of the holes in the netting. I raised it as high as I could and just breathed. I breathed and breathed and breathed, paddling gently in warm calm water. But on the surface: that was the point. I paddled on the surface, breathing the soft warm air and filling up my whole body with it, paddled and breathed until I started sinking again, sinking out of the air. A terrible jolt of something—I wouldn't like to call it fear—shot through me and I thrashed my way back up to the top.

What was going on? Wasn't I a good swimmer? Hadn't Bernie said so? Then that was that.

Think, big guy.

Good idea. I thought. And right away I thought about the

net. It hadn't given up yet, still wanted to carry me down. The net wasn't made of heavy stuff, but taken all together it was heavy enough to sink me if I was paddling gently along. So therefore?

Paddle harder, Chet.

Perfect! And so quick, just when I needed it. Bernie handled the so-therefores, possibly a detail you're familiar with. I paddled harder, all my legs sticking through the net now, and stayed on the surface, no problem at all, although I wished the net hadn't got hold of my tail so tight, keeping me from moving it even the littlest bit.

I turned my head, although not as easily as usual, on account of the net having gotten twisted up in my collar. All I saw was the night, blackness everywhere, not a single light showing—a sight I'd seen once or twice on cloudy nights way out in the desert, so it shouldn't have bothered me. But it did sort of bother me. The desert was my home.

No time for home thoughts at that moment. I paddled, not my hardest but pretty hard, and kept myself, or at least my eyes and nose, above the surface. From time to time a bit of water splashed in my mouth. It tasted salty—saltier than the water in the bayou although not as salty as the ocean at San Diego. Bernie had told me not to drink that salty San Diego water. What about this water, not quite so salty? I tried some—not bad at all—and was realizing how thirsty I was when the clouds parted and out came the moon again.

It stunned me. Had I ever seen anything as beautiful? So big and round and white and shining: it reminded me of Bernie, the shining part. And all around me sprang up tiny moons, bobbing on the water as far as I could see in every direction, beauties piled on beauty.

Whoa: every direction? There was water around me for as far as I could see in every direction? That couldn't be good. I was fine for now, paddling along, but wasn't getting back on solid land the goal? Where was I even supposed to aim for? What if I ended up swimming in the wrong—

I stopped right there, not even letting that thought get a foothold—just another one of my strengths. The point was, I had to keep swimming, and swimming pretty hard, if I wanted to keep my nose in the air. And I did want that, wanted it more than anything. I swam, and swam some more. Not so bad: I had the moon for company.

The moon slid across the sky the way it does, too slowly to see, except whenever you checked it again it wasn't in the same place. Bernie had explained the whole thing to Charlie once, using a basketball, a tennis ball, and a golf ball. The fun we'd had with that, even though basketballs are just about impossible for me. But that day, the great day of the moon explanation, was when I figured out that by curling back my upper lip I could get one of my long teeth—humans called them dogteeth! What a life!—into a nice position for poking it through the skin of the basketball, which promptly shrinks down to manageable size.

Charlie had laughed and laughed. Not Bernie; at least not right away.

I checked the moon. Someplace different, just as I'd thought. A breeze sprang up, and right away waves rose on the water, not too big, maybe as high as my buddy Iggy, back home. The problem was that both the breeze and the waves were in my face. How come they couldn't have been coming from different directions? Not that I was complaining, but with the net trying to drag me down, it was easier to turn around and paddle in the exact opposite way, with the wind and waves at my back. So that was what I did.

I paddled along, glancing at the moon now and then, and after some time realized it was moving right along with me. That felt pretty good: always nice to have a buddy. One funny thing: the water, which had been nice and warm at the beginning, now seemed colder. Not a problem: I was a pretty big dude—a hundred-plus pounder, in case I haven't mentioned that already—and could handle the cold. But what was this? All of a sudden I was shivering? Shivering for the first time in my life: I only knew what shivering even was from seeing Charlie step out of a cold shower, the day Bernie had made a cost-saving adjustment to the water heater pipes, all fixed by the plumber in no time.

I stopped paddling, rose up and down on the waves, and shivered, forgetting for a moment about the net. But the net—which was showing signs of getting heavier—hadn't forgotten about me, and as soon as it realized no paddling was going on, it dragged me down under. I snapped out of the whole shivering thing and got my legs churning. I churned and churned away but didn't reach air. Instead, things got darker and darker. That made me kind of wild, twisting and flailing around in the cold blackness, and in the twisting and flailing I happened to see where the moonlight was coming from: the exact direction I'd been churning away from! How crazy was that! I got a grip, told myself never to lose it again, and swam my hardest toward the moonlight, surprisingly far away. I swam and swam, the chest-crushing now hitting me even worse than before, that feeling in my throat telling me I had to breathe growing stronger and stronger, and all of a sudden it was the strongest thing I'd ever met up with in my whole life, stronger than me. Yes, much stronger than me. I opened my mouth and bubbles flew out and I breathed.

Oh, no: not air, but cold salty water was what I breathed. I choked and gagged and then splashed up onto the surface, felt the air, choked and gagged some more, and finally puked up water, lots of it. And felt better right away, always the way with puking. I paddled on, after a while realizing I was now paddling into the wind and the waves. Hadn't I decided to go the other way? I circled around and swam.

Get the picture, net? I'm swimming

I only forgot to keep swimming a few more times, hard to say how many, but more than two, and always because of getting distracted by the shivering. Would you believe it was the same thing every time: the net pulling me under; swimming in the wrong direction, down instead of up; racing to the surface; fighting the urge to breathe until it couldn't be fought anymore; puking in the warm night air? Although the truth was the air no longer felt so warm on my head—by that time poking completely through the hole in the net where just my nose had been stuck before, but twisted even tighter than ever in my collar—plus the wind was blowing harder and the waves had risen. I checked the moon once more—it was swimming, too, just like me except across the sky!—and maybe on account of waves being on my mind just then I got hit by what Bernie calls a brainwave. Possibly my very first: I couldn't think of another. That didn't matter. What mattered was the brainwave itself: all I had to do was keep my eye on the moon! If I kept my eye on the moon at all times, the net couldn't pull me under. The truth was I really didn't want the net to pull me down again even once more. Inside that truth was another truth I didn't even want to think about, namely the possibility that the next time I wouldn't have the strength to—

I remembered I didn't want to think about that and stopped on a dime. Bernie could shoot dimes right out of the sky: I'd seen him do it. I paddled along, my eyes on the moon and my mind on Bernie shooting dimes out of the sky, and then simply on Bernie. I felt pretty good, maybe not tip-top, but no complaints. After a while Bernie's face appeared on the moon, as clear as day. Then I did feel tip-top. I paddled along and watched Bernie. Sometimes he gave me a smile. My tail would have wagged if it hadn't been so tightly caught in the net. It tried anyway. How crazy was that?

I kept my eyes on Bernie-in-the-moon. His lips weren't moving, but I could hear his voice: *Doin' good, Chet, doin' good.* I got so caught up in that that I forgot the other thing I was supposed to be doing, besides keeping my eyes on Bernie-in-the-moon. What was it, again?

Swim.

Swim, that was it! What was with me, forgetting a simple thing like that? I swam and kept my eyes where they had to be to make sure the net didn't get its way. Also I shivered, an extra thing I didn't actually have to do. It happened anyway. So I was doing one more than two things, which would make . . . Hey! I was right on the edge of what would you call it? A breakthrough? Would the answer be—

On, no. Not a noseful of cold salty water. Was I sinking again? I really didn't think I could—

Churn, big guy, churn! Churn for your life!

I churned, better believe it. I churned up that water big-time with my legs, or at least kept them moving a bit, and my nose rose up out of the waves, and I breathed in the lovely air. I was doing not bad. Getting my legs to cooperate—which I'd never even thought of before—now took some extra effort; other than that, no problems. I told my legs in no uncertain terms, whatever that might have meant, to do their stuff, and they sort of did. But perhaps, what with all that extra effort, it took me longer than it should have to notice that the moon was gone, although Bernie's face was still there, drifting in the sky. Not long after finally getting with the program on that, I also grew aware that the sky itself was no longer dark, but quite lightish, almost like it was day. Right around then a real big wave raised me high up and I saw . . . green? Was green one of the colors I wasn't supposed to be good at? I was pretty sure I saw some green in the distance, and even if not it really didn't matter, because I smelled green: green, green, unmistakable green, specifically the rot all the green had in these parts. Had I ever smelled anything so beautiful? I didn't even try remembering. I just swam toward the green, my legs pitching in on their own when they felt like it. Bernie faded very slowly from the sky. I watched him till he was completely gone and then for some time longer. Meanwhile, the green rot smell grew more and more powerful. I finally took my eyes off the sky and had a look around.

Hey! I wasn't out in open water anymore, instead had green on both sides, and not so far away. I could see trees and that mossy stuff, and even an old falling-apart dock. Plus the waves had died down and the water didn't taste so salty. I was in a bayou! Loved these bayous. What a place! I got myself turned sideways—only one of my legs in on the action at the moment, the others maybe too tangled in the net, or having a nice little rest—and headed for the old dock.

I'd taken a stroke, maybe even two, when I caught my first whiff of that froggy snaky scent with the peppery poopy add-on. The green rot smell came from the land; this other one was drifting up from down below. Kind of interesting, but I had more important things on my mind, namely getting to that dock, so I ignored this smell from down below. Except I really couldn't on account of how it was getting so strong. A bubble popped up right in front of my face and when it burst it was just absolutely full of that smell.

I swam on, close enough to the dock now to make out a few crushed beer cans lying on it and glinting in the sun, a pretty sight. Yes, the sun was up now and shining nice and warm, although for some reason I was shivering harder than ever. I churned away, or at least called it churning, and the dock drew a bit closer. Then came two new things. First, from farther up the bayou, I heard the sound of a boat. Second, I felt a strange tug on the net, like it had snagged on something down below.

I swam on, not my fastest, of course, with just the one paw doing the work. The boat sound got louder, making a sputtering sort of *putt-putt* I thought I recognized. I turned my head to look, spotted a small silver boat rounding a bend up the bayou, not too far away. The driver was a big, gray-haired woman wearing a halter top and shorts. And a patch over one eye? Hey! I knew that woman. Wasn't she—

All at once I plunged down under the surface, so fast the force actually snapped my head back. I was moving faster than I'd ever moved in the water before, straight down, the net pulling tight tight tight now, like some unstoppable force had a grip on it. I hit bottom, felt solid mud under one of my paws, and then I saw where this unstoppable force was coming from. A huge creature rose up out of the murk, right in front of my face, a creature with a long bumpy snout, tiny bumpy eyes on the top of its head, and teeth so big they stuck right out of its mouth. I knew what this creature was from Animal Planet: a gator. And that strange smell had to be gator smell. What we needed was a TV that—

The thought never got finished. The gator opened its mouth—so wide!—and came at me. I pushed off the bottom with my one paw. The gator chomped down—one of those teeth parting the fur on my shoulder—and clamped onto the net behind my neck, just missing me. Then—*whoosh*. I was off on a horrible ride, getting rolled and twisted and shaken through the water, the whole time needing to breathe so bad. All at once I felt my collar ripping right off me and I got flung up to the surface. And what was this? The net was gone? I was free? I was free! I took off toward the dock, got closer and closer, was just a few churns away when I got hit from below, hit so hard I rose straight up in the air, high enough that there was time for a glimpse of the silver boat—much closer—and the woman in the eye patch, on her feet now and facing my direction.

I fell with a big splash. The gator rolled up out of the water right between me and the dock, swung around in one quick snapping movement of its body, so big, so long, and came gliding my way. I got my head up as high as I could and barked my loudest, fiercest bark, all I could think of to do. That got the gator angry: I could see it in those yellow eyes. It kept coming, not scared in the least, and showed me that wide-open mouth again, so huge and pink inside, with all those teeth, on and on, and a thick yellow tongue with a piece of seaweed lying on it. Nearer and nearer, and hissing now—I felt his breath on my nose—and I opened my own mouth, too, ready to bite and fight my very hardest.

Get it on.

Hiss. Hiss.

And then, just as our bites were about to come together: *CRACK!* I knew that sound, took me back to K-9 school and even before: a rifle shot. At the same moment, a bloody hole appeared in the thick green skin behind the gator's head, where the neck would be if it had a neck; I wasn't sure about that. The gator closed its mouth, sank from sight, the tail, so heavy and hard, whacking me in the gut as the beast—yes, a beast for sure—swam away.

I puked first thing, even though there was nothing pukable left in me. Meanwhile, the silver boat glided up beside me, the eye patch woman—Mami, that was it, Mami Boutette—now at the stern, steering with one hand and holding a rifle in the other.

Mami gazed down at me with her one eye, a dark green, bayou-colored eye. "You went one on one with Iko?" she said. "Hell's bells. Liked the looka you from the get-go."

TWENTY-FOUR

We rode up the bayou in the silver boat, Mami and me, both of us sitting in the stern. Mami took out her cell phone, checked the screen.

"Roaming charges?" she said. "They can stick that where the sun don't shine."

Whoa! Had I already figured that one out? Was the answer . . . night? Night! No sunshine at night! What had taken me so long? Mami was saying they could stick whatever it was in the night, plain as day. As for what that meant, exactly, you had to accept that not everything made sense, which I could do no problem, just another one of my strengths.

I was still shivering—although hardly at all, nothing worth mentioning, so forget I mentioned it. Mami patted my head. She had a big hard hand, with calluses and dirty fingernails, but turned out to be a pretty good patter, if not in the class of Autumn and Tulip, those two world-beating patters in the employ of our pal Livia Moon who had a nice setup in Pottsdale, coffee house up front and house of ill repute in the back.

"Would you believe that's the third time I winged Iko in the past twenty years?" Mami said. "Damn gator's gonna outlive me." She slid a bottle out from under the seat, one of those flat bottles, and took a swig—bourbon, a smell with which I was very familiar—and then smacked her lips, one of the best sounds a human could make, in my opinion. She steered us around a big patch of floating seaweed—was that a blackened, twisted-up bird lying in the middle of it?—and from this new angle I could see a town, docks lining both sides of the bayou. It looked kind of familiar. I was puzzling over that when a big bubble broke the surface on one side and Iko's smell came wafting over us.

"Hey, you're still cold, huh?"

Mami gave me a brisk rub up and down my back. The smell faded away behind us. I felt a little better, but not totally better on account of the fact that Iko's scent was on me, actually in my fur. I needed a swim. Maybe not now.

"This detective buddy of yours any good?" Mami said. "That's what I'd like to know."

Detective buddy? Was she talking about Bernie? At that moment I remembered how I'd last seen him, lying motionless on the deck of *Little Jazz*.

"Whimpering?" Mami said. She parted the fur on my shoulder. "Scrape don't look like much. Iko bang up your insides? That it?"

Whimpering? Couldn't be me. Just in case, I shut down any sounds that might have been coming out of my mouth. As for Iko, he hadn't hurt me at all! What a nice realization! Soon after that, I was starting to think I'd gotten the best of our little dustup. A good place to leave it? That was my take.

"You're one tough hombre," Mami said. "Speaks good of him that he hooked up with you, thing in his favor. Then there's Baron's recommendation, but what does that add up to? Dung pile."

Dung pile? Was that what Mami just said? In my mind, I went

back over my dung pile experiences, some of them lots of fun—that time when Iggy and I found our way to the model organic farm!—at least in the beginning. Meanwhile, Mami had her phone out again.

"More like it," she said, and pecked away at the keys.

The town—St. Roch, that was it! I was on a roll, and if not quite there, I could sense one coming—drew closer. At first no one was around and then a car I knew very well came zooming down the road—engine screaming in that voice I loved—and braked to a shrieking stop beside one of the docks. Even before it had stopped fishtailing, a man I knew very well jumped out—yes, jumped—and ran to the end of the dock.

"Easy, fella, easy." Mami put her hard hand on my neck. "Fixin' to dive back into the drink?"

Dive back into . . . I realized I'd shifted position a bit, now had my front paws over the side. Back into the drink? I thought not. Panting started up from deep inside me and wouldn't be controlled.

We glided up to the dock. Bernie! Oh, Bernie! Right at the very edge of the dock, knees bent like . . . like he was going to dive right into the silver boat! *Do it, Bernie, do it!* And maybe he was going to, but before he could I was in midair. Not one of my best leaps, not even close—in fact, a very bad one with me almost not getting to the dock, even though the boat was practically touching it, and falling into the drink instead. Not the drink! Missing a leap like that? What was wrong with me? But somehow Bernie leaned down and caught me, and then raised me up, maybe staggering the least little bit, and held me tight.

Bernie! I licked his face and pawed at him and just went wild for Bernie. He laughed and hugged me and his eyes got damp. Bernie wasn't a crier—not Bernie, better believe it. I'd only see him cry once, the day after the divorce when all Charlie's things got packed up and Leda drove him away—and there'd been no crying until her car was out of sight, making me the only one who saw his tears. Now I saw them for the second time. Second meant two. Two: the best number. It never failed.

At about that point, I noticed Bernie had a bandage tied around his head, and also looked kind of pale, with dark shadows under his eyes. I did some more licking to make it all better.

Meanwhile, Mami was on the dock, tying up the silver boat. She rose and turned to Bernie.

"Hope you deserve all that affection," she said. "What happened to your head?"

"I fell," Bernie said.

He fell? When had that happened? I had a fuzzy sort of idea that maybe I knew something about that, but it stayed fuzzy: my whole mind seemed to be fuzzy. Poor Bernie. I gave him an extra lick or two. He gave me one more hug, then put me down nice and gently. No need for that: I'm one tough hombre. Still, I felt like sitting instead of standing, so that was what I did. Bernie wiped his face on his sleeve, stepped over to Mami, put his arm around her shoulder, and kissed her wrinkled, splotchy, weathered face.

"My, my," she said, her deep green eye opening wide.

"I owe you," Bernie said.

Her eye narrowed fast. "Find Ralphie," she said.

"We're working on it."

Mami clutched the front of Bernie's shirt, not so friendly now. "But are you getting anywhere?"

"I think so," Bernie said, trying to back away and not having an easy time of it. "In fact, I've got something to show you."

*   *   *

She let go of him. We walked to the car. Solid ground felt pretty fine under my paws. Bernie reached down under his seat and took out the thick piece of pipe with the big nut at one end.

"Ever seen this before?" Bernie said.

"No."

"Any idea what it could be?"

"Maybe one of Ralph's gizmos?"

"Most likely."

"Where did you get it?"

"A long story," Bernie said. "Have you heard about Mack Larouche?"

"They say he OD'd up in the city."

Bernie nodded. "How would you characterize his relationship with Ralph?"

"Nothin' now," she said. "It don't exist." Her green eye went darker, almost black. "Unless they're both together in heaven." She turned quickly to Bernie. "Is that what you're telling me? Ralph's dead, too?"

"I don't know that," Bernie said.

"And why does their relationship even matter?" Mami said.

"Might not," said Bernie. "But in my experience cases usually get solved when you reach a sort of information tipping point. We're not there yet."

"They were close," Mami said. "Good enough?"

"Guess it'll have to be," Bernie said. "For now. Does Ralph have a drug problem?"

"Ralph don't even drink coffee."

"Drug users tend to hang out with each other."

"Mack wasn't always a druggie," Mami said. "And I wouldn't even call him a druggie. Mack had it under control."

"Until he didn't," Bernie said.

A breeze fluttered Mami's eye patch. I caught a glimpse of what was underneath. "Believe in heaven, Mr. Little?" she said.

Bernie looked at her, then at me, then at nothing. "I think it's right here," he said. "But in very small moments."

"Better than nothing at all?" said Mami. "Or worse?" She did a dry spit in the direction of the bayou.

Dry spits: so interesting, but no time to go into the subject now, except there's no ignoring that you didn't see it often, and then only from men. Mami: I liked her a whole lot.

"Give me a heads-up next time one of those moments comes around," she said. Her phone buzzed. She glanced at the screen, then up at Bernie. "Anything else? Gotta take this call."

"Is it Duke?"

"No."

"You're aware that Lord took off?"

She nodded. "I shoulda put money on that, maybe got something out of all this shit."

"Would he come back here?"

"What would be stupider than that?"

"Meaning . . . ?"

Mami didn't answer, instead moved away to take her call.

"How about we let Dr. Ory take a quick look at you," Bernie said, "and then find somewhere to chow down? Or," he went on, regaining his balance and wiping away what might have been a paw print on his shoulder, "maybe a quick snack now to tide you over?"

He stepped over to the Porsche, reached into the glove box, took out a Slim Jim. When had that gotten in there? Not on my watch. Also nothing to worry about, or even spend any time on. What was all that talk about heaven and small moments? Totally over my head, or straight through it, but for some reason I remembered it while I was downing that Slim Jim.

We stopped by Dr. Ory's trailer. I didn't want to go in, so she came out.

"Found him, huh?" she said, wiping a wisp of hair off her face.

"Mami Boutette did," Bernie said. "Down the bayou, almost where it meets the sea."

Dr. Ory knelt in front of me, running her hands in that no-nonsense vetlike way over my body. "He swam all the way from here to there?"

"That's not clear," Bernie said.

Dr. Ory glanced at him. "What happened to you?"

"I fell."

"Uh-huh," Dr. Ory said, pouring some sharp-smelling liquid on a cotton ball and dabbing it on my shoulder. "You're going to be just fine, Chet." She scratched behind one of my ears and rose. Iko's scent was totally gone. What a vet! Maybe she'd do some more scratching, possibly until I didn't want anymore, meaning never.

No more scratching happened. I was just thinking that I already felt fine, especially with the sun on me, heating me down deep where the chill still lingered, when a youngish man in a suit and tie came out of the trailer and said, "Last one just died, Doc."

"Damn," said Dr. Ory.

"More birds?" Bernie said

"Four more at last count," said Dr. Ory. "I called in Mr. Patel here from the government. Mr. Patel, meet Bernie Little and Chet."

Mr. Patel and Bernie shook hands. Mr. Patel was a much smaller dude than Bernie, but he had a nice, vigorous handshake, always something I liked to see. Also, he smelled a bit of curried goat, a dish I often enjoy on visits to Mr. Singh, our pawnbroker back home, at present taking care of Bernie's grandfather's watch for us if I was remembering right.

"Call me Jack," Mr. Patel said.

"You with the EPA, Jack?" Bernie said.

"Not exactly," said Jack Patel, flashing a smile, so bright in his dark face. "You from around here?"

"Not exactly," Bernie said.

Jack's smile faded. Weren't we getting along anymore? All of a sudden this wasn't so easy to follow. Instead, I concentrated on the smell of polish that rose from Jack's shiny black lace-up shoes with tiny holes in the front. FBI dudes always wore those kind of polished shoes; other than that, I had no thoughts.

"Mr. Patel's going to have a little talk with Wes Derrick," Dr. Ory said. "See if he can get some better answers than I did."

"The environmental guy from the oil company?" Bernie said.

Dr. Ory nodded, checked her watch. "Should have been here by now."

At that moment a bright green jeep came down the street and parked in front of the trailer. Out stepped Wes, limping—and not just a little but in a pronounced sort of way, a very nice sight.

"Sorry I'm a bit—" he began, and then he saw me. Sometimes the color drains right out of human faces and then they look like they're made of paper and often keel over. Wes didn't keel over. Instead, he backed toward the bright green jeep, kind of feeling for it behind him, his mouth opening and closing. Was he planning to make a break for it? I thought that over. Wes was a perp, no question. One of my jobs at the Little Detective Agency was to never let a perp make a break for it. Also, a savage sort of growling had started up in our vicinity, always exciting, although it meant thinking things over couldn't go on at the same time. Plus, I was in the mood for excitement, big time.

I got my paws under me. I charged. I sprang. I grabbed Wes by the pant leg. More like right through the pant leg—same leg I'd worked on before, at the start of our boat ride, but that was more or less an accident. The other leg would have been just as good, or almost. I worked on the leg I had, did the best job I knew how. Wes fell, screaming in what I think they call agony. The sound made me even more excited! Who knows why?

TWENTY-FIVE

When you're busy like I was, you're hardly aware of, say, lots of human shouting going on, or hands grabbing for your collar—when there isn't one!—or wide-eyed looks on the face of a vet who'd probably thought she'd seen everything. Chet the Jet in action: add that to your list, baby!

But after a while, things settled down out there on the road in front of Dr. Ory's trailer ,and I found myself sitting peacefully at Bernie's side. We watched Dr. Ory cleaning up Wes Derrick's ankle and some of the calf, perhaps, and possibly a touch of above-the-knee involvement—not much more than a scratch when you came right down to it—and bandage up the boo-boo nice and tidy. One thing for sure: Wes was not a tough hombre. Tough hombres don't moan and wince and ask whiny little questions about tetanus and rabies and other stuff that whizzed right by me. Around that time, I realized that Mr. Patel, the government dude, had—would retreat be how to put it?—stationed himself behind the mostly closed door of the trailer, only his head poking out.

"What in hell got into him?" Mr. Patel said.

Dr. Ory rose. "Good question—never would have dreamed he was the type to go off like that."

What was this about? Wes and his wimpiness? That was my guess. I watched Bernie and waited patiently for whatever was coming next.

"Uh," Bernie said.

I happened to notice that he had his hand resting on the back of my neck, fingers sort of curled into my fur—a brand-new thing, first time he'd done that in all our time together, and, of course, it felt good. What a great idea! But that was Bernie.

"Um," he added. "Don't really know." He gave Wes a look like some question was coming, although he remained silent.

"Must be because of my cats," Was said, so weakly he was hard to hear. "I've got cats."

"Ah," said Bernie. "Sorry, ah, Wes. I hope, you know . . . any associated expense, that kind of . . ."

With a groan or two, Wes got to his feet. "Let's just forget it," he said. "The company has an excellent health plan."

Bernie's eyebrows rose. Have I mentioned Bernie's eyebrows? You really can't miss them, and they have a language all their own. Right now they were surprised, plus a little something extra I didn't get.

"Well," he said, "if you're sure you . . ."

Wes started backing toward the bright green jeep. Hey! He seemed to like walking backward: hadn't seen much of that in humans—or any creature, now that I thought about it.

"Wes?" said Dr. Ory. "Where are you going?"

"Think I'll lie down for a while," Wes said, "take some painkillers, put my leg up."

"What about our meeting?" Dr. Ory said.

Wes's eyes shifted to Mr. Patel in the doorway. "Afraid I'm not up to it at the moment."

"But the birds!" Dr. Ory said.

"Happy to discuss whatever may or may not be happening with any alleged birds," Wes said. He opened the jeep's door and slid in behind the wheel, all of it backward. I was impressed, but it didn't make me like him any better. I still didn't like Wes at all, although I no longer hated him: I had the taste of his blood on my tongue. "How's tomorrow, same time, same place?"

Dr. Ory turned to Mr. Patel. "Jack?"

"Guess that'll have to do," Mr. Patel said.

Wes was already driving off, and not slowly. They all watched him go. I watched Bernie. Something was going on in his mind: I could feel it.

"Meantime," Mr. Patel said, "I'll want coordinates for all the bird finds."

"I've got 'em," Dr. Ory told him. They went inside, Dr. Ory pausing in the doorway and turning to Bernie. "I know a very good trainer," she said.

"Trainer?" said Bernie as the door closed behind her. I was with him on that. Trainer? A total mystery. We hopped into the Porsche—me actually hopping, although not my very smoothest—and hit the road. My only sure takeaway was that Wes had no cats. You can't have cats without me being in the know. He did smell like someone who spent time with a member of the nation within. Had I noticed that already? I got a bit mixed up, started thinking about the Isle des Deux Amis, no idea why.

"First," Bernie said, pulling up to a roadside food truck—one of the greatest human inventions, in my opinion, right up there with cars and handcuffs, "let's get you fed." Sounded like a plan to me. And what if after I was done, he said, *Second, let's get you fed again*?

Bernie went up to the guy in the food truck window.

"Got any steak?"

"Just the round, but it's all cut up for the brochettes," said the food truck guy. He wore beaded chains around his neck and was missing a whole bunch of teeth. Getting through life without all your teeth? Hard to imagine anything worse.

"I'll take two pounds."

"How'd you like that done?"

"Raw."

The next thing I knew I was making quick work of the best steak I'd ever tasted, and you can take that to the bank, except you couldn't, the steak being gone. This took place outside the car, right off the paper wrapper, the food truck guy in the window smiling the whole time. After that, I lapped up a bowl of water and another, felt like me. I sat myself down in front of Bernie and waited.

"What?" he said. "What?"

He didn't know I was waiting for him to say, *Second, let's get you fed again*? That had been the plan, at least as I remembered it.

Then from the food truck guy came a big surprise. "I reckon he wants to do it all over again."

"Can't be," Bernie said. "You saw what he just downed."

"So how come he's barking like that?"

Bernie gave me a look. "Could be anything. Cool it, Chet. Let's go."

We went. I tried to cool it but couldn't for the longest time, on account of *it couldn't be anything*! The food truck guy hit it on the nose, whatever that might mean, the human nose being mostly wrong in my experience, or not even in the picture. Finally, Bernie said, "Chet! I can't hear myself think!"

Uh-oh. Bernie's thinking was one of the best things we had going for us at the Little Detective Agency, Bernie having come up with so many thoughts in our career that I couldn't remember any. I got a grip.

"Whew," said Bernie. We turned onto the rutted road that led into the swamp and stopped by the dock where *Little Jazz* was tied up. Bernie switched off the engine.

How nice to sit by the bayou, just the two of us parked in the shade of a skinny tree that wasn't providing much shade at all, but it was still nice. Bernie patted his shirt pocket, took out the cigarette pack he'd bought in the city—I hoped it was the same one—and shook out the last cigarette in there. He crumpled up the pack.

"Final smoke ever, I swear," he said.

I always liked hearing that. Bernie lit up, let smoke curl from his nose and mouth. I felt his whole body relax.

"Time for a mental list," he said.

So exciting! We hadn't done mental lists in way too long. I waited to hear, mental lists being pretty much a mystery to me, and also Bernie's department.

"Item one," he said. "You need a new collar." He gave me a close look. "Sure like to know how you lost the old one." He took another drag. "What went down in the boat, big guy? How many of them were there? Get a good look?"

The boat? What boat would this be? I'd been on so many boats lately, after a whole boatless lifetime, that I couldn't even begin to keep them all in my mind. I took a swing at it anyway: there was *Little Jazz*, of course, and the pirogue. Hey! Was I off to a good start or what? I left it there for the time being.

"Item three," Bernie was saying. I got a vague sort of feeling that maybe I'd missed something. "I don't like getting hit on the head and now it's happened twice." He glanced at himself in the mirror. "Tired of people looking at me funny," he said, losing me a bit more: why would something that crazy ever happen? He opened the glove box, took out the Swiss Army knife, found the scissors and *snip snip* cut the stitches out of his forehead. Bernie kept talking the whole time, but taking in this new side of him— he was as good as any doctor, or better!—used up all my concentration. "Unrelated coincidence?" he might have been saying. "Don't know about you, Chet, but I'm thinking about that Pyro dude who told us Cleotis had split for Houston. Wish to hell I'd seen—huh, literally—what he had up his sleeve, but let's suppose it was a Q. Where does that take us?"

No idea, and all this was impossible to follow. Not only that, but memory of another boat I'd been on was coming to me . . . coming, coming, coming, and boom! There it was: Mami's boat! I could actually see it in my head. Amazing what the mind could do. No comparison to the body's ability, but still it was nice to have both. I'm one lucky dude.

". . . bringing us to item six," Bernie said, mashing the cigarette butt in the ashtray and turning to me. "How come you don't like Wes?"

Bernie gave me a close look. I gave him a close look back. My tail came alive, doing what it could from its somewhat cramped position kind of trapped under me on the shotgun seat. I agreed with my tail, if that makes any sense, not always the case, if that, too, makes any sense: this was nice, me and Bernie just chillin' by the bayou. That was what my tail was selling me and I bought the complete package.

Bernie smiled. "I get the feeling you're way ahead of me, big guy." Me? Ahead of Bernie? Never! We were side by side, to the max. His eyes got an inward look, the way they did when an idea popped up in his mind and demanded attention. "Suppose . . . suppose Wes actually has no cats," he said. "See where I'm going with this?"

I did not, but anyplace without cats sounded good to me.

"And it's testable," Bernie said. "Cats or no cats—either way a solid fact. Which is what we need right now in the worst way."

Bernie reached toward the key in the ignition like he was about to turn it and start us up, and then his gaze fell on *Little Jazz* and he paused.

"I'm an idiot," he said.

Bernie's a great one for jokes. Once we went to a comedy club downtown with some cop buddies and they had a few drinks and some betting went on and all of a sudden Bernie was onstage doing a trick I'd never seen with a tower of beer cans and a volunteer from the audience who turned out to be a safecracker on the lamb. The laughs he got that night! Although he hadn't seemed to recall much about it next morning, and we never visited a comedy club again.

Instead of heading out for a spin, which was what I'd sensed coming next, we got out of the car and stepped onto the dock. Bernie walked along it the whole length of *Little Jazz*, his eyes on the boat all the time, and then back the other way.

"What do I know for sure?" he said.

Give me a hard one! *Everything* was the answer. Bernie knew everything for sure, the whole enchilada, although enchiladas themselves were a bit of a puzzler. I'd once scarfed down not one but two quick whole enchiladas—pressed for time in a restaurant kitchen that might not have strictly speaking been part of the case—and while I had no complaints, there was no comparing enchiladas to lamb kebabs, for example, or baby back ribs.

"I had a picture book when I was a kid," Bernie said, "about these two miners who start digging into a mountain from opposite sides and meet in the middle. Now that I think about it, my interest in mines probably started with that book."

What a great story, probably the greatest story I ever heard! Bernie: just when you think he's done amazing you, he amazes you again.

"Never liked a story with a moral," Bernie said. "Don't like to be hit on the head."

I gazed at his head, still wrapped in the bandage, although it was nice the stitches were gone. Poor Bernie. I hated him getting hit on the head, didn't like getting hit on my own head either.

"But the moral of the miner story is that there are always at least two approaches." He crossed the wooden gangplank to *Little Jazz*'s deck, me following and then somehow ahead. "Can't tell you who we surprised in here, but I know what he was up to—searching the place. Did he find what he was looking for after I was out of the picture? I'm betting you didn't let that happen, big guy. So that's our angle into this particular mine—we're going to rip the place apart."

Little Jazz was a mine? News to me, but I didn't worry about it for a moment. If ripping a place apart is on the agenda, you have my full attention.

TWENTY-SIX

Ripping places apart was a kind of search. We've done searches out the yingyang, me and Bernie, most of them lots of fun, some not. The worst was when we opened up that broom closet in the tidy little kitchen of a tidy little house in Vista City. Too late. Oh, no: too late. I never wanted to think about that, but it came into my mind anyway, sometimes at the oddest times, like when Charlie falls asleep on the couch on one of those days we have him, and I just sit close by, watching him sleep. We've solved every missing kid case we ever took, except the broom closet one. Which was how I thought of it, although the girl's name was Gail. The look I saw in Bernie's eyes: I'll never forget it. Later that night, we'd taken care of justice on our own, which I also won't forget, even though Bernie had said we should. "Lock it in a deep dark place, throw away the key, and never think about it again." I'd tried so many times.

We boarded *Little Jazz*. The sun was high in the sky, a yellow sky, so hot and heavy, and the bayou looked kind of yellow, too. I stuck my head over the side rail, opened my nostrils and did a quick search of my own. Good news: no trace of Iko's scent. Not that I was afraid of Iko. Don't think that for a moment.

The long rubber tube I'd last seen snaking out of a hole in the deck was still there. Bernie knelt to examine it.

"Clues all over the damn place," Bernie said. "Didn't actually check out any of this when I came to—not priority one at that moment."

No? What could be more important than clues? I didn't get it.

Bernie's gaze went to a dark, dried-up bloodstain on the deck. "Who belongs to that?"

Cale Rugh, if I remembered right, and of course I did. When I've tasted someone's blood, he tends to linger in my memory.

Bernie came over to me, gave me a pat, the slow and thoughtful kind. "If there'd been a body on board when we first came here, you'd have known, right?"

What a question! There hadn't been any body on board, wasn't one now.

"So we can rule out the creepy possibility that Ralph's been on this boat the whole time," Bernie said. "But suppose whoever we caught searching it wasn't searching. What if they were bringing him here, step one in a plan that ended in a fire? See where this leads? Even if some remains got found, it would look like the strange but accidental death of a loner no one understood in the first place. So let's go sniff around."

Sniff around? For what? There was no body on board: hadn't we just been through that?

We sniffed around the boat—living room, kitchen, bedroom, bathroom, and through a hatch door on the upfront—bow! I kept forgetting and it kept coming back to me!—part of the deck. Bernie actually sniffed once or twice himself. Even when you were doing something completely useless you could still find lots of fun in life.

"It was a search then, for sure," Bernie said. He went into

the kitchen, knelt by the sink. "So we pick up where the searcher left off. A search," he added, his voice sinking down to muttering level, "a sharper guy would have done the moment we first came aboard." I realized that picking up on mutters wasn't one of my strengths: I must have heard wrong.

The door to the cabinet under the sink already hung open. Bernie gazed inside, then started rooting around, and out came sponges, brushes, detergents, steel wool—big mistake, chewing on steel wool, and there'd be no repetition of that, I wasn't even tempted—paper towel rolls, an old coffee pot, a bunch of rags, a jar full of rusty nails.

"So much junk in life," Bernie said, his head now inside the cabinet, making him a bit hard to understand. "How about we start over, say around ten thousand BC?" Ten thousand BC? That had come up before, a total mystery to me. I moved a little closer in case Bernie was about to explain what it was all about. Instead, he reached in deeper, stretching his body flat out, and said, "Wonder what this thing does? Part of the garbage disposal, or—"

Whoosh! A whole big—maybe not river, more like a fire hose thing—gush of water came blasting out from under the sink, followed by Bernie, his hair plastered flat against his head, the top half of him soaked right through, and then all of him, and me, too! And the gush kept gushing! Meanwhile, how exciting to see Bernie with his hair plastered flat like that! Like he was a different Bernie! But still Bernie! Hard to explain. Next thing I knew, we were crowded under the sink together, Bernie grunting and struggling and using some of the words Charlie wasn't supposed to hear, and me just crowding. Then came a metallic clang and the gushing ramped way up, no question about it. Bernie and I went rolling and sliding across the watery floor. It was almost like surfing!

"The main!" he shouted. "Gotta find the main!"

Did that mean we were done with surfing, so soon? Yes. Things were moving fast, but that was just the way I like them. We ran out of the kitchen, out of the cabin—some confusion in the doorway, me ending up in the lead—onto the deck, back around to the hatch in the bow, and dove right down through it, me actually diving, Bernie sort of falling. Down below—the only light entering through a small round window up high on the wall—he picked himself up, me helping, and looked around wildly. I could hear water flowing across the deck above.

"Where? Where? Where the hell is it?"

Bernie darted into a dark corner, flung some life jackets out of the way, and bent over a whole mess of pipes coming and going in every direction.

"Gotta be this," he said, and started pushing and pulling at some sort of lever. It wouldn't budge. He grabbed a big wrench, swung hard at the lever, missing it completely, the wrench slipping from his hand and spinning across this little below-deck store-room or whatever it was and clanging on the floor. A floorboard broke loose and came whipping right back at us. We jumped out of the way, Bernie losing his balance and crashing into the lever, shoulder-first. It shifted. The sound of running water coming from above and all around us died away.

Bernie rose, rubbing his shoulder, head bandage dangling loose and then falling to the deck, where he left it. No blood was flowing anywhere on his head, a nice sight.

"That was easy," he said.

Which wouldn't have been my take, but if Bernie said so, then that was that. He picked up the loose floorboard, took it over to the hole in the floor, started to lower it in place, and paused. "What have we here?" he said. He reached in and pulled out a very thick and very short piece of pipe with a big sort of nut at one end, a lot like the one we had in the car, or even exactly the same. He turned to me, his eyes glittering in the way they did when we were about to start getting ours.

"Two miners, Chet," he said. What had that been all about again? I couldn't quite bring it back, but the number sounded right.

Bernie brought the other pipe in from the car, set the two pipes side by side on the kitchen counter. By that time, we had all the water mopped up and everything looked ship-shape, as Bernie put it, but wasn't *Little Jazz* a sort of ship? Meaning how could it be car-shaped, or tree-shaped, or any other kind of shape? I puzzled over that and then I didn't. All I knew for sure was that I was Chet-shaped. Good enough for me, amigo.

"Look pretty much identical to me," Bernie said. "But one's good and one's a piece of crap, although that quote is hearsay from Duke, which is like piling crap on crap."

I smelled no crap in the vicinity, none at all, which was actually kind of unusual. Piles of crap would not be something I'd miss. But I believed in Bernie. Crap had to be just around the corner.

"We'll put a black *M* on this one," Bernie said, taking a couple of felt pens from a jar on the counter, "meaning we found it at Mack's, and a red *R* for Ralph on the new one." He raised the pipes one at a time, peering in them like they were spyglasses, spyglasses being something I knew from our pirate-movie-watching period, which had come after our outer-space-movie period and before one of our many Western-movie periods. Westerns were Bernie's favorite, and mine, too, on account of—

"Whoa!" Bernie said. He turned the red-marked pipe this

way and that, squinting into it from different angles. "Something's taped in there? Like a . . ." He opened a drawer, took out a long skewer, the kind for doing shrimp on the barbie, and poked around inside the red-marked pipe. After a moment or two, out fell a small square of folded paper with some torn-off tape across the top. ". . . a note?" Bernie's voice went real quiet.

He sat down at the table, carefully unfolded the small square, ending up with a sheet of paper the same size as what we had in the printer back home—jammed for what Bernie said was the last time and now in pieces in the recycling bin, but forget that last part. Standing beside Bernie, I could make out markings on the page; other than that, I had nothing to contribute.

"X cubed plus 314Y to the . . . and all in a square bracket that . . . forgotten what the sideways squiggly thing . . ." His voice trailed off. "Math, big guy," Bernie said. "Math, math everywhere and not a drop to drink," he added, losing me completely. "Who's good at math?" Or something like that: in my already completely lost state I maybe wasn't paying the closest attention.

Meanwhile, Bernie had pulled out his phone, was tapping at the keys. "No service?" He gave the phone a little smack. Bernie was only human—only human being one of my favorite human expressions—and humans had a habit of smacking their machines around. The machines never smacked them back. I'd seen some very tough guys who did the same thing, just taking it and taking it until their moment came around.

We got in the car and drove down one rutted road and up another, Bernie checking the phone screen from time to time. "Here we go," he said, pulling over. A blob of bird crap fell from the sky and landed on the hood. Crap: just around the corner, making Bernie right again.

"Hey, Prof," he said. "Bernie Little here."

Prof! We had lots of experts for this and that—Otis DeWayne when it came to weapons, for example—and Prof down at Valley College was our money expert. I didn't get to see Prof enough. He had a big round belly that was always making interesting sounds and also jiggled when he laughed, which was often, but his eyes were smart and watchful; kind of like Cleotis's, which might have come up already.

Prof's voice sounded through the speakers. "Hi, Bernie. I've been meaning to call you."

"What about?"

"That router company I recommended in March," Prof said. "Had a nice run-up, but now it's time to cash out and take your profits."

"Uh," Bernie said, "I never pulled the trigger on that."

"No? Next you'll be telling me you took a flyer on that tequila start-up instead."

Bernie said nothing. The tequila start-up? Something about making tequila from this special weed that grew on landfills? I kind of remembered a woman from the company coming over to the house and giving Bernie a taste.

"You can lead a horse to water, but you can't make him drink," Prof said, which couldn't be truer in my experience. Horses were prima donnas and making them do just about anything was impossible. "Any point in giving you another tip, Bernie?"

"Not at the moment," Bernie said. "How's your math?"

"Adequate for my purposes," said Prof.

"I've got a bunch of equations here—mind taking a look at them?"

"They don't teach math at West Point?"

"They do," Bernie said, "but I don't seem to have retained it."

"That's because your life is overbalanced into the physical world. Proust hardly ever left his cork-lined bedroom."

Sounded pretty suspicious to me. I made what Bernie calls a mental note. Proust: possible perp, an orange jumpsuit most likely in his future.

"Can you just take down these numbers?" Bernie said.

"I'll have to go over to the desk." Then came a grunt, which would be Prof getting off the couch in his office, a very comfortable leather couch I'd tried out once myself. "Okay, shoot."

Bernie held the sheet of paper up to the light and started reading to Prof. So nice to hear Bernie's voice. As for whatever he was actually saying, you tell me.

"I'll get back to you," Prof said, just as my eyelids were getting heavy.

I had a quick nap, one of my very quickest, and then we were pulling up to the dock. Another car was waiting. The door opened and Vannah jumped out. She came running over, kind of stumbling in her high heels, like she might topple over any second.

"You bastard!" she yelled. "You're the one who found him and you didn't even tell me! I had to hear it from some goddamn coldblooded cop."

"Um, sorry," Bernie said. "I got caught up and—" He cut himself off. "My apologies," he said. "And I'm sorry for the loss of your brother."

She gazed at Bernie, wobbling back and forth a bit, breathing deeply. Vannah wore a very short skirt and a very little top. Bernie did the best job I'd ever seen him do of keeping his gaze on a mostly naked woman's face.

"And now Lord's missing, too?" Vannah said.

"I'm afraid so," Bernie said.

Her eyes misted over. Was she going to burst into tears? That often came next, but from Vannah? I kind of doubted it, on account of her face, beautiful, yes, but also kind of tough from certain angles, and—

Vannah burst into tears. She threw herself into Bernie's arms. "I'm scared, so scared."

Bernie patted her back. "Now, now," he said, and added, "there, there."

She buried her face on his shoulder, which muffled her crying and also her voice. "Let me stay here with you, oh don't say no." Was that what she said? I couldn't be absolutely sure.

"Ah, um, well . . ." said Bernie. And then I was.

TWENTY-SEVEN

Sometimes a kind of tension springs up between a man and a woman. It's a snap to pick up, since right away—actually even before—they both start smelling different. I began picking up the tension during dinner that night—tuna sandwiches for them, kibble for me—and it got stronger around bedtime. For sleeping quarters on *Little Jazz* we had a real bed in the bedroom section toward the bow, and a padded bench that turned into a bed in the living room part. After some back-and-forth, Bernie got Vannah to sleep in the bedroom, and he took the padded bench.

"A gentleman, huh?" she said. "Haven't run into many of them." A gentleman was a dude who wore a coat and tie, and Bernie was wearing a Hawaiian shirt that night—the one with the coconuts-with-straws-sticking-out-of-them pattern—so I didn't quite catch Vannah's drift. Plus she hadn't seen many dudes in coat and ties? They're all over downtown in the daytime.

I started the night on the floor right next to the padded bench, moved out onto the stern deck and watched the moon for a while, returned to my spot near the padded bench. Bernie was muttering a bit, not having one of his best sleeps. "On the other hand," he said, and later, "if only," both bad signs. I wriggled around, got even more comfortable than I already was, and readied myself for some nice dreams, maybe chasing fat javelinas in the canyon behind our place on Mesquite Road or exploring the inside of Iggy's house with Iggy beside me, an adventure that had really happened once in waking life, a fun day to the max and nothing to feel bad about ever since old Mr. Parsons told Bernie it had nothing to do with Mrs. Parsons ending up back in the hospital. But in that fuzzy time when my eyes were closed but dreams hadn't quite arrived, I heard light, barefooted steps approaching.

My eyes opened but I already knew who it was. Vannah moved through a thin stream of moonlight flowing through one of those little round windows. She wore a T-shirt and that was it, a T-shirt you couldn't call longish. Normally, I wouldn't let anyone near Bernie while he slept, so why wasn't I on my feet, getting between them, maybe throwing in a growl or two? No clue! No clue excepting her hands were empty and just from the way she moved, I knew she meant Bernie no harm. I lay stretched out and motionless on the floor, actually incapable of movement myself, as though I was asleep, and I sort of did feel asleep, but with open eyes.

Vannah stood over the bed. Moonlight shone on her face. She looked a lot older by moonlight, at least to me. Bernie's bare shoulder was sticking up out of the covers. The moonlight caught his shoulder, too, making it like stone. But Bernie wasn't stone, was a flesh-and-blood man, his strong chest rising and falling as he breathed. Vannah reached for his shoulder, ran her hand along it, pulled back the covers, swung her leg up on the bed.

Bernie's eyes snapped open. "Vannah?" he said, sitting up real fast, the way Bernie could move if he had to. "What's going on?"

"Take a wild guess," she said. She laughed a low, gurgly laugh.

"The wilder the better." She lowered her face to his. Bernie's mouth opened and closed, no sound coming out. Their lips were just about touching. At that moment, his gaze shifted and went to me, lying on the floor. He seemed to be looking me right in the eyes. I did the same thing to him, no seeming about it. His expression changed, hard to explain how, almost like he'd given himself a good shake. He held up his hand to Vannah.

"No," he said.

"No what?" she said. "No wildness? Strictly vanilla?"

Vanilla? This was all about ice cream? Ice cream in general I can take or leave, but vanilla I'd just leave. The possibility wasn't even going to arise since there was no vanilla on the boat, the smell being impossible to miss. So: I was actually a bit lost.

Bernie put his hand on Vannah's arm, didn't exactly push her, more like held her off.

"I appreciate the ah, um," he said. "But it's not a good idea."

"How do you know?" Vannah said. "We haven't gotten to the ah, um yet."

Yes, this was impossible to follow. I closed my eyes.

"I have a girlfriend," Bernie said.

"You do?"

"I tried to tell you on the phone. We got cut off."

"How about pretending you don't," Vannah said, "and I'll do some pretending of my own? I can keep a secret, and I'm sure you can, too."

"Yeah," Bernie said, "but I couldn't keep it from myself."

There was a silence, a still moment or two, and then all that tension I'd been feeling in the boat started fading fast. There was no more talk. Vannah's bare footsteps went padding back to the bedroom. Everybody settled down for a nice sleep. Bernie says that sleep knits up torn sleeves, or something like that, although

none of us on *Little Jazz* had on any sort of sleeves at the moment.
I wasn't even wearing my collar! I thought about my collar for a
while. Then I rose and took a little turn on the stern deck, sticking
my nose over the side and sniffing the bayou: no trace of Iko. Not
that I was afraid of Iko, not in the slightest. Don't think that for
a moment. I returned to my spot near Bernie and plunged right
into dreamland.

Bacon! There are smells in dreams, at least the way we dream them
in the nation within. Sometimes I have dreams that are smells and
smells only. Does that happen to you? I kind of doubt it, no offense.

Bacon! The dream smell of bacon got so strong that my mouth
began to water, and when my mouth waters I can't keep my eyes
closed. I opened them—and what was this? Bacon!

Yes, bacon of the nondream type, meaning you could eat it.
In passing, I noticed other early morning details: Bernie at the
kitchen table, checking out those two thick pipes again, a cup of
steaming coffee at his elbow; Vannah at the little stove, wearing
a tiny bikini, and frying up a gently hissing pan of—BACON.
The bacon part was the main event, of course, not part of the
noticed-in-passing details, all of which had already slipped my
mind. Beside that lovely hissing, so full of promise, there was also
the sound of Vannah whistling to herself—and she was good at it.
This was all nice and homey. I rose and was just about to give myself a day-starting stretch—but a quick one, on account of you-
know-what and the need to make plans for getting some—when I
heard someone stepping down on the stern deck. I kind of knew
who it was before I even turned to look, just from the sound of
that footstep—female human, light but firm, strong.

And yes, a woman, light but firm, and strong: Suzie. Suzie!

Those eyes, dark and shining like our countertops back home on Mesquite Road, and just how she stood and moved, more of a pleasure to watch than any other human I knew, except for Bernie, goes without mentioning. I hadn't seen her in way too long. My tail revved right up.

"Hey, there, Ber—" she started to say, and then she saw Vannah at the stove, who happened to be hitching up her bikini top, which seemed to have slipped down a bit on account of maybe being a touch too small for her, which reminded me of a stripper we'd once interviewed on a missing G-string case that I hadn't understood from start to finish, although I'd located the G-string practically from the get-go. But no time for that now.

"Suzie?" Bernie said, rising from the table in a way I wouldn't want to call awkward, although somehow the table ended up overturning anyway, the two thick pipes and the coffee cup crashing to the floor. "What are you, um—?"

"Labor Day weekend, Bernie?" Suzie said. She looked directly at Vannah; the whistling died out right in the middle of things, ending in a harsh way. "Maybe you got distracted and forgot," Suzie added.

"I'm Vannah," Vannah said, waving the spatula, which set off more slippage of the bikini top. "Chief cook and bottle washer. And he's not as distractible as you'd think."

Suzie's eyes went hard and not shiny at all, didn't even look like her eyes. She turned these scary new eyes on Bernie. "I know it's only Friday morning," she said. "My mistake—I thought it would be a surprise." She laughed, one of those abrupt, unhappy laughs that's mostly a snort through the nose. "And it sure as hell is."

"Wait," Bernie said. He glanced at Vannah, maybe looking for some help. Still getting her bikini top squared away, she raised her eyebrows and gave him a bright smile. "This isn't what it looks like!" Bernie said, his voice rising. "I can ex—"

"Let's not embarrass ourselves any further," Suzie said, and in one smooth motion she turned and sort of glided right over the rail, stepping onto the dock and walking quickly to a small car parked beside the Porsche. Without a glance back, she got in and drove away, not too fast, raising only a small dust cloud on the rutted road.

"Wait," Bernie called, "wait, wait." He bolted toward the stern, slipping and almost falling in the spilled coffee. Bernie got himself over the rail, perhaps not with Suzie's ease, but there was always his war wound to consider, and jumped into the Porsche. I found I was already there, sitting high and alert in the shotgun seat. Hadn't Suzie just said something about surprises? And now I'd surprised myself! Chet the Jet, in the picture!

Bernie jammed the key in the ignition and turned it hard. The engine went *whirr whirr whirr*. Uh-oh. I knew that *whirr whirr whirr*, although it hadn't paid us a visit in some time. Bernie tried the key again, stamped on the pedals, shouted the kinds of things humans shouted during this sort of situation. If the car didn't start soon, he'd be banging on it like it was a bad guy, another machine-smacking human moment.

Pretty soon Bernie was really letting the steering wheel have it. Maybe that made the *whirr whirr whirr* go away, but in its place came a quiet *click click click* that to the best of my recollection would eventually lapse into total silence. After that we might see the tools.

Out came the tools. Bernie threw open the hood, leaned way in there, his head disappearing from view, which meant he didn't see a taxi pulling up, and Vannah—now in jeans and T-shirt and carrying a little pink suitcase—getting in the backseat and being driven away. I sat on the dock. Bernie got out some different tools, squirmed under the car. Time passed. An oily blackened hunk of metal fell from somewhere in the engine, rolled across the dock and dropped into the water with a soft splash. Not long after that, Bernie crawled out from under and said, "That should do it."

He climbed back into the car. I got in the shotgun seat. "Odds are she's headed right back to the airport," he said. "If we drive like the wind we can still catch her."

Sounded good to me: driving like the wind was one of my favorite things. Bernie turned the key. Then came an explosion—although it's fair to say not a big one—and smoke rose from under the hood. As for the flames, they were on the small side in my opinion, hardly worth mentioning.

Later that very same day we'd met some cool dudes—tow-truck dude, auto junkyard dude, mechanic dude—and the Porsche was running great, even louder than normal, on a brand-new old engine, and our three shrimpy grand was mostly gone. I felt tip-top, and so did Bernie, and even if he wasn't at his very tip-toppest, he wasn't completely miserable: I could tell from the expression in his eyes, not quite as murky as they'd been the whole after-Suzie time so far.

"Since we're just about in the city anyway," Bernie said as we pulled out of the junkyard, "how about we run down Pyro and see what's up his sleeve?"

I remembered Pyro well on account of the visor that had hidden his eyes, the kind of bothersome detail that sticks in my mind and made me not like him much, but running him over? This was going to be a first. We were up to new tricks at the Little Detective Agency. Bernie? The best.

"Hey!" Bernie said. "What's with you?"

With me? Nothing much. Maybe I'd just given Bernie a quick lick on the side of his face, maybe not. It was also possible that there'd been some swerving. A quirk of the new engine? That was my first thought. No other thoughts came, but in truth I didn't wait for them very long.

Soon we were back in that sketchy boarded-up part of town where we'd first found Cleotis. Now his boxy little shotgun house was boarded up, too, all except for that thick steel front door, which had a big lock hanging from it. We parked out front and stayed in the car. Were we sitting on Cleotis's house again? Any reason not to sit on an empty one? I had a feeling there should be. That turned out to be one of those feelings that didn't go anywhere, often the case and I was cool with it. Bernie took out his phone and tried Suzie again—I could tell because her face came up on the screen—maybe for the zillionth time, which is a pretty big number, certainly way more than two.

"C'mon, pick up," he said.

But she did not.

Bernie put the phone away, gazed at Cleotis's crib. By that time, the sun was going down and the crib looked fuzzy in the dying light, like it wasn't solid. "No Suzie, a complicated case, and we've already spent all of the fee we're likely to get. I'm tempted, mighty tempted." He drummed his fingers on the steering wheel. Tempted to do what? That was my question. I myself knew a lot about temptation, and always ended up handling it the same way.

Bernie never said what the temptation was. "Wouldn't be me," he said after a while. "Maybe I lack the imagination to slip the harness."

Bernie in harness? What a terrible thought! And also a puzzler because Bernie wasn't wearing a harness—today he had on his darkest Hawaiian shirt, the one with the nighttime bongo drums, plus jeans and sneakers—and never once had in all the time we'd been together.

". . . simple curiosity, too," he was saying when I tuned back in. "Suppose, for example, I'm right about Pyro's wrist. If so, then someone didn't want us on this case from the very beginning. Meaning we want to be on it more than ever." That sounded right to me. Bernie opened the door. "How about we see if Cleotis got himself a new tenant?" I was sitting outside the driver's-side door before Bernie had finished getting out. He tucked the flashlight into his belt on one side and the .38 Special on the other. Was there time for him to shoot a few dimes out of the air before we did whatever we were doing? Probably not.

TWENTY-EIGHT

We walked around to the back of Cleotis's boarded-up shot-gun house. The last of the daylight was gone now, the sky moonless and starless, this neighborhood not the kind where the streetlights worked. Darkness, sketchy part of town, backside of a sketchy little house, .38 Special: life was good. I get a feeling when a case is going well, and I had it now. Was it bothersome that the money was just about gone? Only if I thought about it. That was the kind of problem I could solve all on my own.

Bernie approached a boarded-up window by the back door, ripped off the boards like nobody's business, which made no sense to me, this sort of thing being our business exactly. Next came the window. This particular window was pretty much our favorite kind, just one pane. First, Bernie tried to open it: locked. Locked was always my preference—it meant I got to see Bernie breaking the glass. Bernie was a great glass breaker—I'd seen him do it with his head! And more than once! But not tonight. Tonight we were trying to keep the noise level down. I knew that as soon as Bernie took off his shirt and wrapped it around the .38 Special. After that came a quick *tap tap* at the window, practically silent, and the glass broke into two pieces that fell inside and landed on something soft, making the gentlest shattering sounds I'd heard in my career so far.

Bernie glanced around—just an old habit of his, I'd have let him know if anyone was coming—then put on his shirt, picked a few shards out of the frame, and raised one foot as though to step inside. That led to a brief moment of confusion ending with us both safely through the window, me first.

"What a stench!" Bernie said in a low whisper, stench being a smell humans were capable of detecting but didn't like. In the nation within, we have plenty of sounds we don't like, but not really any smells. Smells are too big a world for simply liking or not liking, and besides, we get way too busy breaking down the smells, and breaking down the parts of the parts, and the parts of the parts of the parts! For example, here inside Cleotis's crib we had big-time rotting smells, no longer a surprise to me in this city. You want a part? How about food? We had rotting fruit. How about parts of that? Rotting bananas and rotting pineapples. See the way this works? We also had rotting meat, rotting milk, rotting eggs—even humans never miss that last one. The rotting food part was actually a small part of the big smell picture, which was dominated by toilet back-up. It reminded me of a case we'd once worked involving rival septic tank companies owned by two dudes who hated each other. The ways they had of getting even! But no time for that now. Sometimes the most important smells in our business are the ones that aren't there, and this was one of those times; meaning death was not in the house.

Another quiet whisper from Bernie: "I think I smell rotten eggs." That was Bernie: human to the max.

He switched on the light. We were in the kitchen where we'd had our little face-to-face with Cleotis, but now everything was smashed up, including the fridge, tipped over on the floor. The floor itself was all puddly. I was considering the remains of an almost-floating drumstick when Bernie made a little *click-click* sound in his mouth and moved toward the stairs, the same ones Cleotis's muscle guy Herman had climbed when he went up for his rest after the brief ruckus with Bernie. Bernie and I mounted the stairs, pretty much side by side, although the truth was I nosed ahead as we reached the top.

Bernie poked the light around. We stood in a narrow corridor, the kind you get upstairs in a shotgun house. There were two doors off the corridor, both closed. The first was the bathroom with the toilet back-up problem. Bernie—gun in one hand and flashlight in his mouth—turned the knob and pushed the door open with his shoulder. He glanced quickly around at the wet mess, took the flashlight out of his mouth and whispered, "This is where that stink is coming from."

Or something like that. I was still stuck on the image of Bernie with the flashlight in his mouth, one of the very best sights of my whole life. Was he going to start carrying things in his mouth more often? I hoped so. At that moment something thudded *bump bump bump* against the wall behind me. One backward glance and I knew right away it was my tail. I got it under control pronto: we were in quiet mode and I was a pro. Was it possible that my tail was not a pro? What a scary thought! And now it was drooping? Up, tail, and now! Up it went, nice and stiff, but for the first time I thought that I might be wrong about this case and it was headed off the rails.

We came to the second door. Bernie, about to shift the flashlight to his mouth again—I'd hardly had to hope at all—paused, and bent toward the knob. This was one of those old-fashioned doors with a keyhole—and the key was in it. Bernie looked at me,

his eyes filled with some sort of meaning that didn't come to me
then and there. He turned the key, took a step to the side, keeping me behind him, mostly, meaning away from the door, then
reached out with his hand and pushed the door open. This was
when gunfire sometimes happened—and there was someone in
the room, no doubt about that, someone I knew—but no gunfire
happened. We moved in, the .38 Special pointing the way.

"Drrm froom," said someone inside.

Bernie aimed the beam in the direction of the sound. This
room had nothing in it but a big gas can in a corner and two
chairs in the center, one of which was empty. Duct-taped to the
other chair hand and foot, with one of those horrible ball gags
in his mouth, sat Lord Boutette, his straggly goatee even stragglier than before, and again wearing only his tighty whiteys, except now they weren't so white. Lord's eyes were open wide and
seemed to . . . to be begging for something, the way you might
beg for a treat, which was a no-no in the nation within, at least
at the table.

"Didn't expect you here," Bernie said. "I'm disappointed."

"Hrrum?" said Lord.

"Who tied you up?" Bernie said. "What's the story?"

Lord got louder. "Mrraanf! Frummrr!"

"You want me to take the gag off?" Bernie said.

Lord nodded his head, kind of violently. His neck made a
cracking sound.

"I have no objection to doing that," Bernie said, "on one con-
dition."

"Wrrr?"

"That when you open your mouth, nothing comes out but
the truth."

More nodding. "Rrrr. Rrrr." Lord was actually sounding a

bit like Spike, buddy of mine who hangs out at Nixon Panero's Autobody.

"The moment I hear a false note," Bernie said, "the gag goes right back on. Plus we leave you here for whatever's coming your way."

Head nodding turned quickly, with another neck crack, to head shaking. "Nnnnnrrh, nnnnnrrh." I found myself beginning to understand Lord just about better than any human I'd ever met.

Bernie tucked the .38 Special back in his belt, avoided a little puddle at Lord's feet, and untied the ball gag. He held on to it, the ball dangling within my reach, but that was one ball I didn't want to play with.

Lord made stretching motions with his mouth. "Goddamn nightmare," he said. "Cut me loose, man. Get me out of here."

"How did the nightmare start?" Bernie said.

"Very first time I got married," Lord said. "Would you believe the bride started making out with Duke at the reception? He was fourteen, for Christ sake. Can we finish up with the memories somewheres else?"

"I meant this particular nightmare," Bernie said, waving the flashlight.

"Like how I got here?"

"Exactly like that."

"I'll tell it much better if I can get some fresh air."

"Then we'll settle for the lesser version," Bernie said.

"Huh?"

Bernie raised the ball gag up to Lord's eye level.

"Can't you at least untie me?"

"Maybe in a bit."

"Whose side are you on?"

"That's what I'm trying to find out. I'll need your story."

Lord took a deep breath. "Do my best," Lord said. "Step up to the plate, despite of feelin' like shit."

"Played much baseball, Lord?"

"Never," said Lord. "But I had the rules down cold, back in the day."

"Yeah?"

"Umped Little League games," Lord said. "Till the bastards canned me."

"You took payoffs from some of the dads?" Bernie said.

Lord gave Bernie a sideways look. "Who's been talkin'?"

"Nobody."

"You, like, guessed?"

"It's not important," Bernie said. "Back to how you got here."

"There was only two dads," Lord said. "But their goddamn kids were pitchers on—what's the word?"

"Opposite."

"Yeah, opposite teams. See the problem?"

"The clock is ticking," Bernie said.

A problem, right there. I heard no clock. Was it possible Bernie could hear something I could not? Not a chance. So therefore? Good thing Bernie handled the so therefores, meaning I didn't have to go there, there being the idea of Bernie making a mistake. Uh-oh: did I just go there anyway? Sometimes the mind had a mind of its own, and there was nothing you could do.

"You want to know how I got here?" Lord said. "That it?"

"And fast," Bernie said.

"Then the joke's on you, pal. 'Cause I don't have a clue where the hell I am." Lord started laughing. Laughter is usually the best human sound, but not Lord's, which was high-pitched and squeaky. "Don't think your dog likes me," he said.

"What makes you think that?"

"The look in his eyes," Lord said. "Like he's a stone killer."

Stone killer? Me? I had no desire to hurt Lord the slightest bit; and then, all of a sudden, I did! How about that?

"Chet just wants to hear your story," Bernie said. "And I'd make it quick and to the point. He has zero tolerance for pussy-footing."

Nothing truer than that, amigo. Lord got the idea and started talking fast.

"All I knows is I was mindin' my own business—that's how I am, ask anybody—just sittin' in front of the tube with a cold one and a joint watchin' LSU football—what else'm I gonna do, that son of a bitch shackle around my ankle—when all of a sudden I hear footsteps somewhere at the back of the house. Thought it was Duke, you know? Who else has a key? So I said, 'Duke? That you?' kind of thing. No answer. I took maybe one more hit or two, thinkin' it musta been my imagination. I got a real good imagination—I'm kind of a writer, in fact."

"Yeah?" Bernie said.

"Song lyrics," Lord said. "One thing about Duke is he's musical."

"I've heard him play."

"Then you know. Thing is, he comes up with these tunes, but he don't have the words for them, mind don't work that way. Where I come in. We've been workin' on an album for a year or two or four, should be puttin' some feelers out soon to the industry. Workin' title's *Boomin' You Baby in the Boom Boom Room*— that's also the leadoff song."

For a tiny moment, Bernie got a look in his eyes that made me think he was about to laugh. No laughter happened. Instead, he said, "But it wasn't Duke."

"Huh?"

"Making noise at the back of your house."

"Oh, that. No, not Duke, for goddamn sure. And it wasn't my imagination neither. Problem was, the way I was sittin', had my back to the hall."

"When you were watching football."

"Like I said. LSU Tigers—I'm a big fan. Had a beer or two with Billy Cannon way back when, swear to God."

"But it wasn't him either."

"Huh? Hell, you're pullin' my leg."

I checked out Lord's scrawny legs. Bernie would have no problem pulling them right off him, if they hadn't been tied to the chair.

". . . not Duke, not Billy Cannon," Lord was saying. "But I can't tell you who it was. I called out—still thinkin' it was Duke, understand—'In here, Duke, watchin' the game'—and I remember distinctly leaning forward to crack open another coldie, but after that—blank."

"Blank?"

"Next thing I knew I was in this goddamn room tied to this goddamn chair." He glanced at the boarded-up window. "Where am I, anyways?"

"We'll get to that," Bernie said. "What happened when you came to?"

"I had this terrible headache."

Bernie walked around Lord, peered at the back of his head. "Doesn't look too bad. Won't even need stitches."

"Still got the headache," Lord said. "As if anyone cares, always the way. So I wake up, get smacked by the headache, then the door opens and in comes this masked dude. I start in on makin' what noise I can, lettin' him know I want the gag out and pronto. Sucker comes over, leans in and points his finger at me, points it and points it closer and closer till it's right in my eye. Which I tried to close but too late. So his finger's on my eyeball, not pressing, but right there touching, see what I mean."

"I do."

"So I stopped makin' noise. He took off the gag, fed me half a sandwich and a drink of water, and when he was done with that he gagged me up again and left."

"Did he say anything?"

"Not that time. But he's been back. Same dude, same mask, same thing with the sandwich and the water, but for the once when he brought that other chair and the gas can." Lord jerked his head toward the gas can in the corner. "That was the only time he spoke."

"What did he say, word for word, if you can," Bernie said.

"Word for word?" Lord squeezed his eyes shut real tight. "'Bigmouth'—that's what he called me, Bigmouth—'you'll have company soon but not for long.' That's as close as I can come." Lord opened his eyes. "Didn't know what to make of that. Sounded kind of like a bad fortune cookie."

Bernie smiled.

"What's funny?" said Lord.

"Nothing," Bernie told him. "What did this guy look like."

"He had a mask on! Aren't you listenin'?"

"Did he have a mask on his body, too?"

"Mask on his . . . I get it. Like his build, that kind of thing?" Bernie nodded. "He was short, but real muscular."

"Fireplug type?"

"Exactly."

"Anything you can tell me about his speech?"

"Already gave it to you word for word."

"Did he have an accent, for example?"

"Hell, yeah. You didn't catch it when I did the word for word?"

"Sorry."

"Hispanic," Lord said. "There, that's my whole goddamn story. Now get me out of this hellhole."

"No rush," Bernie said. He got the gag back in Lord's mouth and tied it tight. Lord's reaction wasn't of the pleasant kind, so let's skip it.

TWENTY-NINE

We've been ambushed more often than I want to think about, me and Bernie, but here's the fun part: sometimes we get to do a bit of ambushing ourselves! And this was turning out to be one of those times. First, we covered up our traces, at least in human terms, which meant Bernie had to re-board-up the back window, which he did, sort of, from the inside. "Just a precaution," he said. "Ten to one he comes in by the front door." Who was he talking about? I was considering taking a stab at that when I noticed the drumstick still lying, mostly submerged, in a pool of water. I'd already taken a pass on it, but why? Not a single good reason came to me. Soggy, but so what? I made a quick decision, always the best kind.

Second, we hid out. Hiding out isn't as easy as you might think, at least for me. In between cases, we've done a lot of work on my hiding-out skills. Hiding out means sitting still and quiet until it's time to spring into action. Sounds easy, maybe, but I've had some problems with it in the past. The day, for example, when I'd ended up ambushing the flower delivery lady? "Room for improvement there, big guy," Bernie had said while he was writing the check. Working on hiding-out skills meant sitting quietly until Bernie gave this special little nod. Then came a treat, a rawhide chew, maybe, or a Slim Jim, or even a burger, if we happened to have swung by Burger Heaven. Just between you and me, I actually got the hang of the hiding-out thing sometime back, but I've done what I could to keep the lessons going. Forget I mentioned that.

Only two rooms upstairs, so we had to hide out in the bathroom with the toilet back-up issue. Bernie mopped up what he could using some old towels from under the sink. Then he sat on the edge of the tub. Even though sitting was the right procedure, I stood instead, sitting on those soaking towels seeming not too attractive. My paws have a way of taking care of themselves but cleaning up my fur takes work.

Nighttime with the only window boarded up made for a black as black bathroom, and not much in the way of air. It was kind of nice, just me and Bernie together, not kicking back, exactly, but enjoying a quiet moment. Was Bernie enjoying it, too? I wasn't sure on account of these faint gasping sounds he let out from time to time, but then I felt his hand giving me a little pat on the back and I knew. A little later I happened to find a thickish shred of fried chicken under my tongue. Did I have it pretty good or what?

Time passed, no telling how much. I listened to what was available, such as Bernie breathing, a faint gurgling in the pipes, distant sirens. Then came the amped-down *throb throb* of an approaching motorcycle out front. Were motorcycles in the case? I had a feeling they might be. My ears went up and I almost took a step—might actually have taken a small one—toward the closed bathroom door. I sensed Bernie, already still, going stiller.

The *throb throb* grew louder, then cut out. Silence . . . silence . . . *squeak*. A squeak, specifically the squeak hinges make unless you oil them, and then came what I expected—you start expecting things right when you've cleared all the cases we have at the Little Detective Agency—namely, the thud of a closing door; a heavy thud, on account of that big steel door at the front of the house, just where Bernie said whoever it was would be coming in. My heart got going a bit, the way it does when springing into action is in the near future.

Footsteps sounded on the floor below, changed rhythm slightly, which happens when someone's climbing stairs. This particular someone, a man, for sure—an easy one, men and women moving so differently—wasn't worried about being heard, made no effort to be quiet, sounded strong and confident. I was feeling confident myself: ambushes tended to work out better with unsuspecting dudes like this.

He reached our floor, walked right past the bathroom door. Was he wearing boots? I thought so. Were cowboy boots in the case? Maybe, although these didn't sound like cowboy boots, which change a man's stride a little in a way that's hard to explain. I know it when I hear it: let's leave it at that.

A doorknob turned down the hall, and then came a few quieter footsteps: the man entering Lord's room. He said something I couldn't make out, but he must have thought it was funny because he laughed. I felt Bernie rise. Was he giving me the special nod meaning the hiding-out part was over and springing into action was about to begin? How to tell? I couldn't see a thing. Bernie made a soft *click click* in his mouth. That settled it.

He opened the door. We stepped into the hall, side by side and silent, the only light coming through the open doorway of the bedroom, weak and flickering but enough to glint on the .38 Special in Bernie's hand. I could hear his heart beating, just like mine.

The bedroom door was open. We looked in. A gas lantern

rested beside the empty chair. A short and really wide dude, turned sideways to us, stood over Lord. He wore a mask over his eyes—a black mask like you see on Halloween, not my favorite holiday, lots of masked humans on the loose making me a bit nervous—and had a paper bag in his hand. There was a ham and cheese sandwich in the paper bag and also a dill pickle. Dill pickles don't do anything for me, but ham is another matter. The soggy drumstick from downstairs seemed like a long time ago.

"Hungry, amigo?" the masked man said.

For a crazy moment, I thought he meant me! Then Lord made an annoyed sort of grunt. I took that to mean the sandwich was going to be his in some future time, but Bernie often said that no one can see the future for sure.

The masked dude reached out to untie the ball gag. A movement like that is sometimes a good scent releaser. Now, for example, I picked up the smell of that aftershave I'd been smelling on this case, the one that comes in the square green bottle. Where you saw something or other can be not so easy to remember, but remembering where you smelled something? A different story, although maybe not to you, no offense. I'd sniffed out this aftershave scent twice so far, once on that little island where we'd found Ralph's glasses, and again when—whoa!—when we'd had that meet-and-greet with Pyro, the visored biker right out front of this very house. I checked out the masked dude's footwear: motorcycle boots. All of a sudden I was way ahead of the game: the masked dude was Pyro! Did I have the best job in the world or what?

"Pyro?" Bernie said, speaking in a normal voice, like we were all buddies in this place, just having a get-together. "How about we leave the gag on for the moment, keep confusion to a minimum."

Or something like that. I was still stunned that Bernie knew it was Pyro, meaning he had nosed out that aftershave scent all on his own. But that was Bernie: just when you think he's amazed you for the last time, he amazes you again.

Meanwhile, Pyro had whipped around, seen us, started to reach into one of his pockets and then frozen as Bernie raised the .38 Special. Lord, straining against his duct tape bonds and looking in our direction like he wanted us to do something real bad, went, "Frrrmmimm, frrrmm!"

"Try to relax, Lord," Bernie said. "We'll get to you. First, Pyro needs to toss me that paper bag, nice and easy."

Pyro didn't move.

"He must think I wouldn't just up and shoot him," Bernie said, lowering his aim a little. "Say in his right knee, for starters." He gave Pyro a friendly smile. "Need a second to think again?"

I didn't know how long a second was—pretty short, I thought, probably shorter than the time it took for Pyro to make up his mind. I could tell he was making up his mind from how his eyes shifted in those little mask eyeholes. Hard to explain why I found those eyeholes so bothersome, I just did. My teeth started getting a certain feeling. Pyro tossed the bag to Bernie.

He turned out to be a real bad tosser, sending the bag so wide of the target that Bernie had to make a long reach. Except he didn't: Bernie stood completely still, let the paper bag go right by, hit the wall, and land with the kind of soft thud you'd expect from a ham sandwich. What was up with all that? I had no clue, but things were looking up, and they'd been pretty high already, in my opinion.

"Oops," Bernie said.

Pyro's eyes went through some changes, hard to make out exactly on account of the combination of the low lantern light and those little eyeholes, but one thing for sure: Pyro hated Bernie.

Anyone who hates Bernie has a real big problem with me, case closed.

"Now," Bernie said, "since it's too early for Halloween, you're going to take off that mask and drop it on the floor, nice and slow."

Pyro didn't move. He was a tough guy. Maybe he didn't know we ran up against tough guys just about every day in this job. After breaking rocks in the hot sun for a spell, they're not as tough—a bit surprising, what with all that exercise.

The barrel of the .38 Special tilted up. "At one time," Bernie said, "I wasn't a half-bad shot, maybe could have actually picked that mask right off your face without hardly doing any damage at all. Who's feeling curious?"

I was! I was! Pull the trigger, Bernie! You're still a crack shot! You can do it!

And, of course, Bernie could have done it, but before he got the chance, Pyro took off the mask—didn't whip it off in a panic, although neither could you have called it nice and slow—and dropped it on the floor. We got our first good look at his face, a broad face with a strong jaw and chin, a squishy little nose, small and alert dark eyes.

"Nice meeting you, Pyro," Bernie said. "Now if you'll just roll up your sleeves we'll be all set."

Pyro blinked. "I can go?" he said.

Lord squirmed in his chair. "Nnnrrrr!"

"Go?" Bernie said. "My mistake. I just meant we'll be all set when it comes to building a theory of the case."

Pyro shook his head. "Fuck you, hombre," he said. "Gonna shoot my shirt off?" He laughed.

And was still laughing when—but maybe I'd better back up here. Pyro was wearing a camo shirt, specifically the kind with button-down epaulets, and buttoned down in one of those ep-aulets he had a pack of cigarettes, the same kind Bernie had been smoking the last time he'd quit for the last time. Back to Pyro, still laughing, but his laughter got canceled right out by the crack of the .38 Special. *CRACK!* What a beautiful sound! The ciga-rette pack, the cigarettes, the epaulet with its button: all blown to smithereens, tiny tobacco shreds raining down on my fur. I didn't mind. Meanwhile, Pyro was ripping off his shirt in a hurry. Hadn't Bernie told him just to roll up the sleeves? Was Pyro's messing up on the sleeve instructions a good reason to shoot him now? I went both ways on that.

Bernie didn't shoot Pyro. Instead, he said, "Move closer to the light."

Pyro moved closer to the light.

"Hands up."

Pyro raised his hands. He was scared—I could smell it—but not as scared as some perps we'd had in this sort of setup, not nearly.

"Lord?" Bernie said. "Can you make out that letter tattooed on Pyro's right wrist?"

Lord craned his head—I had an unpleasant encounter with a crane once, never having had much luck when it comes to birds, but no time to go into that now—peered at Pyro's wrist and nodded.

"What letter is it?" Bernie said.

"Grrmmph," said Lord.

"Just to confirm," Bernie said. "We're talking about the first letter in queen?"

Lord nodded again, this time much harder.

"Ever heard of the Quieros, Lord?"

Lord shook his head.

"Pretty new to me, too," Bernie said. "Care to fill us in, Pyro?"

Pyro didn't answer, but his eyes had plenty to say, all about hatred for Bernie.

"What I don't understand," Bernie went on, as if Pyro had in fact made some reply and now it was his turn again, "is how the Quieros fit into this case. You guys are in the drug business. Why bother with a load of shrimp? No real money in that. Help me here, Pyro. Throw me a bone."

Whoa! Bernie had never asked for a bone once, not in the whole time we'd been together. I wanted a bone, too! Tell him to throw Chet a bone, too! That thought zoomed around and around in my mind, even though I knew perfectly well that Pyro had no bones on him—I don't make mistakes on things like that.

". . . which brings us," Bernie was saying, "to this empty chair. Who's it for?"

No answer from Pyro, just that hot darkness in his eyes.

"Maybe you're too far down the depth chart to even know," Bernie said. "Boss keep you out of the loop?"

A vein throbbed in Pyro's neck. "I got no boss."

"Make you feel better to think that?" Bernie said.

Pyro spat on the floor. Human spitting: a whole big subject of its own, and no time for it now. "Think you're tough with that piece in your hand," Pyro said.

"Nah," said Bernie. "I'm a softie." Oh, Bernie. Have I mentioned what a joker he can be? "My whole goal here is making sure everybody gets out of this room in good health—including whoever's coming to sit in this chair." Bernie raised his eyebrows, like he'd had a sudden thought. "Oh, my—any chance it's Ralph Boutette?"

Some perps were pretty good at hiding what was inside. Pyro was one of them. His eyes barely shifted. His mouth hardly fell open at all. "Don't understand you, hombre," he said. "My English is bad."

"Don't be self-critical," Bernie said. "Your English is the best thing about you." He gestured to the empty chair. "Take a load off, let's get to know each other a bit."

Pyro looked at the chair like . . . like it was dangerous, kind of a puzzler to me, and shook his head.

"Prefer to stand?" Bernie said. Probably a puzzler to him, too. We're a lot alike in some ways, in case that hasn't come up already.

Pyro nodded.

"Something about that chair troubling you?" Bernie said.

Pyro stopped nodding.

"Got any ID on you?" Bernie said.

Pyro laughed that kind of laugh humans call laughing in your face. I'd never realized how bad human laughter—normally one of my favorite sounds—could be until that moment.

"Don't particularly care what your real name is," Bernie said. "I'm just betting it's not Pyro."

Angry eyes, yes, but not out of control: Pyro was watched Bernie carefully and his mind was working hard.

"More of a nickname is my guess," Bernie said.

Where were we going with this? I had no clue, just trusted Bernie, always the right move.

Still not looking away from Pyro, not even once, Bernie said, "What's the word *pyro* mean to you, Lord?"

"Frrmpf," said Lord. "Frrmpf mmrrcc."

"Fire maniac?" Bernie said. "Nice way of putting it. Lighting fires is Pyro's vocation and avocation."

"Hrrh?" said Lord.

"Meaning he has a thing for starting fires and he gets paid for it. Didn't you wonder what the gas can was for?" Bernie made a slight chin movement in the direction of the gas can in the corner.

Lord nodded.

"Spell it out, Pyro. What's the gas can for?"

Pyro didn't answer for what seemed like a long time. At last he nodded. "I want a deal."

"What kind of deal?"

Pyro made a gesture with his hands, still keeping them up but not quite as high. Bernie didn't take his eyes off Pyro's hands and neither did I—keeping track of perp hand movements being at the top of the list in our line of work—which was maybe why we were both late picking up on Pyro's booted foot, swinging real fast and kicking the lantern right at Bernie.

Pyro turned out to be aces at kicking lanterns. The lantern hit Bernie hard on his gun hand and the .38 Special went flying.

"Gun!" Bernie yelled, meaning it was my job to grab the .38 Special and give it up for nobody except Bernie; can't tell you how many Slim Jims I've gotten working on this particular trick. I sprang for the .38 Special, still clattering across the floor. Two other things happened at the same time. One was Pyro springing at Bernie. The other was the lantern going out.

THIRTY

Back in complete blackness again, but we had plenty of sound: thumping and grunting and smashing and smacking and whacking, a cry of pain—that last one coming from Pyro, goes without mentioning. Would I even know what a cry of pain from Bernie sounded like? I'd never heard it. The point was we had a knock-down drag-out fight going down, and if there's a fight going down—visible or not—I want to be in on it, especially if Bernie's involved. My problem was the .38 Special, at that moment gripped securely in my mouth. Bernie calling "Gun!" meant part one: get the gun; and part two: bring it to him. I was all set on part one, but part two was shaping up not as well. Maybe a bark or two would get his attention, but that meant dropping the gun, a no-no. Then came a fresh idea: how about just plain dropping the gun and diving right into the fight? I went back and forth on that one, back and forth, back and forth—and then found that I was actually racing back and forth across the floor, and soon around and around, faster and faster, bumping into this and that, possibly knocking over Lord in his chair—"GRRRMMPH!"—leaping high and by sheer good luck landing on Pyro's back—"Chet! For God's sake!"—or perhaps

Bernie's as it turned out, and then we were all—Pyro, Bernie, me—spinning in a sort of black tornado, and I was part of things, amigo, and still had the .38 Special in my mouth. Best of both worlds! Maybe even having my cake and—but let's not go there.

An unseen fist whizzed past my nose—although not so fast that I didn't pick up a whiff of aftershave—and thudded into human flesh. Then came a grunt from Bernie, followed by more flesh thuds from all directions, the whole tornado spinning faster and faster and faster and—

CRASH! I heard shattering glass, and almost at the same instant, the splintering of wood. Light entered the room at once, weak night light from outside, but enough to make out the window—glass now broken, boarding-up boards now knocked out—and beyond it, framed by the empty window and still spinning, although slowly, and hanging outside in midair: Pyro.

But you can't hang in midair, not for long, not humans, not us in the nation within. From the look on Pyro's face I got the feeling he was thinking that very same thing. And the thought was just starting to scare him when he dropped out of sight. Nothing . . . nothing . . . *thud.*

Bernie and I rushed to the window—Bernie jumping right over Lord, still in his chair now lying sideways on the floor for some reason—and looked down.

Pyro lay in a bad position in the small paved-over yard behind the house. He crawled for a tiny bit, and then he didn't.

"Is he, ah, like . . . ?" Lord said.

We stood in the paved-over yard behind Cleotis's place, me, Bernie, Lord—now ungagged—all looking down at Pyro, lying in the circle of the flashlight's beam.

"What do you think?" Bernie said.

Bernie was angry at Lord? I wondered why, found no reason, but got ready to be angry at Lord myself.

"What do I think?" Lord said. "I think you're way scarier than you look."

"Shut up."

Lord swallowed whatever had been coming next, a lump of words I could actually see bob up and then down in his scrawny neck. Meanwhile, Bernie was squatting close beside Pyro, taking Pyro's hand in his, turning it palm up.

"Dincha already check for a pulse?" Lord said, forgetting about the shutting-up thing pretty fast. "Or maybe it's gonna start up again? Saw that in a movie once."

Bernie didn't answer. He was peering at the big muscle at the base of Pyro's thumb.

"Mighta been with Vin Diesel," said Lord. "The one where he . . ." Lord moved in closer. "Hey—dude wrote something on his hand? Used to do that myself back when I was a kid." He squatted down beside Bernie. "Looks like a phone number, huh?" he said. "Seven one three—that's Houston."

"Seven one three," Bernie said in this low voice he has for speaking to himself, including me in it, too, of course, goes without mentioning. And then came a bunch more numbers.

"You can memorize phone numbers?" Lord said. "Just like that, I mean, no going over and over and—"

"Shut up," said Bernie.

"Can I squeeze in a question first?"

"What is it?"

"Headed back down to St. Roch by any chance? I could use a lift."

Bernie gave him a long look.

"What?" said Lord. "What did I do?"

*   *   *

"What did he do?" said Henry, the big cop who was Bernie's friend on the force in these parts. Lots of people had joined us in the paved-over yard, most of them in uniform.

"Got framed for a shrimp heist he knew nothing about," Bernie said. "And then got separated from his ankle monitor, also not his doing."

Henry gazed down at Lord. "What's up with you?" he said. "Bad karma?"

"For sure," Bernie said. "But he is alive."

Henry turned toward the body. "This the guy you were searching for?"

"No."

"Just another dead man turning up in the course of your investigation?" Henry glanced around. "Also interesting is the fact that the first one OD'd on heroin and until recently a smack dealer name of Cleotis Moore was operating out of this house. Feels like I should be putting some pieces together."

"Maybe we can have a word," Bernie said.

"I'd like that," said Henry.

Meanwhile, Lord was kind of drifting away in a direction that might take him around the house and out on the street. That didn't feel right, although I didn't know why, confusing me a bit, and in my case confusion sometimes leads to growling. And what was this? The remains of the ham and cheese sandwich slipping out from between my jaws? How had it even gotten there? Plus a scrap of the brown paper bag was hanging from my chin? I got rid of it pronto. *Get it together, big guy! We're on the job!*

"What the hell?" Bernie said, glancing around and spotting Lord. "Get back here!"

Lord paused, one foot in the air, for a strange moment somewhat resembling a member of the nation within. "Thought I'd be moving on," he said. "On account of what you were saying to the lieutenant here about my innocence and all."

"Wouldn't be in your best interest," Bernie said.

A long discussion got started on the subject of Lord's best interest, impossible to follow, but it ended with a cruiser coming up through an alley, Lord getting helped into the backseat, and then he was off to central booking, a real unhappy look on his face.

"I'll spring him soon as I get to the bottom of all this," Bernie said. "Right now he's in danger."

"From who?" said Henry.

"The Quieros on your radar?"

"Central American drug gang? I heard they've expanded on up to Houston."

Bernie pointed at Pyro with his chin.

"Telling me they're here?"

"He is."

Henry sighed. He glanced over at the house. "And Cleotis Moore?"

"They either paid him off, ran him off, or shot him."

Henry looked down at his shoes, highly polished shoes, shining in the night. "Any chance these Quieros turned up here in my town on account of you?"

Bernie didn't answer.

"Have a safe trip home, Bernie," Henry said. They didn't shake hands.

"Are we the common thread, big guy?" Bernie said. "That's a disturbing thought."

I took a swing at feeling disturbed, couldn't quite manage it. Might have done better if I hadn't been in the shotgun seat at the

moment, and us rolling down a quiet street under clear skies, the
night warm and soft: hard to feel disturbed at a time like that,
beyond my capabilities.

"But maybe it gives us a chance to work backward," Bernie
added after a while.

Working backward! One of our very best techniques—don't
look my way for an explanation—and we hadn't used it ages. This
case was as good as solved, maybe even better. I tried to remember
who was paying.

"... means they're going after our sources," Bernie was saying,
"starting with Mack Larouche. That led them to Cleotis—kind of
peripheral in their eyes, unless I'm slipping up on something. So
either he's not peripheral or they're not that good. Am I missing
some other alternative?"

Bernie missing something? The answer to that was always the
same: impossible.

"Then there's Lord, not peripheral." He fell silent, but I could
feel his thoughts, going deep and coming back up. "... and Pyro's job? Burn down the house—just another crazy drug thing,
optics-wise—with Lord and one other person in it. Who else but
Ralph?" His hand tightened on the wheel. "Or is that wishful
thinking? Don't those glasses of his make him a goner already?"

A puzzler. Was there a kind of thinking that wasn't wishful?
I found myself . . . wishing the answer would come to me, and
began to feel vaguely disturbed after all.

Bernie banged the wheel, disturbing me even more. "Shrimp?
We ate the damn shrimp!" He glanced at me. "You think it's
funny." Huh? I wasn't thinking about anything at all, except for
the taste of shrimp, and I wasn't really thinking about it very hard.
"Maybe it is funny," he said, and laughed, a laugh that started out
as more of a grunt but soon turned loud and lovely. I stopped feel-

ing disturbed. Everything was . . . not peachy, exactly, on account of those huge pits peaches had inside them, always spoiling the experience; let's just call it pretty good.

Bernie's laughter faded. "Tired of getting pushed around, big guy?" he said. "I sure as hell am." Uh-oh—we were getting pushed around? Time to put that to bed, and pronto. I waited to find out how. "Seven one three is Houston," Bernie said. He took out his phone and began pecking at the buttons, then paused and put the phone away. "Need a payphone, Chet. Keep your eyes peeled."

My eyes peeled? That sounded too horrible to think about. And payphones? A new one on me. I sat up straight and tall in the shotgun seat, on alert for I didn't know what, a total pro, on the job.

We drove around for a while. "Used to be a payphone on every corner," Bernie said. "How about we all ratchet back to nineteen fifty-nine and live there from now on?" What was this? Moving from the Valley? I wasn't so sure about that, was still trying to get my mind around the concept when Bernie pulled over in front of a convenience store.

"You stay here," he said, scooping up a bunch of coins from the cup holder and getting out. A few moments later, I hopped out myself, not certain I'd heard right and afraid of making a rookie mistake. Not afraid, exactly, the truth of the matter being I'm not afraid of anything. Then I thought of Iko.

I followed Bernie up to a sort of open metal box hanging on the wall of the convenience store. Hey! It had a phone inside! I'd seen these before! Chet the Jet, on top of his game!

Bernie shoved some coins into the slot, punched the buttons, put the receiver to his ear. Instead of sitting beside him, my usual spot, I kept a little distance between us; it seemed the way to go, hard to explain why. But I had no problem hearing what was happening on the other end. First came a single ring, and then a click, followed by a man saying, "Yeah?" I was pretty sure I recognized the voice. Bernie said nothing. The man said, "Hello? Hello?" and then came another click and the hum the phone makes when the call is over, and now I was totally sure.

Bernie hung up the phone in a slow, thoughtful way and turned. He noticed me, maybe where I was I supposed to be, maybe not, one of those gray-area type of things, and said, "You'll never guess who that was."

Guess? I didn't have to guess. When someone tries to hurt me, the sound of his voice stays in my memory forever.

"Cale Rugh," Bernie said.

Meaning we were on the same page. My tail started revving.

Bernie gave me a look. "Think you got away with something, huh, Chet?"

That friendly if puzzling little message—I could tell it was friendly from the way his face wanted to smile even if he wasn't letting it—went right over my head, zip and gone, leaving nothing but a nice warm feeling. I was ready to take on anything. Perps and gangbangers: time's up!

THIRTY-ONE

"Step one," said Bernie, as we crossed back over the mighty Mississip and headed down to bayou country, "let's rerun Fleurette's story." Sounded like a good step to me: although I hadn't the slightest difficulty remembering Fleurette, especially the taste of her tears, any story she might have told us had vanished.

"Specifically," Bernie went on, "her description of the scene outside Rooster Red's in the predawn hours when the stolen shrimp arrived. Too dark to really see the guy who brought the shrimp—all she said was that he was tall and quote walked like a cowboy. So where are we?" I waited to find out. This was kind of interesting. "Cale Rugh stole the shrimp, Chet, or at least masterminded it. After he left, Fleurette saw Mack come outside. By then it was getting lighter and she saw he was counting money. Not only did Rugh not charge Mack for the shrimp, or even just give them to him—he paid Mack to take them. See what this means?"

I saw right off the bat: Cale Rugh wasn't good with money, kind of like . . . us. Uh-oh. I didn't want to be like him in any way.

"Means the shrimp heist was definitely a smoke screen, start to finish. The question is why."

We divide up the work at the Little Detective Agency, just part of our great business plan. Bernie handles the whys. I bring other things to the table.

There was a long silence. We drove through the night, so pleasant. We do a lot of driving through the night in our line of work. It always ends up the same: your eyelids get heavy and do what they have to do. Then there's nothing but the feeling of Bernie's thoughts flitting all around, and the lovely motion of the Porsche from underneath. Did I hear him say, "Wonder if Vannah got hold of that money, even used it to . . . ?" Maybe, maybe not.

Eggs and bacon? I opened my eyes. We were parked in a roadside turnout in open country, sun just coming up, mist rising over a bayou that glinted through the greenery, the first rays of sunlight glowing through the mist like it was lit from inside. All of that quite nice, I suppose, but even nicer was the sight of a food truck—our food truck!—open for business and only steps away.

Bernie looked over at me. "How about some chow, big guy? Shaping up as a long day."

Putting those two things together like that? Just another example of Bernie's brilliance. Pretty soon Bernie was leaning against the hood, munching on a bacon and egg sandwich and sipping from a paper cup of steaming coffee, me beside him, keeping busy with a fat sausage that made wonderful sausagey explosions in my mouth with every bite I took, plus my water bowl, of course, and from time to time, whenever I looked at Bernie in a certain way, a torn-off bacon scrap.

"I'm starting to think it's true what they say about the food down here," Bernie said. "You can't get a bad —"

A black-and-white pulled in, parked not far from us. A trim, fit-looking cop stepped out, eyes and hair the color of ginger ale, although the hair was graying: Sheriff Robideau. He went up to the food truck window, ordered something, then turned to take in the scenery while he waited, and saw us.

"You still around?" he called over.

"And we will be till Ralph Boutette turns up," Bernie called back. He took another bite of his sandwich, kind of eating it in the sheriff's face, if that makes any sense. It does to me. Who wouldn't love Bernie at a moment like that?

Sheriff Robideau turned back to the window. The food truck guy, the one with all the bead chains and the missing teeth, handed him a sandwich and a can of soda. The sheriff cracked the can open with a real loud crack that sounded almost like a gunshot in the still morning air. Then he tilted his head back and drained the can, that thing in his throat that men had and women didn't seem to—some kind of apple, was that it? having an apple in your throat all the time sounded unpleasant, but maybe it's just me—bobbed up and down. The sheriff crushed the empty can, tossed it on the ground, and came our way.

He looked at us. We looked at him.

"Your dog's not wearing tags," he said.

"He lost his collar," Bernie said. "Lost maybe not being the right word. More like Iko tore it off him."

"Iko the gator?" the sheriff said.

Bernie nodded. "How Chet got all the way down to open water is another question—that's where the human part comes in."

"Got anyone in mind?" the sheriff said.

There was a long pause before Bernie said, "No."

"Whatever the cause, if you're staying in the county you'll have to get tags on him. It's a safety issue."

"I'll make it a priority." Bernie took another bite of the

sandwich—a real big one—and said, "How's the canvass coming along?" Or something like that—hard to tell, what with Bernie's mouth so full.

The sheriff's eyes narrowed in an annoyed sort of way. Maybe he didn't like listening to mouthful talk, having something in common with Bernie's mom in that respect. Has Bernie's mom come up yet? She's a piece of work. Hope we have time to go into that later.

"Canvass?" the sheriff said.

"Wasn't your deputy canvassing the citizenry regarding news of Ralph?"

The sheriff nodded. "The citizenry had nothing to say."

"Meaning no one knew anything, or they knew but were too afraid to say?"

"Strange question," said the sheriff. "Especially coming from an outsider unfamiliar with our ways."

"Consider it withdrawn," Bernie said.

This seemed like a nice, polite conversation, no raised voices, no threats, no angry body language—and I don't miss that one, body language being one of my specialties at the Little Detective Agency. At the same time, I got the feeling Bernie and Sheriff Robideau wanted to kill each other.

"Anything else I can help you with?" the sheriff said.

Another long pause from Bernie. "Wouldn't want to trouble you."

"You're no trouble," said the sheriff. He walked over to the black-and-white and drove away. Bernie picked up the soda can the sheriff had tossed away and dropped it in the trash barrel beside the food truck.

The food truck guy leaned out of his window and said, "Hey!"

Bernie turned to him. "Yeah?"

"Couldn't help but overhear some of your palaver with the sheriff."

"Uh-huh," Bernie said.

"Had me a dog once myself."

"Uh-huh."

"Name of Doc, on account of he was so goddamn smart. Ten times smarter than yours truly."

Which left me no wiser, the only Truly I knew being on the staff at Livia Moon's house of ill repute back in Pottsdale, and she'd always seemed smart enough to me.

"Nice name," Bernie said.

"Thing is, Doc's passed on."

"Sorry to hear it."

"'Preciate that. Do you believe in the rainbow bridge?"

"I'd like to."

The food truck guy thought that over. Were we talking about the bridge over the mighty Mississip? I believed in it totally, having already been on it several times.

"Thing is," the food truck guy said, "Doc left behind somethin' I want you to have."

"What's that?" Bernie said.

The food truck guy held up a collar. "I like the look of that dog of yours. And his appetite—reminds me of Doc big-time."

"Very nice of you, but—"

"Doin' it for myself," said the food truck guy. "Would make me feel good, like Doc's still out there, havin' adventures."

"All right," Bernie said, his voice turning gentle. "Thanks."

We went to the window. "Killed it myself," the food truck guy said, handing Bernie the collar. "Out bow-huntin'—that's my relaxation."

Bernie examined the collar. "Alligator hide?" he said.

"Totally legal," said the food truck guy. "Kick in the twenty-five bucks for my license every year."

"It's not that," Bernie said. "I'm just wondering whether Chet might not . . ." He . . . he sniffed at the collar! Oh, Bernie. Then he held it in front of my nose, maybe thinking that would help me get a good sniff, too. How nice of him, but I'd already sniffed all there was to sniff on the collar, which included gator smell, but toned way down, and also the smell of a member of the nation within, plus some food truck smells, of course. In short: a great collar. Hadn't I ended up doing sort of all right with Iko, coming pretty close to at least holding my own? I wouldn't mind being reminded of that, although I had no plans for more swims in the bayou. You can put that right out of your minds, pronto.

"When his tail gets goin' like that it means yes," the food truck guy said. "Doc was the same way."

"Cool collar," Bernie said, as we drove away from the food truck. "Maybe the coolest there is."

Plus it felt good around my neck. And then there was the fact that I'd just downed a first-class breakfast. Who wouldn't have been feeling tip-top?

"What now, you may be wondering," Bernie said. Which I hadn't been in the least. What I'd been doing was watching the telephone poles zip by and that was about it. "All I can think of is driving to Houston and marching right into Cale Rugh's office at Donnegan's. Or maybe the office of the CEO—why the hell not?" Telephone poles zipped by, faster and faster. "I'll tell you why the hell not. One, it's too goddamn clumsy, even for me. Two, it means moving away from the locus of the case." Locus of the case? I'd never been more lost in my life. The telephone poles started going by more slowly. I spotted bullet holes in more than two.

The phone buzzed. Bernie hit a button and a man's voice came through the speakers.

"Bernie?"

"Yup."

"Prof here. I showed those equations of yours to a very sharp friend of mine in the engineering department. They're stress calculations."

"Stress calculations?"

"Critical in all sorts of design and construction. In this case, he says we're dealing with stress induced by pressure, specifically liquid pressure."

"I don't understand."

"Why not? I'm talking in plain English. Do you see what's happening here, Bernie? We're on a forced march all the way back to the dark ages."

"Try to make it plainer."

"A pleasure. Our celebrity madness, mixed with the leveling desires of powerful opinion-setting segments of society, plus near total amnesia regarding the past and—"

"I meant this pressure business."

"How can I make that any plainer?"

"Pretend I'm your dumbest student."

"Don't have one. The dumb ones stay away because of my reputation for actually handing out F's if deserved."

"Prof?"

"Yes?"

"We're dealing with high stakes here."

"You're referencing in contrast the notoriously low stakes of everything academe?"

Bernie didn't answer. Prof went on, his voice now a little softer. "Suppose you were designing a pressure gauge, for example."

"A pressure gauge?" Bernie leaned forward, hands gripping the wheel so hard his knuckles turned bone-colored.

"A deliberate choice on my part," Prof said, "since my friend tells me these are pretty much classic pressure gauge calculations, as least as they apply to problems involving liquid pressure. Suppose—to instance a common real-life situation, according to my friend—you wanted to measure pressure build-up at a well head. Obviously, you're dealing with a multivariable calculus involving forces and material compositions, but you've also got to factor in certain dynamic—"

"Well head?" Bernie said, his voice rising.

"At an oil-drilling platform, for example."

Bernie spun the Porsche in a screaming U-turn that just about brought my breakfast back up into the world. The telephone poles started zipping by the other way, so fast they almost blurred into one.

THIRTY-TWO

Were we flying or what? If I stuck my head above the windshield my ears snapped straight back, flat against my head. I stuck my head up and kept it there, squeezing my eyes almost shut against the wind.

Bernie glanced at me and shouted over all the noise, which actually just added to the noise: I would have heard him just as well, or even better, if he'd spoken at normal volume. I was so busy considering this interesting noise issue that I kind of missed what he said, perhaps something about Wes and cats.

It was still pretty early when we swung by Dr. Ory's trailer. She was just going inside, a stack of files under her arm and a big bag of kibble—the kind in the blue bag, not bad at all—in one hand. Bernie hurried forward, got the door open for her. Dr. Ory had deep purple patches under her eyes, a sure sign of a real tired human.

"Anymore dead birds?" Bernie said.

"Eleven yesterday," said Dr. Ory.

"What did Wes have to say about that?"

"Haven't discussed it with him yet. He's coming in this morning."

"From where?"

Dr. Ory blinked. "From where?"

"Just so I can gauge when he might here," Bernie said. "I'd like to sit in if you don't mind."

"Don't mind at all. The truth is, I'm confused about what's going on. Confused and frustrated."

"How do you mean?"

"I hadn't had a single bird brought in for months, and then up goes number nine and in they come."

"Number nine being the new platform?"

"That's right," Dr. Ory said. "What's frustrating is that Wes swears up and down they're not leaking a drop out there. So where's it coming from?"

"Maybe another platform?" Bernie said.

"I asked Mr. Patel from the government about that," Dr. Ory said. "Apparently all the other platforms are much farther out, meaning birds would be turning up east of here on account of the current, maybe all the way to Mobile, and that's not happening."

"I'd like to talk to Patel."

Dr. Ory shook her head. "He got called back to Washington. He didn't seem too happy about it." Bernie's face hardened. Dr. Ory was watching. "What's that look?" she said.

"No look," Bernie said.

"No?" said Dr. Ory. "I think it means some fix is in and you don't like it."

"What kind of fix?"

"You'd know more about that than I would. I'm just a vet. But you're a fighter, that's plain to see. Wes is renting a cabin at the fishing club south of town. You can't miss it."

*   *   *

We drove out of town, came to a sign showing a fish leaping over blue waves. Bernie turned into the next lane, a narrow unpaved road lined with white-painted stones. Ahead stood a big yellow building up on stilts. We followed the road along a canal with some boats tied up to the side, including a green one I knew well.

"There's his boat," Bernie said, slowing down. "Hey, what are you barking about? I see it. Chet! Easy, big guy. Calm down." I calmed it down to a low growl, best I could do. Bernie glanced over at me. "What's on your mind?"

What was on my mind? I hadn't liked getting rolled into a net and tossed into the water: that was on my mind. Wouldn't you be thinking the same?

Some little yellow cabins appeared, clustered in a grove of trees; all except for the last one, kind of off on its own. That last cabin had a green SUV parked out front. All the other cabins seemed empty. Bernie pulled up beside one of them, turned to me and made the quiet sign, finger over his lips. The low growling that had been accompanying us faded out.

We left the car, walked up to the SUV. Bernie took a quick glance inside—all about grabbing the keys if they were in the ignition, which they were not in this case, too bad because it was one of our coolest moves—and walked up to the front door of the cabin.

A screen door, as it happened, meaning you didn't need to have much going on in the hearing department to pick up Wes's voice from inside.

". . . but, with all respect, Mr. Sim, that's not my job. I never expected that—" Silence. Then: "Yes, sir." And the click of a phone call ending.

Bernie pushed the door open with the toe of his sneaker. Wes was standing in front of a curtained window, gazing out as though the curtain were open, his back to us.

"What's not your job, Wes?" Bernie said.

Wes whirled around, mouth and eyes opening wide.

"What the hell—" he began, his soft brown eyes not quite so soft at that moment. "What are you doing here?"

"Thought we'd come see the cats," Bernie said.

"Cats?"

"We're cat lovers, Chet and I."

Had I ever been more shocked in my life? For a dreadful stretch of time that felt like forever I got all tangled up in the idea that I didn't understand anything about anything, not one single thing in the whole wide world. Then I noticed a glint in Bernie's eyes—very faint but I knew all the signs to watch for in Bernie—that meant he was enjoying a little private joke, which he sometimes did at unexpected times, such as in a serious interview. Ah ha! This was a serious interview. No holds barred in a serious interview—that was basic—meaning sometimes you had to do some wacky things, like posing as cat lovers. Now we were cooking, me and Bernie.

"I don't understand," Wes was saying. "I don't have cats."

Which had been clear to me from the get-go on this case. Not only that, but a member of the nation within had been in this cabin and not long ago.

"No cats?" Bernie said.

"Uh," said Wes, his eyes shifting and shifting again, like he was trying to remember something. "Not here, is what I meant to say. No cats here. I leave them at home when I'm on a remote assignment."

"Where's home?"

"Houston."

"What are their names?"

"The cats?"

Bernie nodded.

Then came a very brief pause, hardly noticeable, but any pause at all at a moment like that caught my attention, why I couldn't tell you in a million years, which is probably a lot, but don't bet the ranch.

"Babe," Wes said. "Babe and Ruth."

Bernie smiled. "You a baseball fan?"

"Matter of fact, yes," Wes said.

"And a pretty quick thinker."

"Not sure what you mean by that," Wes said. "And I'm sorry to disappoint you on the cats. But if you'll excuse me, I've got a big day coming up."

"Meeting with Dr. Ory?" Bernie said.

"That's on the agenda."

"She's got more birds to show you."

"Sorry to hear that."

"What do you think's going on with all these birds?"

"I believe I've already explained," said Wes.

"You're talking about the natural seeps theory?"

"It's more than a theory. Natural oil seeps are established fact in these parts."

"No way any of the platform wells could be leaking?" Bernie said.

"Absolutely not," said Wes. "We monitor them twenty-four seven."

"What about the number nine rig?"

"Least of all."

"Why is that?"

"Because number nine isn't even operational yet."

"What does that mean?"

"We're not pumping."

"Why not?"

"It's a new installation," Wes said. "Drilling was only completed last week and the structural test results didn't come in until yesterday."

"And how did you do?"

"Huh?"

"On the test," Bernie said. "Gentleman's C?"

"We don't joke about things like that," Wes said. "The tests were perfect. We don't pump an ounce until they are."

"When will pumping start?"

"Soon."

"Today? Tomorrow?"

"That's confidential information," Wes said.

They gazed at each other. Bernie's eyes were hard; Wes was back to the soft brown look.

"I assume pressure measurements are part of the testing," Bernie said.

Wes flinched, just the tiniest bit, as though Bernie had finger-flicked him on the tip of the nose. "Wouldn't know about that," Wes said. "I'm not an engineer." He took a long look at his watch. "And now I've really got to get moving."

Bernie nodded, turned toward the door. The interview was over? That didn't seem right. Wasn't Bernie going to finger-flick him on the tip of the nose? I'd gotten that lodged in my mind, wanted to see it in the worst way. But it didn't happen. We walked out of the cabin, headed toward the Porsche.

And that would have been that, except on the way to the Porsche we passed a scrubby little bush, probably of no interest to you, but you would have missed the fact that it had been marked very recently by a member of the nation within, no offense. I got busy with some thorough sniffing, then laid a mark of my own on the bush—Bernie calls them Chet marks and seems to think that's pretty funny, no telling why—higher up and . . . decisive, in a way that's hard to describe. After that I sniffed all around the bush in a circle, easily picking up the trail of whoever I'd just overmarked— loved overmarking, one of my very favorite activities—which led around the cabin to a little shed at the back.

"Chet?" Bernie said, trailing after me. "What's going on?"

I trotted toward the little shed, not much in mind, except I hadn't had a fun play with a buddy in some time; and one other shadowy thing having to do with the Isle des Deux Amis and the day we'd found those glasses—whose glasses they were not coming to me, if the fact had ever been there at all. Not to worry.

Bernie caught up to me, walked by my side, not saying a thing. We came to the door of the shed, a windowless door padlocked shut. I made a low rumbly bark.

From inside the shed came an answering bark, also low and rumbly, almost—but not quite—as low and rumbly as my own. I got ready to meet a pretty big dude.

"What the hell would I do without you?" Bernie said.

I didn't understand the question.

Bernie glanced around. The cabin was quiet, the curtains closed in all the back windows. Bernie grasped the lock, gave it a shake: nothing doing. He raised his leg and in one smooth motion—making it look easy, Bernie-style—kicked in the shed door. Loved those splintering sounds, could have listened to them all day. Did I have the best job in the world or what? All of a sudden I was in the mood for Bernie to smash the whole shed to smithereens! Oh, the fun we'd have! But something told me this wasn't about smashing the shed. It was about . . .

This little dude who came stepping slowly and carefully—
like his paws were too precious to touch the ground—out of
the shed. A grumpy dude, which was easy to see from the way
he eyed us, like we were annoying him just by being there. Hey!
Who broke you out of the shed, little grumpy dude? Ever think
of that? I like just about everybody, including most perps and
gangbangers, but I was having a problem with this dude, whoever he happened to be.

Bernie squatted down in a crouch, held out his hand toward
the new guy. "Let's have a look at your tags, little fella, just to
confirm the obvious."

All that got Bernie was a hard stare and some strange sniffling
and snuffling from a squashed-in nose that reminded me of Snaffles Ferolli, this washed-up boxer who worked as a bouncer at a
club in South Pedroia that we no longer frequented, or even went
to a single time after a certain incident, never mind frequently.
But forget all that, the point being that the flat-faced grump made
not the slightest move to help Bernie with the tags.

Bernie reached for them. What was this? The little bugger
gave him a nip? And Bernie chuckled? I saw nothing funny, found
myself crowding in. Someone had to take charge. The solution
was obvious. We had to lock this guy back up in the shed and
forget all about him. As if he was reading my mind, he rounded
on me—if any move so slow and clumsy could be called rounding—and bared his teeth, which were already sort of bared on
a full-time basis, surprisingly sharp-looking teeth, and a point
of difference from Snaffles Ferolli, who had none. With all this
going on, he forgot about Bernie, who caught hold of the tags,
gave them a quick once-over, avoided another one of those nips,
and said, "Nice to meet you, Napoleon. Been looking forward to
this."

Which made no sense to me. What was nice about it? And what I was looking forward to was locking him back in the shed and going on with the rest of my life, Napoleon-free.

Bernie reached out again and . . . oh, no: gave Napoleon a pat? All that did was make Napoleon growl. A pleasant development, and just in time to stop me from pushing in between. And then Napoleon made an up-from-under head twisting motion and I realized he wanted . . . more.

"Ooomph," said Bernie. "Easy there, big guy. Sit down for a minute."

I sat down, if sitting down could include butt not actually in contact with ground. As for how much time a minute was, my impression had always been hardly any at all.

"Chet! We're working here."

This was work? The case had something to do with Bernie patting Napoleon? I wasn't seeing that, not the least little bit. But it was the kind of thing Bernie would know. I sat back down, my butt practically grazing the ground.

Bernie gave Napoleon one more pat, real quick and with his eyes on me. Napoleon pressed his head up against Bernie's hand with all his puny strength. Bernie's gaze shifted to him. "Been through a tough time, huh, little fella," Bernie said. "Where's Ralph?"

Ah! I'm not saying I began to get it, but all at once I knew for sure that something gettable was going on. And it was coming to me—coming, coming, coming, right on the edge of where my mind grabs things and doesn't let go—when I heard a sound from the cabin, specifically the sound of metal curtain rings sliding on a metal curtain rod. I whipped around and there was Wes at the window, eyes, eyebrows and mouth all taking the position of human alarm.

Wes was not my favorite guy to begin with and now I got the feeling he was even worse than I'd thought. I barked. Bernie turned, maybe just in time to see Wes vanishing from the window.

"Let's go," Bernie said.

We took off toward the cabin. I heard the screen door slap open, followed by the sound of running footsteps. As we—or maybe just me—reached the side of the cabin, Wes came into view, sprinting toward the green SUV, now just steps away from it.

"Get him, Chet!"

Which I did. In fact, Wes still had one more step to go, meaning he didn't even have time to grab hold of the door handle; too bad, since that often led to the kind of pulling contest I particularly enjoy—tug of war, really, except it's done with a perp instead of a rope.

THIRTY-THREE

B abe and Ruth," Bernie said. "Complete fiction?"

We were back in the cabin now, Wes sitting on the bed, Bernie leaning against the wall across from him, me sitting beside Bernie, Napoleon asleep on a footstool that he'd clawed his way up onto, barely. Wes was as scared as any human I'd ever seen, the smell of his fear filling the room, plus he'd pissed his pants the tiniest bit.

"No," he said. "They're real, just not mine. They're my mom's cats."

"Where does she live?" Bernie said.

"Omaha."

"You close to her?"

Wes's eyes filled with tears. He nodded. Bernie gazed at him, his own eyes hard and also making some kind of point.

"I'm a good person," Wes said.

"That remains to be seen," said Bernie.

"What are you saying?"

"Think about it."

Wes made a motion to wipe his eyes, not so easy on account of the cuffs. "You want something from me."

"Everything," Bernie said. "We want everything. This little scheme you got yourself involved in is falling apart. People are going to jail. I can maybe keep that from happening to you, unless you had anything to do with killing Mack—"

"No, no—that wasn't me!"

"Who was it?"

"That crazy gangbanger."

"Pyro?"

"Yeah, Pyro. But he won't admit it. Those guys never talk."

"I don't expect he will," Bernie said. "How about the night I got knocked on the head and Chet was kidnapped?"

"I had nothing to do with that either."

The feeling of needing to bite took over my teeth at once, and completely.

"See," Bernie said, "that just doesn't add up."

"I don't understand."

"You don't have cats, Wes. And Chet doesn't like you, went after you on sight the morning Mami pulled him out of the water. Why would he do that?"

"For Christ sake—you're valuing some sort of dog behavior over my word?"

"Way over, Wes. And how this is playing out, there'll be plenty of proof. The FBI will be camped out on *Little Jazz*. You comfortable betting you left no DNA behind against twenty years on a cell block?"

Wes's mouth opened and closed.

"Here's a tip," Bernie said. "Totally undeserved. Anyone who gets into a scrap with Chet leaves DNA behind."

A new one on me, and I'd been in plenty of scraps. I'd be on the lookout for DNA the very next time, whatever DNA happened to be.

Wes's eyes dampened up again. "All right," he said. "I was there."

"Were you the one who hit me on the head?"

"No. I hate violence, that's the horrible part about all of this."

"Is it?" Bernie said.

Wes tried to meet Bernie's gaze, ended up gazing down at his feet. Bare feet, as it happened: Bernie had made him take off his shoes, which he sometimes did in situations like this, for reasons I didn't know. Was it so there'd be more smells for me to enjoy? That was as far as I could take it, maybe too far, if that made any sense, which it didn't really, not to me. Taking something too far: my mind isn't the kind that can get around a concept like that.

"Just one of the horrible things is what I meant," Wes mumbled.

"Was it Pyro, then?" Bernie said.

"Pyro?"

"Who knocked me out."

Wes shook his head, gaze still downward.

"Cale Rugh?"

Wes looked up. "You know about him?"

"You do the answers, Wes. I do the questions."

"Sorry."

"Tell me about Cale."

"He's a cold-blooded bastard."

"What's his role here?"

"Security. But he's not a Green Oil employee. I got orders to cooperate with him."

"Orders from who?"

"Houston."

"Meaning headquarters?"

"Yeah."

"And what Cale mainly needed from you," Bernie said, "was your boat and your knowledge of the waters."

Wes nodded.

"Is Ralph alive?"

"I think so."

"Where is he?"

"I'm not sure."

"But you were in on the kidnapping."

"I didn't even know that was what it was, man. You've got to believe me."

"I don't have to believe anything," Bernie said. "You're still not getting it, Wes. This is the most important day of the rest of your life."

Wes went real pale, the way people do when they're about to keel over. "But it's true," he said in a weak, low voice, like all his strength was gone. "Cale said we were just going to talk to him, find out why he was making trouble."

"This was out on Isle des Deux Amis?" Bernie said.

"How do you know all this?"

"Just answer the question."

"Yes. Sir."

"Sucking up won't help you," Bernie said. "Where's Ralph's Zodiac?"

"On the bottom of the lake," Wes said. "That was Cale's idea. It was all Cale's idea."

"You're repeating yourself."

Wes's eyes did more of their dampening thing. "Sorry," he said again. Round about then was when my teeth lost the biting urge. Wes wasn't worth it.

Bernie went to the window, pulled back the curtain a bit, looked out. "What kind of trouble was Ralph making?" he said.

"He's a total whack job, thinks he's some sort of scientist."

"Actually he's an established inventor with over thirty patents to his name," Bernie said.

"Not how I heard it," Wes said. "Ralph's a garage hobbyist kind of guy, according to Cale, and he came up with a crazy theory that all the new pressure gauges we're putting in are flawed. He wanted to sell us some homemade replacement for a million bucks. Company turned him down, of course, which was when he started making threats."

"What kind of threats?"

"Whistle-blowing stuff. Going to the Feds, shutting us down, all that."

"Name Patel mean anything to you?" Bernie said.

"Not really," said Wes.

"Unacceptable answer."

"Christ, you're just as bad as—" Wes swallowed whatever was coming next, took a deep breath, and went on. "Ralph mentioned the name out on the island. That's what set Cale off. But when I asked him about Patel, he told me to shut up."

"What does that mean—set Cale off?"

"He just lost it."

"I got that part."

"You want the gory details?"

"That's where the devil is."

"You're so right." Wes took a deep breath. "Cale's one of those real strong, raw-boned types. Ralph's just a fat little guy." He shook his head.

"Go on."

"Cale beat the crap out of him," Wes said. "I mean literally. After that, whatever plan Cale had in mind—maybe paying Ralph off, maybe just throwing a scare into him—was out the window."

"Meaning you had to kill Ralph or take him somewhere," Bernie said.

"Not me," Wes said. "It was all Cale, making the decisions."

"Don't want to hear it," Bernie said.

"Sorry."

"If you say sorry once more you'll be sorrier than you ever dreamed."

"S-s—"

Bernie got a look in his eye that made me think something very bad was about to happen to Wes. Wes shrank bank on the bed.

"I'm trying to help, I swear," Wes said.

"Then help me understand why Ralph's still alive."

"That's all about Ralph being sort of crazy like a fox, maybe. Cale's worried he left some clue behind, hidden like, that had to be found before anything, you know, happened to . . ."

"Which is why you were searching the boat," Bernie said.

"Ralph kept saying that there were no clues, but Cale didn't believe him."

"Kept saying when Cale was trying to beat it out of him?"

"But I got the feeling he didn't want Cale to believe him," Wes said. "Ralph's kind of . . ."

"Smart?" Bernie said. "Brave?" He glanced over at Napoleon, still fast asleep, snuffling and sniffling away. I could feel him thinking, meaning Bernie, not Napoleon. As for me, I wasn't sure how we were doing on this interview. Hadn't it been going on a for a long time? I was ready for action.

Bernie turned to Wes. "Was that Cale on the phone when we arrived?"

"Someone else. They want me to—" Wes took another one of those deep breaths. Sometimes humans did that when they were getting ready to puke. I inched backward a little.

"Want you to what?" Bernie said. "Finish the sentence."

"I'm not sure what they wanted, exactly."

"That's a lie, Wes. They wanted you to do something. You said it wasn't your job. So let's hear it."

Wes licked his lips. "The boat."

"They want your boat?"

"And me in it."

"For more dirty work at sea?"

Wes did some more of that awkward dabbing at his eyes with the back of his wrists.

"What kind of dirty work?"

Tears started flowing now. Bernie watched them, his own eyes like ice. "Take Ralph way out," Wes said. Or something like that, his voice hard to understand, being so choked up.

"Then weigh him down and dump him?"

"No one said anything about weighing down."

Bernie gave Wes's bare foot a soft kick, hardly touching him, but somehow that made Wes stop crying at once.

"Where's Cale got him?" Bernie said.

Wes raised his head, all of a sudden looking like he wanted to try giving us some trouble. The criers were that way sometimes, given to wild mood swings. "Suppose I tell you. Can you sweeten your offer?"

"What offer?"

"About keeping me out of prison."

"Sure," said Bernie. "Tell us where Ralph is and I'll let you walk out of here alive. That's as sweet as it's going to get."

Wes's mood began swinging back to the teary side. "Number nine," he said.

"The platform?" said Bernie. "Ralph's been on the platform the whole time?"

"I don't know about the whole time."

"So all those people are aware of what's going on—the drillers, the roughnecks, the tool pushers?"

Wes shook his head. "Maybe the captain, but no one else. Cale's got a separate pod on the south end, gated off and out of bounds. Cale or Pyro is always there and Ralph doesn't come out. The crew thinks they're guarding the platform."

"From what?"

"Eco terrorists."

Bernie made a snorting kind of laugh, not my favorite laugh type, but it sounded just fine coming from him. He went to the window and peeked out again.

"What's changed?" he said.

"I don't understand."

"Cale's decided not to keep Ralph alive anymore—how come?"

"Number nine's going operational tomorrow—sometime tonight, actually," Wes said. "Could be something about that, but more likely it's you."

"Me?"

"You're pissing him off."

"So he's taking it out on Ralph?"

Wes shook his head. "You've got him hearing footsteps, in my opinion. He wants to close this out. That's what he said—'we're closing this out tonight.'"

Bernie turned from the window and took out his phone. "Dr. Ory? Bernie Little here. I've got Napoleon." He listened for a moment. "I'll explain later. Can you come get him? Last cabin. I'll leave it unlocked." He clicked off.

"What's going on?" Was said.

"Call Cale," he said. "Tell him you're on."

Over on the footstool, Napoleon stretched his stubby legs, sighed in a snuffling way, and slept on.

THIRTY-FOUR

Here's how much I was loving boats: even though I'd had no desire to ever get back on this particular boat—meaning Wes's—after not long at all I was having the time of my life, and if not that, at least a pretty good one. The motion, the soft night air, the salty smells—we were out in the open ocean now—the moonlight, the starlight, Bernie's strong hands on the wheel, the .38 Special glinting in his belt: what more could anyone ask for? As for what we were actually doing, all I knew was that it had to be the exact right thing. For a little while I worried about who was paying, and then a wavetip came slopping over the side and smacked me on the face. What fun, and totally unexpected! I shook off the water.

"Hey!" Bernie said. "You're getting me wet, big guy." But he was smiling.

Wes was doing the opposite of smiling, the corners of his lips bent down, his eyes worried and scared. This boat of his had a small covered space in the bow, a sort of little cabin, and Wes was sitting in it, on the deck, hands cuffed in his lap. He didn't appear to enjoy boating. So how come he had a such a nice boat? A puzzler. No reason to puzzle over most puzzlers for long, so I turned and watched the spreading white wake the boat was making, a sight I could watch forever. When I'd had enough of that, I raised my gaze to the land we'd left and all its twinkling lights growing smaller and smaller. I'd seen sights like this in the desert, although not quite the same, with some difference I was considering thinking about when all at once a huge creature rose up on the surface of the sea, just off to one side of the boat.

Had I ever seen a creature this big? Not even close. It seemed to be sort of shaped like a fish, but not really. That head! So enormous. Its eye, so huge, saw me, no question about it. Not just saw: the creature was watching me, watching me kind of like . . . Bernie does sometimes, meaning in this very nice way that says, "Hey, Chet, you're a fun dude to hang with." This creature—a really smart creature, although not in Bernie's class, goes without mentioning—was giving me that kind of look and also keeping up with us no problem while not making any effort I could see. Then through this sort of hole in the top of its head, the creature shot a tall jet of water straight up in the night sky, a gleaming fountain in the moonlight. A creature that could make its own fountains! Now I'd seen everything.

"Chet! What are you barking at?"

I swung around to Bernie and barked some more. He had to see this.

"What? What?"

I turned back toward the water, Bernie following my gaze. The creature was gone.

"Easy, big guy. Need to be on the top of our game tonight."

But—

Sometime after that, the moon now lower in the sky, some lights rose up ahead, a small group of lights and not very bright. Bernie slowed the boat, and as he did I picked up the distant *whap whap whap* of chopper blades. The *whap whap whap* grew louder, became *WHAP WHAP WHAP*, and then high above appeared two white lights with a flashing red one at the back, which was all you saw of choppers at night. It made a big circle out past the small group of lights, came back toward us, maybe dipping down a little, and then zoomed off in the direction of land.

"Who's that?" Bernie said.

Wes gazed at the sky. "Don't know," he said. "Maybe one of ours?"

Bernie throttled back a little more. We bobbed up and down in the water in a soothing sort of way. I was considering a brief nap when Bernie left the wheel and walked up to the cabin, crouched in front of Wes.

"You understand how this is going down?" he said.

"I take us in at the south end," Wes said. "I don't tie up. Cale brings Ralph down in the lift. I act normal."

"You're leaving out an important detail," Bernie said.

"If I screw up, you shoot me."

Bernie nodded. He took out a key, removed Wes's cuffs. Wes rose, rubbing his wrists, and went to the wheel. Bernie made the little *click-click* sound meaning "come," and the two of us moved under the cabin roof in the bow. A roof is always nice, makes you feel safe. Bernie sat on a boat cushion. I curled up beside him. From there I had a good view through a small round window.

"Now," Bernie said.

Wes hit the throttle, his face green in the light of the console dials.

Through the small round window I saw the group of lights drawing closer. They began to come together in a shape that reminded me of things Charlie built with his Erector set. This particular thing was a sort of big steel deck perched on beams that rose up out of the sea. There was a whole little camp on the deck with some buildings, a crane, and lots of battered and dirty-looking equipment. The smell of the sea changed a bit, became more oily. Hey! This had to be the oil platform everyone kept talking about! Chet the Jet, in the picture! Bernie made a motion with his hand and Wes throttled back. I sat up.

The platform, much bigger than I'd thought, loomed high above us. Wes, going real slow now, took us on a long curve out past the platform and then back around and in from the far side, steering between two support beams and cutting the engine when we were right under the high steel deck.

It was quiet under the platform, just a low machine hum coming from above, plus the sounds of the sea sucking at the support beams, which were actually like huge legs. I had a crazy thought— the sea wants to suck this whole thing down off its metal feet— which I forgot right away, and then Wes was watching Bernie. Bernie pointed his finger at Wes in the signal for go. Wes looked up in the direction we couldn't see, and called, "All set."

A long pause, followed by a voice from above, Cale Rugh's voice, in fact, which didn't surprise me at all, now that I was in the picture. "Sending the lift."

Wes glanced at Bernie in surprise. Bernie gave him a hard look. "Huh?" Wes called. "Aren't you coming down with . . . aren't you coming down?"

"Need your help up here first."

Wes looked at Bernie again. Bernie gave him a nod.

"I'll have to tie up," Wes called up.

"Then tie up, for Christ sake," Cale told him. "You're wasting time."

Wes moved to the stern, reached toward the nearest support beam with a boat hook, pulled the boat closer, tied up. Then he let out some line and the boat drifted back to where we'd been. Meanwhile, a creaking machine started up somewhere above, the sound getting louder. A freight elevator came into view. This particular freight elevator didn't seem to have any walls. Its roof was attached to a thick cable that passed on through and connected with the steel floor. The freight elevator came to a stop right beside the boat and hovered there.

When humans get close to panic, a wild look appears in their eyes. It was happening to Wes at that moment, but not to Bernie, whose eyes were calm. He made a little motion for Wes to come. Wes left the wheel, made his way under the little cabin roof. Bernie put his hand on Wes's shoulder, kept it there until the panicky look left Wes's eyes. Then he cuffed Wes to a handrail—but in the friendliest way, like they were buddies and Bernie was looking out for him—and mouthed something. Wes nodded and called up: "On my way."

Bernie and I moved to the front of the cabin, right to the very edge of the part covered by the roof. Bernie put one hand on my collar—which sometimes happened when he thought I might: actually I didn't know what he thought—and peeked out. So did I. And what we saw was that the roof of the freight elevator blocked any view from above. We slipped over the side of the boat and got on the elevator. A little box with a button on it dangled from the elevator roof. Bernie pressed the button. The elevator jerked and started creaking up. Bernie took the .38 Special out of his waistband. I felt so alive!

Up and up we went, real slow. We reached the platform and kept going through a hole made to fit the elevator. A man began to take shape from the bottom up. First came his feet in cowboy boots, shiny boots gleaming in the moonlight, then—

But before any sort of thing could happen, the man bent down, so quick, and there at point blank range was Cale with a gun in his hand. "Love the brainy types," he said. "They do all your work for you." Bernie was still raising the .38 Special when Cale pulled the trigger. Crack of the shot, thud of the bullet—oh, no—hitting Bernie in his gun arm just above the elbow, blood seeping out right away, and the .38 Special fell to the floor, bouncing, bouncing, and over the side.

When things are happening fast in this business, you have to be faster, which turns out to be one of my specialties. I sprang out of the elevator, right at Cale. He swung the gun in my direction. But Cale proved to be one of those many fast dudes who couldn't ramp it up to my kind of faster. I hit him on the chest and we went down, rolling across the deck, and in midroll I caught a glimpse of another man close by, a roly-poly garlicky-smelling man with his arms tied behind his back and a black bag over his head. Maybe because of that sight, a bit disturbing, I got distracted, because all at once Cale had a tight grip on my collar—he was a real strong guy, no question about that—and was wrenching me around. I didn't like that, and twisted backward, trying to bring my teeth into play. He wrenched. I twisted. We rolled some more, me on top, Cale on top, and then all at once we rolled right off the platform.

We fell, a long long fall, Cale still gripping my collar. His eyes were full of scary things, too many to keep track of. All I knew was that I didn't want to be so close to that kind of scariness. With one final twist I got free enough to sink my teeth into his arm. Cale started to cry out and then we hit the water, the ocean swallowing up his cry, and swallowing us up, too. Down and down we sank, down into darkness, where I didn't want to be for a single moment on account of Iko, and I bit harder into Cale's arm, tasting blood and oil. Cale let go. A faint ray of moonlight lit his face, mouth open, silver bubbles bubbling out. I shot up to the surface.

And there was Bernie, treading water with one arm! He wrapped it around me and hugged me tight. I licked his face. We treaded water together, meaning I sort of herded him back toward the platform. A light shone down from the deck, found us. Then came a *WHAP WHAP WHAP* and a chopper flew out of the sky and hovered right above. Mr. Patel leaned out and gazed down at us. So much going on! What else? Oh, yeah: Cale Rugh didn't come up. And one more thing. I forgot to add that I'd held my own with Iko. Sort of.

Not long after that, we were back on the platform, me and Bernie. And not just me and Bernie, but kind of a crowd, including Mr. Patel, who'd landed in the chopper, and Ralph Boutette, the roly-poly man, the hood now off his head and his arms freed. Bernie was explaining things to Mr. Patel and Mr. Patel was explaining things to Bernie, all way too hard to follow. I stuck close to Ralph, on account of him being our meal ticket, if I understood the case right. And besides, I'd taken a liking to Ralph. His very first question had been about Napoleon.

"Almost forgot," Bernie said, turning to Ralph. "Brought you these." He took Ralph's glasses from his pocket, kind of awkward with his arm in a sling, and handed them over.

"Blind without them," Ralph said, putting them on. Next would come some sort of thanks, right? But no. Ralph marched immediately to the edge of the platform and peered down. "You see!" he said. "You see!"

We joined him. Ralph pointed down. The rig was all lit up now and the look of the ocean reminded me of the day Bernie decided to save money by taking care of the Porsche's oil changes by himself.

"This isn't just about the fact that their pressure metrics are bound to be screwed," he said. "Look at that—seabed's like a sponge cake." He pointed his fat finger at Mr. Patel. "How can you let them go operational? Answer me that!"

"We can't," said Mr. Patel. He went over to a group of men in hard hats.

"We didn't know anything about this," said the only one wearing a tie.

"All that'll get sorted out later," Mr. Patel said. He took out a sheet of paper and handed it to the tie-wearing guy. "Right now I'm shutting you down."

Around that time was when Bernie told Ralph about Mack.

Ralph went still.

"Can't prove this," Bernie said, "but at first he must have thought the whole shrimp business was just more nonsense between the Boutettes and the Robideaus, with Rugh some sort of hired hand. That changed when I showed him your glasses." There was a long pause. Then Bernie added, "Which got him killed."

"I don't see it that way," Ralph said. "And neither should you." He moved off to a quiet spot by the crane, stood there by himself. I stood by Bernie. He gave me some nice pats, but he was looking kind of pale and I kept a close eye on him. Other than that, my mind was on sponge cake.

They took the slug out of Bernie at the nice little hospital in St. Roch. After Bernie got bandaged up, Mr. Sim, VP, Consumer Affairs of Green Oil, paid us a visit. He was a distinguished-looking dude with silvery hair, smooth skin, and a nice suit.

"Can't thank you enough," he said.

"Huh?" said Bernie.

"Talk about going rogue," said Mr. Sim. "Enlisting the help of some Central American drug gang—can you imagine? Naturally, Donnegan's denies all knowledge—as if that'll stop us from suing the pants off them."

"Uh-huh," said Bernie.

"But none of that concerns you," Mr. Sim, reaching into his pocket. "Here, as a token of our appreciation, is a check for fifty thousand dollars."

Fifty grand! Had I ever even heard of so much money? I actually didn't know.

Bernie shook his head. "No thanks."

Mr. Sim rocked back. "I'm sorry?"

"We've already got a client."

Mr. Sim tilted his head in a way that actually reminded me of Bernie. "Kind of easy, isn't it?" he said. "Maybe even lazy, from an intellectual point of view."

"What are you referring to?"

"Hating the oil business."

"I don't hate the oil business," Bernie said. "I hate what you did to Ralph Boutette."

We had a client? That turned out to be the Boutettes, a fact that kept slipping my mind. They threw a big party for us at Rooster Red's with the whole town coming, the exception being the Robideaus, who had all left suddenly on a long vacation, and Lord Boutette, who turned out to have some outstanding warrants up in the city. Bernie laughed a lot, especially when he realized our three shrimpy grand, all gone, had come from Cale Rugh originally, by way of Mack and then Vannah, or something like that, not so easy to track, and laughed even harder when he learned for sure there'd been more originally, before Vannah did a little skimming. We got to sample Mami's sweet potato pie, and the

Boutettes took up a collection for us. We walked out of there with eight hundred dollars and seventy cents, not too shabby, unless I was missing something. Did I mention Mami's sweet potato pie?

On the way home, Bernie finally reached Suzie on the phone.

"It's crazy to let silly misunderstandings come between us," he told her.

"How about serious misunderstandings?" Suzie said.

Bernie laughed. "Them, too."

Then they were both laughing. What was funny? Don't ask me. But the sound of Bernie's laughter couldn't be beat, and Suzie had made it happen, so therefore . . .

Almost forgot: Bernie handles the so therefores. I bring other things to the table.

ACKNOWLEDGMENTS

Many thanks to my wife, Diana, and my sons Seth and Ben for first getting me interested in Louisiana. And I'm deeply grateful for Atria's enthusiastic support of the Chet and Bernie series—special mention to Ariele Fredman.